The Knowledge Well

Book 1 – The Genius Threads

Chris Haught

CHAPTER 1 — SAVING BRILL

Five-year-old Brill Everly *tried* to listen to the gentle autumn rains as he laid in bed, hobbled by some illness that left him barely able to walk. What he was really listening to, though, was the conversation Mom and Dad were having in the kitchen, which was several doors down from Brill's room. It was about him and something they called their "last option." Brill could hear Mom's voice floating on the air, reminding him of the birds singing their praises to the late afternoon sun. Her voice was always one of comfort, though this discussion was a somber one.

Brill loved the summertime, and longed for the days when he and his best friend, Sirum Lars, would go fishing at Grandpa's farm. He'd finally learned enough patience to wait until the bobber went under before tugging on the line, and now he could catch lots of fish! The thought of those fish diverted him until his ears picked up Mom's voice saying the alarming word "cancer." Dad was a cancer doctor, so Brill knew what that was, and he'd watched enough YouTube to know that cancer was a very nasty thing that nobody wanted and most people couldn't get rid of.

Dr. John Everly, a renowned oncologist and Brill's Dad, had run the final tests himself several times to be certain the lab results were correct. Brill had shown symptoms of tiredness for the past six months, which was highly unusual for a five-year-old, and it just kept getting worse. Even physicians have hope when their own children have a potentially terminal disease. The tests kept coming back as a potential leukemia and tomorrow would either confirm or deny that. His hope tended to focus on the latter, despite what the data said.

The next morning, John met with his assistant, Amber, to review the final round of testing. The prognosis was grim. He stared at the ceiling as she recited the results. John was trying to find the right words between thoughts of Brill, and finally blurted: "It's Acute Myeloid Leukemia, then."

Amber looked away with tears in her eyes, "Yes."

"This the part of the job I've always hated. I never dreamed it would land on one of my own."

Though he had delivered grim news many times over the years, he had no idea how to break the news to Jenna. Brill was her baby, the apple of her eye since the day he was born, and he was certain it would devastate her beyond recovery. He didn't know how he was going to survive it himself, much less shatter his wife's world with the news.

#

Six Years Before

John Everly had always admired the creativity of science fiction books and movies. The idea of nanomachines that could enter the tiniest of spaces and build from the molecular level up was intriguing from a medical perspective. The idea of treating diseases inside cells could revolutionize medicine, but the nanomachines in and of themselves could also present new problems to the body. As he thought through the possibilities, it occurred to him that a nanomachine might be built in a way similar to how cells constructed themselves, out of carbohydrates, starches, and proteins, using DNA and RNA to direct where and what you wanted the tiny device to do.

When he had begun his career as an oncologist at Stanford several years before, he had realized that to distinguish himself from the other staff, he would have to run a research program in addition to his surgical duties. Just recently, he had learned that the DOD was offering research grants to physicians who targeted their research toward battlefield injuries and other much-needed military medical advancements. So John had reached out to the DOD directly via their website.

Within hours of submitting his request, a major in the U.S. Army called him to set up some time to discuss his research plan further. John thought this would be a phone chat to discuss the requirements of such a research program. To his surprise, the major, Liam Rhett, indicated he was already headed to the Bay Area and would be there by evening. Thinking this was a positive sign, John arranged to meet with Major Rhett the following day at his home.

Just after breakfast, the doorbell rang and John sprang off the sofa to welcome his guest. As he opened the door, Major Rhett boomed in the most southern accent John had heard in a number of years, "Good morning, Dr. Everly, it's a pleasure to meet you in person," with his hand extended.

"Good morning, Major Rhett, please come in out of the fog," John said, as he shook Rhett's proffered hand. "Would you like some coffee?"

"Yes sir," Major Rhett answered with conviction.

As John handed Liam his coffee, he said, "Let's go in the den, as I find the fire to be comforting on these foggy days. The dampness of the morning chills me to the bone."

After they finished the small talk, John said, "I'm curious as to why my proposal prompted such a quick response. I had the impression the government moves at a snail's pace."

Major Rhett smiled. "Dr. Everly, do you recall when we met during your residency at Emory University?"

John responded, "Please call me John, Major. 'Dr. Everly' is a formality reserved for my patients and students. You do look familiar, but I don't recall meeting you."

Rhett relaxed a bit. "Sir, please call me Liam. My training will make it difficult for me to address another by his first name; the best I can do is reference you as sir."

Laughing, John replied, "Not a problem, I've been called worse."

Liam continued, "We met when you were treating my father, Colonel Jackson Rhett, for thyroid cancer. I only had a few days of leave from the Academy, so my visits were infrequent. My dad was a patient at Emory on and off for five years before he passed. I was highly impressed with the treatments you suggested, and could see your work was

~~helping him live easier. I knew a cure for his stage~~ of cancer was unlikely. He knew it too, and was happy to have the extra time, always speaking highly of you."

John expressed his condolences for Liam's father before Liam indicated there was a second time they'd met. "We also shook hands very briefly at your wedding. Your wife's dad was a good friend to mine, and Jenna and I knew each other growing up."

"Wow, it really is a small world," John said.

"Now to the business at hand, sir. You indicated in your grant application that you could design a bio-machine without any actual mechanical parts. The idea is very intriguing, and immediately caught the attention of my superiors. Designing something that could work inside the body to impart healing or other instructions would be of a great benefit to the Armed Forces, since combat injuries sideline many a soldier."

John was cautious with his next words. "Yes, the idea came to me as I was thinking of the cell itself. I could go into the biology of it, but those details are all in the application. What would you like to hear from me?"

Dr. Everly, "You mentioned in your application that this could be applied to injured cells. What would you envision as an application to injured soldiers?"

"These pseudo-cells can be tailored to anywhere in the body. They would be a great improvement over other treatments, as the manufactured cells could be instructed to complete a specific job and only that job to any spot in the body. Imagine a bullet that has ripped up the muscle. These could be injected into soldiers so that when they are injured, the repairs would begin immediately."

After a pause to sip his coffee, John continued, "Nature is efficient with all orders of life, this would be one small step forward, using natures tools. In order to progress this to human testing, though, I need money and access to government supercomputers, so I submitted the grant proposal."

After Liam pondered what he'd just heard, he said, "My superiors were so interested in what you proposed that they diverted me here to see if we can come to an agreement. I might have the ability to open the government's checkbook and give you what you need whenever you ask for it. The amount is irrelevant, as long as you can show steady progress. However, the government will own all the high-profile results and it will be top secret."

John looked a little stunned. "How will that help me if I can't publish?"

Patience Dr. Everly. "I was getting to that. We will help you start your own side-business to conceal our involvement. That work will be considered top secret, but you'll be allowed to be share certain elements with the scientific world and the public to help you gain the credibility you need to advance your career."

"Sounds too good to be true."

For a brief second, a smile crossed Liam's face. "The company we'll help you start will be made public from the beginning, and the government will own none of it. You'll be the sole proprietor, as this will help you gain the wealth you'll need later in life to properly influence the world we live in."

John sat for a long while without saying a word, deep in thought. Then he finally said, "What other strings are attached? If I don't agree, what are the ramifications?"

Liam answered solemnly, "You're wise to question the golden goose, sir, since nothing is ever as it appears, especially with intelligence agencies. I'm just the messenger for now, and I know of no negative ramifications if no agreement is reached."

John thought briefly but deeply, then reached out his hand to shake Liam's and said, "We have a deal. Let's draw up the paperwork and make it official."

After Liam shook his hand, he said, "This project will be handled out of a new agency called the Homeland Intelligence Agency, or HIA, sir, and I may or may not have contact with you again. That's up to my superiors."

From that moment on, John would always be on his guard, for he was wary of his new masters. The term he thought of at that moment for his company was *Vassal*, as he would be ruled by an overlord, the government. At first he dismissed the name, but it stuck with him, and eventually became the name of his government-sponsored company.

#

Present Day

To celebrate their 10-year anniversary and to spend time with Brill, the family had taken a long-planned trip to Santiago Chile. Two days before they were scheduled to leave, they went on a short hike to the thermal springs up in the Andes mountains. Brill was swimming gleefully in the springs when he spotted an odd looking rock jutting out of the water near the shoreline. Curious as he always was, Brill reached his hand under the rock. As he got a good hold on it and started pulling it out of the dirt, a sharp stabbing pain tore through his thumb. With his prize in hand and tears streaming down his face, he ran to his mom to show the prize. Halfway to his mom, he let out an ear-piercing scream and fell to the ground.

With Brill unconscious and unresponsive, John called for an ambulance and immediately spotted the problem. Looking at Jenna, John exclaimed in a nervous voice, "It seems Brill was stung by a scorpion. Due to Brill's leukemia, his response looks like a complete systemic shutdown. They rushed him to the hospital where he began to recover.

Jenna was in a state of shock as John stroked her hair.

"We have to get him back home. I've contacted the pilot and he will be here by nightfall. Once Brill's ready, he'll be taken to the plane in an ambulance, and we'll head back home, okay? I've prepped my staff to get Brill treated as soon as he stabilizes. I'd hoped to wait a few more weeks for that, but this event has moved up the schedule."

He put his hands on Jenna's shoulders. "Honey, there's more. Their scans have detected a tumor in Brill's abdomen, and I'm concerned." She looked at him, horrified, and he tried to soothe her. "Don't worry. I'll operate on him and get it out right away once we're home."

None of them slept that night. They all stayed the night in Brill's room, with John consulting with the physicians there, offering his help where he could.

They loaded up within the hour, and were airborne by mid-morning.

On the way home, Jenna handed John the rock that had cost Brill so much to get. As he inspected it, he realized it was more than it seemed. The rock was the size of a small dinner plate, but light as a feather. It bore glyph-like inscriptions, with the tree of life prominent in the first images, indicating a Mayan origin. *Odd*, he thought; the Mayans were never thought to have visited South America, yet the symbols were clearly of the Mayan genre. As he tried to decipher the script, he saw what appeared to be a group of Mayans, either worshiping or praying, with the next glyph somewhat difficult to understand. It resembled a great hand reaching out from the heads of those individuals into the cosmos, or the thirteenth level of the tree of life.

John knew a bit about Mayan religious practices and how they believed that one neither died nor was born. There was a constant balance in the flow from life to death and back again; yet this script indicated something entirely different. Puzzled, he packed the stone in his bag, intending to give it to Brill when he graduated from college. If that day ever came.

#

The tension was high on the ride back home, as John and Jenna clung to each other, expressing their grief and gaining strength from each other's comforting. After fifteen hours, they taxied up to their hanger in Santa Clara, readying themselves for the trials yet to come. The air was heavy with fog, the scent of cypress trees tickling the nose as they exited the plane and thanked Captain Lawrence.

Heading to the waiting ambulance, Jenna and Sam piled in with Brill, while John retrieved their luggage and vehicle.

On the way to the hospital, he mulled over some of the exploratory research Vassal was developing that might help Brill. As he pondered on those possibilities, his thoughts centered on the immediacy of getting the tumor out of his son. Radiation therapy was likely needed as well, and he'd prepare Brill as best he could. Ultimately, Brill would need a bone marrow transplant; that would be the most difficult of the treatments, since matching donors were rare. Interim stem-cell therapy would have to do.

He so lost in thought that he was surprised to find he was at the hospital, having driven on autopilot. "Welcome back, John," Dr. Lest greeted him at the door of the emergency room. "We've missed you here. Sorry to hear about Brill. He got here about half an hour ago and is being prepped for surgery now. I know he's your son, but it may be best for the attending surgeons to take on this one, as it's a fairly routine abdominal surgery. Are you sure you want to do this?"

John replied, "Wouldn't you? Him being my son means I'm going to do more than my best, and give him every attention to detail. I can't sit back and turn this over to anyone else. I have to be in there. I will, however, let you take the lead, since I haven't had much sleep these last couple of days, and I don't want to make any mistakes."

Dr. Lest nodded. "I appreciate your confidence in me. It's not misplaced."

After a week in the hospital, Brill's healing from the surgery was progressing well, though they had to take extra care, as his AML was also progressing. John had prepared Brill for the bone marrow transplant, hoping a donor could be found soon; the stem-cell therapy would only last him so long. The screening through the national database had yet to yield a compatible donor. John was getting discouraged when Nurse Sam rushed in, shouting that a donor had been found. The person with the closest match was Brill's best friend, Sirum Lars!

John wasn't sure he could convince Sirum's parents to let him undergo the transplant procedure; bone marrow aspiration was a long and painful process, and Sirum was thought to be autistic, so he wasn't sure they would consent. Sirum was brilliant at music, art, and math, and considered a genius savant. His speech had taken longer to develop than in most children — not unusual with autistic kids — and it was his mispronunciation of "Bill to Brill," Bill was what his parents had originally called their son, that became Brill's nickname. After a year of hearing "Bill" pronounced as "Brill," the name stuck, because Bill was adamant about using the nickname. He thought it made Sirum feel better.

Sirum's DNA confirmed that his mutation on Chromosome Fifteen gave him autistic tendencies. Sirum, however, was more determined than most autistic kids, and was able to develop behaviors similar to those of typically developing kids of his age. His brilliance helped him adapt to every situation quicker than most.

After a short wait, Sirum's parents consented to the transplant, and following four weeks of intensive treatments, the transplant finally took place. It worked. Brill was slow to recover, and spent the better part of a year in the hospital.

From his perspective, life was always the only option. He could never understand why the adults kept telling him he was only going to live another year. That year had now passed, and he was still alive, after all.

#

Nonetheless, the marrow transplant proved to be too little too late. It slowed the progression of Brill's leukemia, but a different treatment was needed to stop it altogether, or Brill would die. John had already begun to develop an experimental treatment through Vassal Biogenetics. The treatment he was seeking would revolutionize cancer treatment if it worked as intended; and by this point, he was desperate enough to try it on Brill.

John brought it up at his next meeting with Major Rhett. The meeting was ostensibly a review of current progress, but John had included the code words to indicate a special request. As they settled into a secure room at Vassal HQ, he began with a rundown of the progress they were making on battlefield enhancements for repairing damaged limbs. The last topic was John's special request. "Now, to my topic of need. I've been working on a prion modulator. You may have heard of prions in the negative sense, due to Mad Cow Disease, but I've found a way to use them strategically. I just need a clear path of approvals to get them into human testing."

Liam's eyes narrowed a bit. "This has to do with your son, doesn't it?"

"Yes. Am I that obvious? I've run out of options, and Brill has only months to live if I don't make some sort of Hail Mary play."

"My superiors have been following your work," Rhett said slowly, "so we know about the prions. Nothing you do goes unnoticed, John. They have concerns about the first human test being a terminally ill seven-year-old, however."

"Don't they realize the upside? *Complete control over any cell in the body*. Being able to eliminate aged cells and encourage the growth of young, healthy ones."

"John, many people in history have used the ends to justify the means. If you're wrong, you walk a perilous path to ruin — not only of your reputation, but of your family. I've ordered many men into battle, knowing they might give their lives for the cause. It's never easy to bear that kind of responsibility. I don't think you could live knowing you hastened your son's death."

"Liam, please. Open the path for me to try."

"Dr. Everly, you know as well as I do that this is beyond my authority."

"Please, just ask."

"I understand your pain. Though I don't have children, my brother's daughter, Liora, would drive me to any means to save her if she were in the same peril. I may have an option for you, but time may not be on your side, and it may cost you dearly."

"Anything, I'll try anything. I'm at the end of my rope."

Liam leaned toward him. "Dr. Everly. This stays within these walls, and everything you do after I tell you this will be on your conscience."

"Tell me," John eagerly replied.

"A special detention center at Guantanamo Bay, Cuba houses the worst terrorists we've ever captured. Some have been infected with a modified hantavirus, and are in various stages of decline. If you can heal just one, to prove your treatment works, then you'll likely get your approval."

Liam rose to leave without another word. Before he stepped out of the room, he slipped a scrap of paper onto the table. The note was a simple cypher that indicated a geolocation and time of day. Once John plugged the coordinates into his phone, he saw that he had two weeks to arrive at Moffitt Field before the plane — at least, he assumed it was a plane — would depart.

He began preparing his prion treatment to find and reprogram hantavirus-infected cells.

The prion modifier John's team had developed would target cells that matched part of the protein code that made up the prion. Within the prion shell was a modified RNA strand that would enter the cell and begin producing the desired peptide, be it a protein or enzyme. In this case, the enzyme it produced would seek out the shell of the hantavirus and insert the code for the enzyme itself. Then every hantavirus produced would seek out other hantaviruses and reprogram them, until every hantavirus in the body was eradicated. Additionally, he would put code into the prion to encourage cell growth to replace the cells already destroyed by the virus. It was, John thought, quite an elegant design, but extremely powerful.

The two weeks passed in the blink of an eye. John's cover story was that he was traveling on Vassal business to the Dominican Republic. He let them know his business would take him to the remote regions of that country, and he would be out of contact for three weeks.

When he arrived at the airfield, John wasn't sure exactly who or what he would find. At the exact spot the coordinates indicated was an unassuming black SUV with completely tinted windows. As he approached with his equipment in tow, a window rolled down and someone motioned him to enter the truck. John climbed aboard, and as soon as the door was shut, the truck took off. Not a word was exchanged until they arrived at a hidden coastal airfield. John was greeted by several airman and ushered aboard a jet. Once he settled in, the craft took flight. At cruising altitude, the pilot made his way back to John, and was immediately recognized.

John exclaimed on seeing the pilot that flew them out of Chile, "Captain Lawrence! I'm surprised to see you here."

Lawrence smiled tightly. "Dr. Everly, the world is smaller than you think. I might show up in the least-suspected places. Welcome aboard; we have many hours of flight time ahead. This craft is military issue, but untraceable by radar. You won't see me again on this flight. When we land, please depart the plane as quickly as possible, and hurry into the waiting vehicle. Don't delay. Your presence won't go unnoticed, so stay alert and be on guard."

The flight was turbulent, and John was queasy when they finally landed. This wasn't the smooth Learjet that the Captain had previously piloted. The waiting vehicle was a less-than-stellar but rugged-looking jeep. The ride was rough, the terrain inhospitable. If their vehicle were to break down, John thought, the countryside would swallow them up. After what seemed like an eternity, gates festooned with barbed wire became visible in the pre-dawn light. They exited the vehicle and hurried through the checkpoint.

Once inside, John realized that he was in an old fort dating from the 1800s: no air conditioning, and few amenities. Swatting mosquitos, he reached into his bag for water and pulled out something else. A giant spider had decided to make a home in his bag, and nearly bit his finger as John shook it off. From then on, he was much more cautious of his surroundings.

He was told by an anonymous soldier that the prisoners he would experiment on were housed in the other wing of the fort, but that was all he knew.

John had been shown to his room and was preparing to bed down for the night when a knock on his door startled him. A young soldier was waiting on the other side when John opened the door. He said stiffly, "Dr. Everly, your work is to begin immediately. Please pack your things and follow me. You'll find a cot and latrine near your subjects."

At a loss for words, John did as requested. As he passed from building to building, the security grew tighter, until he felt like he was being crushed by security personnel; there wasn't a place he could turn where a soldier was not. Finally, arriving at what looked to be a makeshift lab, he was instructed to place his bags near the wall and begin his work. He shrugged and began doing as instructed when he heard footsteps behind him. As he turned, a familiar face greeted him: Major Liam Rhett. "Dr. Everly, I hope you've found

Guantanamo Bay to your liking thus far. It was the best we could do on short notice."

That was the first time John ever saw Liam crack a smile, and it would be quite some time before he saw another. "Major Rhett, I'm here to work," he replied calmly. "As you indicated, time is not on my side. Please bring me the charts for the patients I'm supposed to cure. I need to know how bad their prognoses are."

"Certainly. If you find you don't have the equipment you need, please let us know, and it will be at your disposal within a day." With that, Liam turned and exited the room. John didn't see him again for weeks.

When the charts arrived, John began reading through them. Several charts into the stack, John slammed down the packet, cursing himself for the involvement he would have in this, this... The only words that came to mind were *cruelty* and *torture*. He had been thoroughly deceived. These prisoners had been purposefully infected with a virus that permanently amplified the pain centers of the brain, so that even the slightest sound or touch resulted in excruciating agony. They were then systemically infected with additional engineered viruses, *nine* in total, so the only parts of the brain left were the deep memory, speech, and pain centers. No other emotions, no purpose left in life. Hideous. *I'm a doctor, sworn to heal and protect. Not this,* he told himself.

As he read on, he landed upon the reason they'd brought him here. The virus cocktail didn't stop at the brain; it rapidly degraded the subjects' internal organs, so much so that after the last treatment, the prisoners lived only a few weeks. The last treatment was necessary, as it tied together all the previous iterations, making torture very simple. One spoken word triggered pain that brought up a specific image, and the prisoner involuntarily described that image. Sounded efficient, until John realized the challenge: it was like describing a twelve-hour movie scene-by-scene. Then someone had to figure out where that movie had taken place and in what context, as the prisoners had lost the cognitive ability to tell them. Imagine trying to figure out the image of a dog, when the description is teeth, sharp, brown hair, toenails, tail, drool, and so on — but with those images associated with specific people and places. John realized that they wanted him to do two things. First, stop the organ deterioration; second, maintain the cognitive centers of the brain.

He threw up his hands in exasperation. "This was *not* what I was prepared to find! How can I heal Brill when this has *nothing* to do with his disease?" he growled to himself.

John was hard-pressed on where to start, and on whom. These were hopeless cases, and he realized he was in over his head, now completely alone with just two or three weeks to make progress — or else. After reviewing the files, he settled in for the night; maybe an idea would arrive in his subconscious. He drifted off to sleep with troubled thoughts.

The morning didn't find him in better spirits. Going for a run had always cleared his head, but this was the devil's house filled with demons, with nowhere to go. He found a path that let him gain a glimpse of the sun, stopped, and stared as long as he could. With dark spots obscuring his vision, he leaned against a tree, deep in thought. Those spots, images burned on the retina, caused his mind to begin racing from idea to idea. The images the brain sees are mirror images translated by cells in the eye, then stored deep in the brain for processing later, usually during REM sleep. The analytical side of the brain will then associate the right language with the imagery for later recall. His prion treatment could access the fundamental neural pathways to rebuild damaged cognitive centers. The subjects would be akin to grade-school kids learning to read and write. Once taught the proper skills, they could describe the images the questioners sought; but he would have to deactivate the pain response for that to work. At this stage, it served no purpose; these men were already stripped of their identities and loyalties, left only with their memories.

The second problem was more challenging, and might be what Brill needed. The prions would have to go into each cell and reprogram them to fight off the viruses from the inside out. He just needed the viral cage to imprint it into the prions for recognition and repair.

The tools on the base were limited mainly to those used for torture. However, one remnant from a previous use of this location was still intact. This place had once housed a thriving university before the U.S. military had acquired it, and the previous inhabitants had left everything in their haste to depart. One thing John found was an intact transmission electron microscope; not an easy instrument to use, but ideal for imaging the viral cage.

After two days of trial and error with the TEM, he finally had the image he needed and began coding his prion treatments to target the brain and organs. In his haste to perfect the organ treatment, however, he left some extra peptide codes in the brain prions. He noticed this later, but dismissed it as nonsense code that wouldn't be worth the effort to remove. He was ready to begin his experiments, realizing he would no doubt have several failures — deaths — before he hit upon a success. This struck him to the core.

His thoughts oscillated between doing what was right, and healing his son. The latter won out sooner than his conscience would have led him to believe going into this.

John tried every combination possible, with each attempt resulting in the acceleration of the prisoner's' deterioration. After the fifth death, he began to lose faith in his ability to heal Brill. During his autopsy of that body, John's scalpel slipped as he was excising the heart. The scalpel dug deep into the spine, almost taking John's left thumb with it, and he found it was jammed in tight. He was ordered by his minders to remove the scalpel, no matter how time-consuming it was. He would have left it and moved on, but apparently it created a security risk in the morgue. So he reached for a cranial saw to cut out the segment of the spine in which it was jammed. He was in a hurry, and didn't have time for delays.

Upon removing that piece of spine, he found something unexpected: what should have been nothing but nerves, bone, and clear fluid turned out to contain something thin and shiny. He checked the prisoner's chart, looking for anything he might have encountered or experienced that would explain this. It was too much of a mystery to let it go, so he took up the saw and tried to section the spine. The saw should have sliced right through it, but instead, it deflected and broke the blade, which flew across the room, slicing through a computer screen before it landed on his hotplate. His curiosity now fully piqued, he used tweezers to pick up and put the spinal segment under the microscope.

The revelation was startling: he found tiny, microscopic machines in the subject's spine! They had gotten clumped together, forming a solid mass of metal that the saw somehow hadn't been able to cut through. John was curious to learn if the nanobots, which were mechanical rather than the biological ones he'd envisioned years before, used sugars in the blood to power themselves, as that was what he would do. He rounded up some sucrose and introduced it to the bots. No response. Trying different biological fluids from the patient on the table had no response, either. Everything he could think of, except — no, it couldn't be. The thought racing through his mind was *neurotransmitters*. He would need a live patient to acquire those, so he had him minders bring in the patient he was supposed to treat next. He extracted the needed cranial fluid and had his answer almost immediately.

The bots from the spinal section readily separated to form liquid islands and began consuming the fluid, which was unexpected. This begged another experiment, though it would be costly, as the man involved would surely die. He accelerated the next treatment on the next prisoner. He didn't wait for the outcome, since he needed the cranial fluid. He was curious whether it would elicit another response from the bots, and the result confirmed his suspicions.

He had one more gruesome task to perform that literally went against everything he had ever been taught: performing a live autopsy, an actual vivisection, like something out of a horror story. He needed to see what was killing these patients, and could only do it as one of them was dying. Worse, he couldn't administer any anesthesia or even pain medications; he needed to watch the man's death unhindered from the inside out. Before he began cutting, he put in earplugs, but the screaming was still too loud for him to endure. He wiped tears from his eyes; cutting into the spine of a living man who wasn't under anesthesia was almost more than he could bear.

There was one last thing he had yet to observe, and he guessed he would find his answer there. He did. Furious, John screamed at the guard outside the door, "Get me Major Rhett. Now!"

After what seemed like hours, Liam appeared. "How may I help you, Dr. Everly?"

"What the hell, Rhett! You failed to tell me how you modified these prisoners' brains! Your omission completely fucked up my tests! I have been at my wits' end, thinking I was failing, but it was *your* handiwork that caused the failures!"

"Dr. Everly, please sit. My work here is as a liaison. I can neither confirm nor deny your suspicions. Please, enlighten me."

"Don't give me that line of bullshit, Major. You're as connected to this evil experiment as anyone here. I am *not* a novice at reading who's in charge. From the moment we got here, you were always the one who drew attention, even from the commandant of the base."

"Again, Dr. Everly, please share with me your concerns."

"I had to do a *vivisection* to get my proof. That would cost me my medical license and land me in jail if anyone found out. I'm certain you've recorded everything I've done. Your hidden cameras haven't gone unnoticed. I found your nanobots by accident."

"Nanobots? Science fiction, don't you think, Dr. Everly?"

"Don't play stupid with me. Now I know why you jumped on my proposal so quickly!"

"And if these men *were* infected with nanobots, what concern is it of yours?"

"Every concern! They're responding to the prion treatment by condensing in the spine."

"I fail to see the problem, Dr. Everly."

"Because they eat neurotransmitters for energy, they're depleting the patients of needed neural signals, and the patients die, you idiot! Their brains can't command any organ to keep functioning, so they just shut down!"

Rhett lifted an eyebrow. "We seem to be at an ending point for your time here, Doctor."

"Dammit, my treatments *worked*. They fixed the problem — which was your *bots*, not the viruses! Every patient had healthy organs at the end — better than when they started. I watched this happen, and confirmed it during the, the live autopsy."

A smile crossed Liam's face. "Then, Dr. Everly, you've completed your mission here."

"Have I? Now what?" John demanded as he threw up his hands in exasperation.

"Now it's time for you to go home and cure your son. Your plane leaves in two hours."

As John began to gather his experimental data, Liam Rhett put his hand over the microscope slides John was about to put away. "Dr. Everly, some things are best left unanswered."

John put the microscope slides back on the counter and collected his prion treatments, along with their designs.

#

After returning to Stanford, John checked into a hotel to recuperate for a few days before heading home. Having cleaned up and regained his composure, he put on a facade of just having had a Eureka moment to fool his wife. Bursting through the door, he shouted, "Jenna, Jenna!"

Running into the room, she saw the excitement on his face. "You're home early." She hugged him and planted a huge kiss on his lips.

"I think I found a cure for Brill!" he said enthusiastically.

"A cure?"

"Yes, a cure! I know it sounds impossible, but the guys at Vassal completed animal studies with complete regeneration of the mutations, using a treatment I invented!" A partial lie, but one he could endure without sharing secret information. "I have special approval to begin human trials immediately. In two days, Brill will be the first subject!"

Suddenly angry, Jenna yelled, "*What*? You should have discussed this with me!"

"Jenna, he only has a few weeks left to live, which is why I went ahead and scheduled him first. The treatment is real. It works. I have proof, and he *will* survive."

She sagged, like a marionette with cut strings. "Do it. What choice do we have? He dies for sure if you do nothing. But what if...?"

They hugged and cried for hours, preparing for the possibility that John might be wrong.

Chapter 2: Liam Rhett

Eight Years Ago

Colonel Jackson Rhett had returned from his final tour in the Middle East five years before, planning to spend time with his wife and sons — only to receive a diagnosis of cancer just a few years into his retirement. He had always tried to be a good father, but military conflicts had pulled him from one area of the world to another. His wife was an incredible woman who loved him, despite the military loneliness. She was dedicated to raising her boys to be men who respected authority, and they eventually followed their father into the service. The older boy, Liam, went into the Army, while the younger, Andrew, went into the Marines.

In the fall of his first year at West Point after his Dad came home, Liam was eager to prove himself, as he lived under the shadow of the great Colonel Rhett. He soon found it wasn't easy to be great on his own, not when everyone in the command structure knew or had served with his father.

The classes were of little challenge and he was already soldier trained, which made the rest of the experience a formality on his way to his career. Specializing in military intelligence, Liam's first commission as a second lieutenant had him stationed in Greece, where he got his first foray in battle. By then, Andrew was stationed in Lebanon.

#

The Kafr militants, as they had renamed themselves in honor of their recently slain leader, were a stealthy bunch of rag-tag ex-soldiers who had cobbled together a loose army across much of the Middle East, with their headquarters thought to be in Faiyum, Egypt. Their mantra, *Islam Commands Western Eradication*, was spray-painted on nearly every free surface in their territory. The governments of these lands gave lip service to the UN-backed troops tasked with controlling the militants, claiming they were happy to allow those troops to fight on their behalf, but intelligence sources painted a different picture. At the root of the Kafr's organized resistance was the Saudi Arabian government, especially several younger sheiks who had quickly risen to power after the suspicious deaths of their elders.

#

The sunrise cast a red glow over the pyramids at Giza as the heat of the day steadily rose. Liam's squad had made progress from Crete to their landing in Alexandria the night before, and now were making their way through Cairo, using the cover and cool of the night to cross the city undetected — or so they thought. During the last trek of the night, a sleep-deprived Sergeant Chase had ordered privates Sosh and Rivers to scout ahead down to the banks of the Nile.

Giza was mostly sand and buildings, with the only cover being the vegetation near the riverbank and the darkness of night. Getting to the river undetected would be a challenge; when the sun rose, everything was visible. Private Sosh, who had been ordered to scout to the riverbank, did just that; but he unwisely stopped at the river's edge to relieve himself instead of fading back into the brush first. How many

American servicemen could say they'd pissed in the Nile, right?

Across the river, an early-morning fisherman spotted him. Had he not been in camo and urinating, he might have gone unnoticed. Sosh soon headed back to camp, two hours away, where he and Rivers reported the path ahead clear.

The mission of Liam and his squad was to ferret out the militants who had reportedly made a base in Faiyum, 100 kilometers south of Cairo. It would be several more nights by foot, at least, before they could make camp at Lake Qarun, the saline remnant of ancient Lake Moeris outside Faiyum; so they needed to move faster. That night, they made their way to the river, hoping for better cover as they headed south. They had just acquired a local boat, unbeknownst to the owner of that craft, when the first shot rang out. Liam's squad quickly made for cover, leaving the boat where it lay; then Liam ordered scouts into the cover of the surrounding buildings. Sergeant Chase spotted three snipers on a rooftop. Regrouping and outlining their options, Liam decided the best course of action would be to mount an offensive. If these were scouts for the militia, then their mission would be compromised if he left them alive. He ordered an assault to take out the snipers as quietly as possible, since the locals were preparing to go about their daily business.

Liam had identified an underground entry into the snipers' building, no doubt meant for deliveries, and decided that was their best bet to get inside undetected. Once they made their way up the stairs to the rooftop, though, the options became limited. There was only one entrance to the roof, which would surely be guarded. *Time for another plan*, Liam thought.

The eighth floor presented itself as the best point of entry to the roof, via a fire escape. Quickly entering the rooftop, the Americans ghosted up behind the snipers and simultaneously, on Liam's command, slipped hands over the militants' mouths and swiftly snapped their necks. They hid the bodies amongst the air-conditioning equipment, adding their weapons to their own. They then retreated to the boat they'd liberated and made their way downstream to Al Wasta.

Toward evening the next day, they disembarked and began the trek to Lake Qarun. It was 65 kilometers by car, and even longer by foot, given the intervening wadis and salt flats. The only road to Faiyum was riddled with checkpoints, as the militants had a stronghold in this part of the country. But they flagged down a local with a large covered flatbed, aiming to get a ride. After some bargaining, for the right money — anything could be bought in this part of the world — they had a ride with no questions asked. They hid themselves under several layers of tarps layered with horse manure on top to discourage the guards from looking underneath. What should have taken an hour by truck took three hours. After nine checkpoints, they finally reached the shores of Lake Qarun. They found a secluded spot near the water, and the tarp was pulled off. After the manure hit the ground, the squad piled out, ripe with the scent of days-old horse shit. Money changed hands, and they were soon left to their own.

Liam led them off the road and into the cover of an olive orchard on the lake's southwest shore. They set up camp, readying for what was to come, and found time to relax a bit as the sun set. Soon the night was deepening, requiring night vision goggles to progress. The infrared switch was accidentally switched on as Liam settled his goggles over his eyes. Reaching up to switch it off, he caught a glimpse of a thermal trail over the lake. Instantly, he signaled for the squad to be silent and take cover. They soon picked up the thermal trace again. Zooming in, they spotted several drones heading up the lakeshore their way. Liam ordered them to grab their gear, and they scurried ahead to find cover.

They were hustling through an unplanted area when they literally fell into the entrance of some old ruins — an unexpected twist of luck, though it cost Chase a twisted ankle. Being underground would completely cover their heat signature, allowing them to wait out the drones. As they waited, Liam began inspecting the ruins with caution, unsure about what they would find; snakes seemed likely. Everything in this part of the world seemed determined to kill them, after all. As he scouted, he couldn't get the picture of Indiana Jones having to cross a floor covered with snakes out of his head. But the ruin was empty of life, and very dusty, indicating that they were the first to visit in a long time. It was a good place to set up camp, so they established a bivouac from which they planned to conduct reconnaissance into Faiyum to locate El San Suhain, the reported leader of Kafr.

The next day, they cautiously exited the ruins and inspected their surroundings in the light of day. This structure was surrounded by seven-foot stones all the way around. From a distance, they looked like random boulders. Had they not fallen into it in the dark, they would never have seen the entrance.

Liam marked the entrance with his GPS, and they moved on, trying to minimize their occupation of the area. Covering their footprints as they entered the brush that covered the fertile area, they eased along the lakeshore, looking for their route to Faiyum. A small tributary provided a means to get into Faiyum undetected. Donning their camouflaged wetsuits and snorkel gear, they formed a human log, utilizing mini-jets to propel them along the surface of the water. Their hopes of finding a boat heading that way diminished as the day passed, hampering their progress. The light of day would provide no cover in the city, so they located an alcove off the main waterway to wait for darkness. After sundown, their wetsuits readily converted into light-absorbing night suits, enabling them to slink along the shadows to seek out their target.

The outskirts of the city flourished with the bustle of people going about their normal business. Avoiding those areas, they carefully trekked into the city center. Rounding a corner of what appeared to be a deserted alleyway, they came face-to-face with a Kafr militant. Liam's reaction was one of years of training in hand-to-hand combat; he had the soldier unconscious within seconds. Knowing there would be more patrols, they pulled him into a darkened building, securing the area.

His senses were on high alert. His thoughts were frantic, analyzing every detail of their passage through the city and this random encounter. Something seemed off. Interrogation was new for Liam, but he had to learn somewhere. This was his first prisoner, and he doubted it would be his last. Information was at a premium in this city, and they had to obtain it at all costs. Routine interrogation techniques were of little value for this war-hardened soldier, he knew, so he applied some of the chemical means he'd brought along — chemicals that increased pain and decreased willpower — in addition to a few rough tools.

After a few hours of treading lightly, Liam injected the prisoner with the chemicals and began a slow torture. Even the sturdiest of men will crumble under intense, enhanced pain. This one held up longer than Liam expected, but then, he had little experience to back up those expectations. The information came in spurts, as Liam's Farsi was middling at best. Drilling past the firewalls the brain uses to protect sensitive information, he finally got the answer he was looking for. "El San Suhain, him you seek? He is just an image! Everyone here is El San Suhain!"

Puzzled, Liam countered, "If I wasn't clear on who I want to find, it is the *man* El San Suhain, not the group," he said slowly in Farsi.

"El San Suhain is like Allah, one and all! You will find the image at Sultan Square!"

Liam figured his translation must be off. "An image is not what I seek."

The prisoner started shaking uncontrollably, blurting, "You should fear them! They are coming for me!" as he lay dying.

Thinking he must have given the man too much of the chemicals, Liam dismissed his final statement. Finding Sultan Square wasn't easy, it not being on any map. They had laid out their map to the city on the floor, looking for a central square, when a canister crashed through the window, filling the room with tear gas. "We're compromised. Follow me!" Liam ordered. But before they could regroup, they were hit with tranq darts. The effect was nearly instantaneous; all of them slumped to the ground.

Regaining consciousness, Liam found himself stripped of his gear, dressed only in a traditional local tunic. Oddly, he was unbound. He could only locate Sergeant Chase, and spent a few minutes helping him come to. The room was locked, indicating they were still prisoners. An intense search of the room revealed no way out. Giving up on escape for the moment, they settled in chairs set against the far wall, waiting for whatever came next.

After several hours, the door opened, and a man dressed in a flowing robe entered the room. "Lieutenant Rhett; Sergeant Chase. I fear you and your team have trespassed on holy ground. That required a price, which those under your command have paid with their lives."

A chill ran down Liam's spine. His men were dead? "We know nothing of holy ground. Under the UN charter, we are authorized to apprehend El San Suhain," he intoned.

"Follow me, and keep your eyes on the floor. If you raise your head, you will die. This is a temple of El San Suhain; we are all El San Suhain. Who among us do you seek?"

Entering a large sanctuary moments later, Liam observed hundreds of men lying prostrate on the ground, unmoving. Liam whispered to the militant, "Are they dead?"

"This is the Temple of …" The man said something Liam couldn't translate. "In English, the Temple of the Mind."

Chase, who was still limping, nearly stepped on one of the prostrate men, causing him to fall to the side. Reaching out to catch himself, his hands landed on the man beside him. Within seconds, the Sergeant's head was rolling across the floor, as his body collapsed. Liam's instinct to help his soldier was halted by his guide, who promptly gripped Liam's shoulder to hold him back. "As I said, this is a temple; if you defile it, you pay with your life."

Liam asked gruffly, "Why am I still alive, then?"

"To deter further efforts. You see these men on the ground? Some have been here for months, in that very position, never getting back up. They don't eat or drink or move once they drink the living water. Together, we form a mind-link with the community around us. We brought you here to show you that we are nonviolent. We pray for peace, and use our will to project it."

"Your definitions of 'peace' and 'nonviolent' and the rest of the world's are completely different, then," Liam grumbled.

"Well, peace is a means to an end, a beginning of new horizons, and requires a cleansing, yes? You were brought here to observe our skill and to gain respect for our power."

What Liam observed was a half-filled vial of some sort near the body of Sergeant Chase. Chase must have kicked it out of the hand of the man lying on the ground next to him. Seeing an opportunity, Liam asked if he could pay his last respects to his fallen friend. Granted that request, Liam knelt next to the Sergeant, with the vial positioned in between his legs. Lowering his head as if to pray, he placed his right hand on Chase's back, while his left hand moved to the vial. In one swift motion, the vial was inside his sleeve, and then he was standing. Suspecting he would be set free, since these fanatics seemed to want someone to hear their message, he wept, feeling for the vial, hoping it would provide some clues to what they were doing.

Later that evening, his captors loaded Liam into a helicopter and dropped him off at his predetermined rendezvous spot. Perplexed, Liam asked why they had chosen that location.

His guide told him, "Lieutenant, we knew when you arrived, what you were going to do, and your complete orders. Why do you think it was so easy for you to get to where you were going?" The man glared at him hawkishly. "You have heard and seen. Now go and tell your U.N. We are in control here, and we will protect our lands. Leave now, forever."

Back in Greece, Liam reported all that had happened, highlighting the vial as a potential key to this Kafr group's mass hysteria. Within an hour of submitting his report, he was whisked away by a group of non-uniformed officers — intelligence geeks, he suspected. From there, he was shoved aboard a transport plane headed for Germany, and then onto another headed to D.C. Not a word was said to him the whole time, just grunts and gestures when he asked questions. Sensing he had stepped into some international spy mess, he became very cautious of his words, very aware of his surroundings. After several plane changes, vehicle swaps, and base-to-base transports, he thought he might have arrived in the Pentagon E-Ring, but wasn't sure.

He was finally brought to table surrounded by drones in black suits. He bellowed out a laugh. This was entirely too much of a cliché, and he'd had enough. "Since nobody's gonna talk," he said, "I'll say everything. I put everything I know in my report, and know of nothing more."

The silence was too loud for him, but he endured. The door opened, and an aging Lieutenant General he didn't recognize entered the room with the vial he had acquired. It was empty now. After he stood at attention and saluted, she led the conversation with a greeting, and asked him to be patient a while longer. "This vial. You said it was from what you called 'the Temple of the Mind,' yet you saw no signs of any other vials?"

"I didn't have time to inspect every person lying on the ground, ma'am. The man leading me around said they drank 'the living water' before falling into their catatonic state."

"You didn't mention they were catatonic."

"I mean the state of not eating or drinking or getting up," Liam replied cautiously.

"We've analyzed what you brought back, Lieutenant. It contains highly complex nanotechnology, unlike anything we've ever seen. Your story doesn't fit the technology in this vial. How could such simpletons as those design and utilize such technology?"

Liam stared at the table, hands clasped, "I don't know, ma'am. My report is the truth. I know only what I observed, and did not have the luxury of looking around their quarters or the temple."

Many hours of questioning the veracity of every detail of his story ensued, followed by chemical interrogation. The latter was a turning point for him. When had the government started doing this to their own?

When he awoke in a hospital bed days later, the same general approached his bedside. "Now that we know who you are and whom you serve, we have a proposition for you," the hard-faced woman said. "The technology you found is one of the many new threats this country faces. You had the foresight to retrieve it, not knowing what it was or if it would cost you your life. I'm offering you an opportunity to become part of a new organization called the Homeland Intelligence Agency. You will lead the HIA's antiterrorism efforts, and help advance the cause of freedom around the world."

Liam thought for a moment. "Everything has a cost, ma'am. I doubt you would have told me all you have if you didn't expect me to say yes. Do I really have a choice?"

"You always have a choice, Mr. Rhett, though the alternative may not be what you like."

"Then I accept. What now?"

"You've already been advanced to the rank of major and will have an office and staff here in D.C.," she told him, as she handed him his new oak leaves and walked out.

In his new role, the first assignment he received was a grant proposal from a pioneering researcher in California, one Dr. John Everly, who had proposed the use of biological nanotech for treating illness and battlefield injuries. His orders were to leave immediately and enroll Everly in the program.

Chapter 3: Vassal Biogenetics

John sat quietly in his study after Major Rhett agreed that the government would bankroll his business, thinking of the road he must now travel. His ideas were excellent, he thought, but they were just that: ideas. What if he couldn't deliver? Would he be forever under the government's thumb? Was retirement ever in his future, or would he suddenly disappear or die at the government's whim? *Deep thoughts for this early in the day,* he mused.

Clearing his mind was nearly impossible. He wasn't going to waste even a second. As he rose, he noticed a folder tucked into the chair where Major Rhett had been sitting. A sticky note was attached to it with the words: "Thought you might need this." Thumbing through the folder, he found a dossier on a building that had the complete lab setup he needed, with what was described as "Pentagon-like security." The folder also contained a badge with his picture on it, though the name of the company was missing. He would have been shocked had they picked the name he had just thought of. Apparently the lab was already staffed with military doctors and researchers. Another note instructed him that the additional information he needed would find him later in the day.

#

The "information" was actually a military escort to his new company. He was taken to a nondescript building off the coastal highway. As the car pulled up, the guard checked their identification and ushered them through, though the guard himself was in plainclothes and did not appear to be military. The first floor of the building was bustling with office activity, and that continued to be true until they proceeded down two levels. This was where the real lab began, and where John was introduced to his new staff.

Entering a plainly decorated conference room, an Army captain without a name tag told him that everything he would hear from this point on would be national security secrets, as he slid a keycard across the table. The instructions were clear: he would be told what he needed to know when he needed to know it, no more. This wasn't his show to run; that would have to be earned through trust and sacrifice. The public story of this company would be shrouded in some truths and much subterfuge, making it impossible for outsiders to determine the reality of the situation. This would give him the cover he needed for public success, money, and publications. The latter, he thought, would be the most important for any physician aiming to become a highly-regarded expert in his field.

Curiously, a tour of the building had him bypassing many locked doors, making the show-and-tell of little importance. After a brief lunch, the role of puppet finally began. By then, he was regretting his deal with the devil. The staff showed him some of their work, all relating to the story he'd be telling in about two years regarding his company's first success. The invention was real; at least, it would be if what they were sharing was the complete truth, which he suspected it wasn't. The announcement he would make in two years was that he had created a T-cell therapy to cure certain types of cancer. Though it would in fact do as promised, he was never quite sure how they had accomplished the feat. It would be an eloquent story, with a call for clinical trials, though nobody would ever be entered into them, since the data was already sitting right in front of him. Then the FDA would announce the approval of a new treatment that would revolutionize cancer therapy.

Two Years Later

Just as planned, the story unfolded without any deviation after two years. Dr. John Everly was nominated for and received the Nobel Prize for Medicine three years after the announcement of their miracle treatment, shortly before his son's fourth birthday. His speech was handed to him a year before he even knew he'd be nominated. With the script already written, John had only lackluster enthusiasm about contributing anything significant to Vassal's affairs — that is, until the following year, when he was pressed by the need to develop a real cure for Brill's AML.

John began vetting his original idea for a bio-based nanomachine through the rigors of animal testing at Vassal. This eventually morphed into a prion-like programmable device. The programming would consist of genetic code, peptides, that would drive an intended response. *He kept this hidden from his staff until the need arose to put these into action.* In general, prions were regarded by the medical community as transmissible diseases, including what was publicly known as "Mad Cow Disease," or Bovine Spongiform Encephalitis in medical parlance. Prions typically consisted of misfolded proteins that had unintended consequences. Using this concept, John could link peptides and fold them in a way that would impart an effect anywhere in the body he wanted. By fooling the body's cells into taking up the misfolded peptide, as those cells would normally view them as damaged and try to destroy them, he could then unpack the instructions hidden inside the prions. The body used peptides to communicate many different signals cell to cell; John saw the opportunity there, and capitalized on it.

#

John was back at the lab just one day after his hellish trip to Guantanamo Bay, recreating the cure he'd paid a high price to unravel. He was eerily surprised that the staff at Vassal not only knew every detail of his prion treatments with the prisoners, but had actually begun to tailor them to treat Brill's leukemia. He received multiple compliments on the genius of his work, something they said none of them could have fathomed had they not seen it in action.

There were some sticking points in the treatment, involving the random code John had hurriedly left in during his rush to perfect the protocol. Since it had been built to drive the treatment to target bone marrow cells, the random code couldn't be removed without starting over. The code, however, shared a close resemblance to the transmitter peptide of the cerebrum, and the P3 beta-amyloid peptide of the right temporal lobe. Since John had been trying to cure the brains and bodies of the prisoners, he'd mashed together two treatment regimens into one. Fortunately, as the prion treatment's modification grew more specific to bone marrow, those unintended pieces of peptide code became less of a concern.

Or so he thought until he learned, to his horror, that the first test cases had been a disaster. The chimpanzees Vassal was using to mimic human leukemia began to exhibit paranoid behavior, attacking each other in fits of rage, then falling into a catatonic state, never to awaken. The staff had conveniently omitted this from their report to John on their early progress. Later experiments built steadily upon his refinements even as he was experimenting on the prisoners. They quickly engineered improvements, and now that John was here to guide them, were close to perfecting the treatment. The one hurdle they couldn't overcome was how to fix the cells that weren't dividing — the legacy ones. The radiation should have killed all targeted cells and the chemotherapy all the cancer, so any cells that evaded the treatment would be problematic later.

John's guidance gave his "prion-eers," as they referred to themselves, the direction they needed. Within days, they had solved the most glaring issues and most of the minor ones; those left untapped were the mood changes and increased physical strength, neither of which were life-threatening. So they moved on to perfecting the treatment regimen. John soon had a protocol that would be approved by the FDA (though the approval was a non-reviewed signature). They had devised a series of incremental prion builds, as they couldn't get one to do everything. This required about six months of treatments, along with some genetic engineering of the chromosomes, specifically chromosomes Fifteen and Thirteen. The marrow that Brill had already received from Sirum provided the genetic template they could use to modify all of Brill's cells, including those in the brain that had long since stopped dividing.

Brill became a regular at Vassal for the next few years. He showed up every Wednesday and Saturday for tweaks to his treatment. He was the one and only patient to ever receive the prion treatment, though thousands had signed up for the clinical study that never happened. His treatment was completed with a high level of success, though at first the prions were continually adapting and causing Brill to exhibit unusual symptoms; when they did, they had to be stopped. Like viruses, though, once in a living system, they were unstoppable. To stop the unstoppable, you have to use it to your advantage and let it keep going. To do this, John introduced a new viral prion into Brill's cells. Its main function was to seek out any free-flowing prions and destroy them.

Brill enjoyed visiting his Dad's company. He learned quickly and was soon picking up complex skills and an advanced education, as the scientists were eager to explain their work. They never considered a seven-year-old a security risk. Brill was eager to spend time with his Dad, relishing every moment. They played many games while he was undergoing therapy. His dad often created new games, due to Brill quickly tiring of the old ones. One game he invented was a secret code only the two of them knew. This game they only played at home. John crafted a complete language in this code, which only Brill could decipher.

Brill began learning at an accelerated rate; sometimes, he seemed to know things without being taught. One weekend, John and Jenna decided to have Brill take music lessons. They wanted him to experience some culture, and figured playing the piano would be a great skill for him to learn. The instructor, knowing it to be Brill's first lesson, started with the basics. In the background, Mozart's masterpieces were playing softly. The instructor was chatting with John when Brill slipped onto the bench and began playing Mozart's Fifth perfectly, without missing a beat. Later, as the stunned adults listened, Brill proceeded to play a complex, haunting piece none of them could identify. It was the most moving piece they had ever heard. John apologized to the instructor, explaining that Brill had never had any lessons, and he didn't understand how Brill could play like he did. As John was speaking, Brill made his way to a violin and began to play the same pieces he had just performed on the piano.

This was their first introduction to Brill's incredible abilities.

#

Ten years into the company, John was greeted by now-Colonel Rhett as he entered Vassal one sunny spring morning. *Liam must be doing the right things if he's moving up in the ranks*, John thought bitterly. That day, Liam invited John into a room in his own lab that he had yet to enter.

It was filled with monitors and a large boardroom-style table. "Please sit, Dr. Everly."

"Gee, thanks, Colonel," John said, a bit sarcastically. "Congrats on the promotion. You've done well since we last met."

"Dr. Everly, I didn't invite you here for pleasantries," the Colonel replied solemnly. "My time here is limited, so please pay attention."

"Always."

"Ten years may seem like a long time to you, and you've helped the team here make excellent progress on their work, as well as on your own special projects. When you went to Guantanamo several years ago, however, you stumbled on some of the top-secret work taking place here at Vassal. Work that you have not been allowed to see yet."

"Well, enlighten me," John snapped. "It pisses me off that you'd hold back that tech."

"That wasn't in my decision space, Doctor."

"Oh? You made me torture men to get what I needed. You realized that if I could've walked away, I would have?"

Rhett fixed him with a serious stare. "We needed you to show us your character and how far you would go if necessary. You went that extra mile, as any good soldier would."

"I'm not a damned soldier. Don't patronize me. I did what I had to, and I'd do it again if it was necessary to save my son."

"Exactly, sir, which is why you're now going to have everything unveiled to you."

"Really," John sneered. "Is it the whole show? Or just enough to whet my appetite?"

"Dr. Everly. John. In time, we *will* unveil what is needed, as it's needed."

John shook his head, frustrated, as Liam directed his attention to a monitor. The video he was finally allowed to view was on par with the best science fiction movies he'd seen. The image showed a tiny machine linking up to other machines inside a cell, one that looked like a neuron, given the branching filaments that had to be axons. If he understood what he was shown, the nanomachine intercepted the electrical signals that passed from neuron to neuron, changing them somehow. Liam explained how the neurons could be modulated to change thoughts, or to increase or decrease pain. The nanomachines themselves were "simple" designs that acted as conduits for signals passing through the neurons. As the nanos connected to each other, they could change the signal or insert a new one into the synaptic flow. This allowed them to drive the response the programmer wanted, making them the perfect tools for interrogation.

John left the demonstration wondering what the hell he'd gotten into, but knowing that it was worth the cost of his soul if it helped him save Brill's life.

#

The revelations were harder to understand than he had expected; he had a decade of work by the clandestine branch of Vassal to catch up on. A few months later, he was still learning how the machine-based nanotechnology worked, frustrated that it only worked on neurons. Surely they could have generalized them during the developmental process. An avid learner, John wanted, *needed* to understand when the nanos were invented, who invented them, and how they worked. That information seemed to be nonexistent, or still classified. The microscopic machines had just seemed to appear about ten years ago. The early experiments in the files indicated the scientists didn't know what they had, or how it worked. John wondered if the government had stolen the technology and then reverse-engineered it somehow.

Initially, they injected mice with the nanobots, and soon they were all paralyzed. Some unnamed scientist then decided to inject them into the brain of a mouse. That mouse survived, piquing their curiosity. When they gave the mouse a CT scan, it went into convulsions. From there, they began to figure out uses for the devices. One oddity that kept being reported was that multiple mice in the same cage with the nanobots in their heads would exhibit simultaneous behavior, indicating a shared psychosis. The phenomenon couldn't be reproduced in humans, but they had other uses in the human brain. The side effect, though, was irreversible brain damage.

John was eventually allowed into a laboratory previously closed to him, one filled with sophisticated tech. This was where the nanobots were created and refined. In time, he became an expert at modifying the tiny machines. He professed that he wanted to use them to work with his prions and cure many diseases. John was only allowed to work with a simplistic version of the nanotech, however. He had directly observed the more complex bots during his time at Guantanamo, and it was obvious to him that those he had access to were the child's toy versions of the real ones, though he kept this to himself.

He was fast becoming suspicious of his staff. He caught them monitoring his movements and constantly observing him, though they tried to mask this with other activities. He knew he needed some of the advanced bots to give Brill an advantage, if his son ever became the object of the military's programs. John suspected he could reprogram the bots to give Brill some protection against the interrogation techniques that he had personally observed, but first, he needed to catch some of the complex models. Knowing the advanced nanos used neurotransmitters as an energy source, he felt confident he could devise a trap. His actions would be captured on the surveillance cameras, of course, so he would have to make it non-obvious that he was trapping them deliberately.

Acquiring the neurotransmitters was the difficult part. Utilizing the supply at Vassal would draw attention to his intentions.

John struck on the idea of capturing neurotransmitters from the patients upon whom he was performing neurosurgery in his private practice; that was the best hope he had of obtaining the bait for the bots. The tricky part here would be keeping his hospital staff out of the loop; they had to be, for their safety. A course of action popped into his head: the aspirator the nurses used to clean the surgical area of fluids. John invented a control mechanism to divert the fluids from the suction to a jar behind the scenes, actually at the feet of all those in the room. He would place the controller for the diversion on his fingernail. It would be a simple task to tap that finger to activate the switch, tapping it again to switch it off; nobody would be the wiser.

The vials of neurotransmitters John collected by doing this over the following months were more than enough to set the trap. He used just half of one of the vials, freezing the rest for use at a later date if necessary. In his mind, this would be a delicate operation. Making the scene that played out in the surveillance feeds look as natural as possible was going to be a challenge.

The next day, while working in the bot lab at Vassal, he set the trap. A Petri dish in his main lab had the neurotransmitter fluid loaded onto it, and he carried the dish with him into the bot lab. This next part would have to look natural. John had several dishes that all looked the same, with the trap having a slight chip out of the top rim. That one he placed closest to the adjoining workbench. The timing would need to play out perfectly, he knew, as that scientist wouldn't show until later in the afternoon. This meant he needed to continue his work in the bot lab until well after that point.

As John conducted some routine tests on his simplified nanobots, the scientist with the advanced bots started his own work across the way. John let his dishes sit out for another hour as he kept busy with his efforts to adapt the simple bots to somatic and blood cell use. By then, he figured he must have captured at least a few of the advanced bots, so he carefully sealed up all the plates after dosing his nano-cultures with a sterile saline solution.

Later, he discovered that he had indeed captured some of the complex nanos he was after. He set out to reprogram the bots and smuggle them out of the facility. That should be easy to do, he figured, since nobody could actually *see* them. The bots were more of a challenge to reprogram than anticipated, though, as they used deep learning to constantly rewrite their code and create their own. John managed to strip the code down to just its functionality. After some very late nights, he was able to write his own code and upload it to the bots; it told them how to keep the brain functioning, resisting interrogation while minimizing pain. After further thought, he dismissed the idea of smuggled the bots out. Getting them directly into Brill was easier.

John planned to "accidentally" introduce the bots into Brill during his next adjustment at Vassal. He'd have to lure them into Brill in a way similar to how he'd trapped them in the first place. His plan was simple, and should go unnoticed by the constant surveillance. He had surreptitiously placed some of the neurotransmitter solution into an isopropyl alcohol bottle. When Brill arrived at the lab, John said he could look at some cancer cells under his microscope if he liked. As expected, Brill was excited by the idea. Before allowing him at the microscope, John dabbed a bit of the neurotransmitter solution onto a sterile cloth, then wiped the eyepieces with it, as if he were cleaning it off with alcohol. This was the easiest way to seed Brill with the bait for the nanobots. He dropped the cloth into the incinerator chute and washed his hands thoroughly, as he did many times a day. He looked into the baited eyepieces, needing to dose himself first to be certain they were not of harm to Brill. He set the stage for what would happen next.

Brill, now almost nine years old, was eagerly examining the cells under the microscope when John cracked the lid of the dish containing the bots, which he'd placed right next to the 'scope. He knew it would only take minutes for the entire host of bots to move to Brill's eyes, as they would quickly consume the neurotransmitter fluid on the eyepieces; and once in Brill's eyes, they would be drawn into the brain. John realized that the risk was high; if detected, he would never be able to break free of the government. He might even be imprisoned or killed. His need to protect Brill was too great, though, and outweighed the risk of him getting caught.

Without any evidence of the bots in John's lab, the staff would only have their suspicions once they discovered them missing. If they ever did.

#

A month after he infected Brill with the nanobots, the confrontation John was dreading actually occurred. Colonel Rhett had arrived for an update the evening before, which usually didn't involve John. He rarely saw Rhett these days, given that he was only at Vassal when he could fit his research in around his surgical schedule.

This time, it was clear that something was off. John was summoned into Rhett's office about an hour after John arrived at the lab. He entered the office expecting just him and the colonel, but this time there were two other Army officers present, both captains. One had a laptop open, ready to transcribe all that was said. The other never said a word; he just watched John. *Must be a psychiatrist,* John thought, *trying to read my body language.* Colonel Rhett motioned for him to take a seat at the chair in the middle of the room. "Dr. Everly, welcome."

"Thanks. Will I be long? I have some experiments running that I need to address shortly."

Liam brushed the question aside and jumped right into interrogation mode, "Dr. Everly, two months ago, you were working in the nano lab when some experimental bots went missing. These were special nanobots. A new breed, if you will."

Addressing me formally. Must be a serious matter, John thought.

"A review of the surveillance footage shows you working directly across from the area where the nanobots went missing. We're not accusing you of anything, Dr. Everly, just trying to get to the bottom of this. What experiments were you performing that day?" Rhett specified the date.

"Ah. I'll have to check my notes, but I believe those were my first attempts to merge the prion and nanobot technologies. I still have those experiments going, if you would like to see them. They're promising."

"Please explain to us every detail of what you were doing."

"I had engineered my prions to fuse with the nanobots to which you had recently given me access. In my Petri dishes, I had a type of brain cells called glial cells. They insulate neurons, basically. Those cells are particularly problematic in neurodegenerative ailments, such as Alzheimer's and Parkinson's diseases. I was trying to see if I could reprogram the nerve impulses to be more uniform, a first step toward treating such illnesses."

Rhett scowled thunderously. "Dr. Everly, you were given explicit instructions to keep living cells *out* of the nano labs!"

John sat up straight and glared at the man. "No, Colonel Rhett, I was *not* given any such instructions! It was the other way around. I was instructed to never remove the nanobots from the lab, and I didn't. Completely opposite of what you just said."

"Hardly a difference in the end, Dr. Everly."

"It's a *huge* difference. Colonel Rhett, if I'm to utilize the nanobot technology to cure diseases or to help with battlefield injuries, I *have* to have them interact with living cells. Since I couldn't remove the bots from their lab, I brought the cells to them."

Rhett's mood lightened a bit, and he nodded thoughtfully. "Well then, Dr. Everly, thank you for your time. In the future, please clear all experiments on the nanobots ahead of time. I will send an officer to your lab to inspect the dishes to see if those missing nanobots hitched a ride somewhere."

"Fine."

That was too easy, thought John as he went back to work. Within ten minutes of getting back to his work, several soldiers entered his lab with equipment unlike anything he had observed at Vassal. The equipment appeared to be some species of locator — and they should shortly find the leftover nanobots, right where John had left them. He had used a fine needle to poke microscopic holes in the bottoms of two of his Petri dishes. This would cause the glial cells he was working with to leak neurotransmitters, leaving the complex nanobots clinging to the bottoms of the dishes. A well-designed decoy, but John was a bit too proud of himself.

As expected, the soldiers located the bots and immediately began questioning him. Oddly, they appeared to have no idea the nanobots were attracted to neurotransmitters. They believed the nanobots derived their energy from sugars in the blood. Wrong as they were, it would help to clear John and provide a cover of mistaken attraction of the bots to the dishes. After an intense round of questioning, they left the room with the nanobots. *Whew,* thought John, *I may have dodged a bullet there.*

Several days later, John was summoned back to Colonel Rhett's office right after he entered the building. His silent watchers were there again. "Dr. Everly, as you know, we found the missing nanobots, but there was a problem with them."

"A problem?" John asked with as questioning a look as he could muster, since he already knew what the problem was.

"Yessir, a problem. The nanobots are dead. In all the years we've been working with them, we've never been able to shut them off. They're always active. These, however, are not."

"You mentioned these were special, a new breed. Maybe they behave differently than your previous versions."

"Dr. Everly, you're not here to play detective. Somehow, your experiments caused these nanobots to deactivate permanently. What happened to those Petri dishes when you brought them back to your lab?"

John shrugged. "I still have them, as your men found, but I destroyed the merged prions before I even left the nanolab. The bots you were letting me use needed to be deactivated, so I tailored an electroprotein solution to react with them that I added to the colonies before I left the lab. Check your video; you should see me doing so. Once that protein bound to the bots, I hit them with theta waves in the 1-4 hertz range. The proteins were designed to modulate the theta waves into directed pulses that would destabilize the core of the nanobots. I knew this would also keep the glial cells alive, and allow them to keep functioning."

The questioning went on for some time, but John felt he handled it well. He sensed some skepticism from those fielding the questions. Eventually, though, they let him go back to his lab; and from that time on, he had very little interaction with Colonel Rhett. From time to time, John noticed things missing from his lab, and realized that other items had been moved. His suspicions began to grow.

At home, he kept a special log of everything he had done, using the special code he and Brill had developed years earlier.

#

By the time he reached adulthood, Brill Everly was miraculously cured of AML, and by the time he followed his father's footsteps into medical school, the threat of it coming back was past.

At his father's urging, Brill never worked at Vassal during his medical-school years, though he wanted to. Brill's area of specialty was neurology rather than oncology. After completing his medical degree, he planned to do his residency near home at one of the local university hospitals.

He was visiting home one evening when his Dad called him into the study. The discussion was a somber one. John began writing on individual sheets of copy paper in the code they had developed years earlier. As he was writing, the conversation centered on John's fears. "Brill, when you look at the world around you, things are not all as they seem."

"Not sure I follow you, Dad."

"I've been working at Vassal for decades now. The security is always tight there, but lately it feels like a noose around my neck."

Brill just sat and stared, not sure what to say next.

"Colonel Rhett has changed his behavior around me. He acts suspicious, more so than usual. I have to watch what I say now. The staff doesn't freely ask me for advice like they used to, and I get the sense they're distancing themselves from me." He handed Brill the coded papers.

Brill read through them, translating every word in his head.

"When the time is right, son, the information you need will find you," John said heavily. He got up and lifted a painting off the wall, motioning Brill over to him. Laying the painting on the desk, he picked up a device hooked into his computer that looked like an endoscope and aimed it at a specific spot on the back of the painting, highlighting an odd flaw. The monitor proved the "endoscope" to be an advanced microscope. The image soon clarified to show something that looked like a microchip. It zoomed in even further to show advanced circuitry, like a miniature cell phone on that tiny surface.

"Brill, caution is your best friend. Use it frequently and wisely. Once you graduate, please go far enough away from here that you can come into your own," John stated, putting the painting back on the wall. Brill nodded somberly, getting the message.

He graduated a few months later, and began looking for a residency anywhere but near home, as his Dad had urged. Shortly after, he learned that his father was being honored by the state for his accomplishments, with an awards ceremony followed by speeches from multiple high-level politicians and military leaders. During the event, Brill was seated next to John and Colonel Rhett on the stage, along with a few dignitaries and politicians. The speeches were rather boring to Brill, except for his Dad's; Brill listened intently, watching him from stage right.

When it all fell apart, it did so suddenly. Movement from the left caught Brill's eye as all hell broke loose. His Dad had just finished thanking multiple people, as the crowd and those on stage rose to give applause. The applause hit its crescendo when gunfire rang out, and Dr. John Everly's head snapped back as blood gushed from a wound in his forehead.

Instinctively, Brill tried to rush to him, but a strong hand from Colonel Rhett latched onto his shoulder, bringing him to the floor of the stage. Within seconds, Brill was pinned down by two other people, ostensibly for his own safety, but nobody was helping his father! Brill's screams to let him up went unanswered as he laid there for what seemed an eternity as medical personnel struggled to reach the elder Dr. Everly through the panicking crowd. Meanwhile, every other VIP was rushed off stage, while his Dad just lay there bleeding.

Brill's eternity ended after five minutes, when Liam Rhett released his hold on Brill and the other men released his legs. Brill's suspicions of the military were cemented at the core of his being right then, for he firmly believed he could have helped his father. They had just let him die, as if they had *wanted* him to die.

Paramedics carted his Dad to an ambulance, and that was the last Brill saw of him until the funeral.

Chapter 4: Liora Abrams

Liora Abrams was a little shit of a kid with a mouth that would shame a sailor, a kid who would rather roam the streets of Jerusalem than sit in school. The daughter of an American Marine, Andrew Rhett, and an Israeli, Sharon Abrams, her life could be little more than one of worry and heartache. Her early years saw her Mom and Dad in an on-again, off-again relationship, never cemented as a marriage. At the age of eight, her Mom became her sole parent when her Dad met a fiery death at the hands of terrorist IED. She and Sharon retreated into the heart of Jerusalem, more for the protection and the structure that the traditional Jewish neighborhood provided than anything else. During this time, they survived several suicide bombers' intentions, only to pay a price in the end.

In her sixth year of only having one parent, Liora's world came crashing down when her Mom was caught in a blast that instantly turned Liora into an orphan. She became a ward of the state. Anger and hate became a way of life for her.

Word soon reached Colonel Liam Rhett about Sharon's death and Liora's predicament. He'd kept tabs on his niece as a favor to his brother, and now felt a deep obligation to help. He was the next of kin and only family Liora had, though she wouldn't likely see him in that light. Fortunately, a year before his brother died, Andrew had set up a will that would give Liam custody if something were to happen to both him and Sharon.

Liam had never met Liora, nor any child like her. She was a hellcat wrapped in the body of a fourteen-year-old posing as a woman in her early twenties. He arranged for the state school to hold her until he arrived, since Liora had a habit of disappearing on a daily basis. When they met at last, the silence was deafening until Liam finally spoke. "Miss Abrams, you seem to live for trouble. The administrator and I have discussed the options you have left."

"Who the hell cares? I have no family, so I'm nobody's fuckin' problem."

"Maybe. My guess is that the moment you hit eighteen, you'll be *somebody's* problem, if not before. You had better hope it's not the Palestinians, as they don't take kindly to Israelis."

"What's it to you, Mister?"

"Miss. Abrams, Liora," Liam said as softly as his military training would allow. "I'm the only family you have left. I'm your uncle. Your father's brother, Liam Rhett."

A stunned look crossed her face for a moment before she spat, "So you think you can just walk in and take over after all these years? Do I look like I *need* help?"

"You do, actually. Everyone needs help sometimes, Liora. I made a promise to your dad that I would look out for you if he and your mom weren't around, and I intend to keep it."

"What took you so long? Sounds like the only help you provide is when someone begs for it."

"Your mother didn't want my help, but I've kept tabs on you and your mother. When I heard the news about her death, I dropped everything, and here I am. That was my deal with Andrew."

The conversation continued for some time, with Liora lobbing many curses and epithets at Liam. In the end, whether she wanted to or not, she left for the States with Liam, and was now officially his problem. But even as they were making their way back to his home — an Army base in North Carolina — Liora was planning her next move. She didn't consider the brilliant strategic mind of a career military officer in her plans, though, as he anticipated her every move.

Life in North Carolina was rough for both Liora, who had to adjust to a structured military life as well as the discrimination that came from being a foreigner in the Deep South, and for Liam, having to raise a defiant adolescent. After six months, she'd had enough. Planning her escape was the challenging part, since she was deep in a military base on a very routine schedule. Her free time, though, proved to be her undoing. Growing up on the streets of Jerusalem did not avail one of the First World privileges that many Americans take for granted. The one she most cherished was her smartphone. It opened up a whole new world to her. She lived without fear, and openly posted about her dissatisfaction with her current state. Snapchat was her favorite social media site.

Her life appeared boring, until she met someone who said all the things she wanted and needed to hear. He said he was the same age as her, and the photos he posted did not contradict him. The conversation built over time, and she reached out to him for help in her escape. They planned a location to meet up, a place Liora thought would be far enough away from Liam that he would never find her, and she could lose herself in this great big country.

The photos she posted of herself were more revealing than a girl of her age should ever post. She was easy to spot in a crowd, and wouldn't go unnoticed. Thinking she needed a disguise, she found a cowboy hat and sunglasses. These did little to hide her beauty, only magnify it, but in her mind, it was a disguise. She found her route of escape over the next few days, and asked "Brad" to be there to help her out. He was more than eager, though his request was odd, she thought. He wanted her to leave all her belongings behind, to not bring any jewelry and wear flip-flops rather than normal shoes. That was an odd request for late March, since it was still cold out at night; nevertheless, she followed his instructions.

The ride she found was a flatbed pickup as it departed camp, unbeknownst to the occupants of the vehicle. She only had the geo-coordinates to Brad's location, and had to use her phone's GPS to know when to jump out of the truck. It was nearing dark, so she was able to exit the vehicle at a stop sign without being seen. An hour's hike found her in a remote location. There was a small travel trailer with a blue car in front of it, just as Brad had described.

Liora approached the door and knocked, nervously, an unusual feeling for someone normally so self-confidant. The door cracked open, and a voice invited her in. Slowly, she pushed the door wide and entered, the hair on the back of her neck telling her this might not be such a good idea after all. Her limbic system should have taken over at that point, but Liora was determined to see this through.

As she entered, the door slammed shut. Startled, she turned to see what had happened, but the only light came from the table in front of her, with a single chair waiting. The voice asked her to sit and have a drink — the alcohol she had posted she wanted to drink, Kentucky bourbon. Following directions, she sat and started to sip the drink. The voice from the background kept urging her to enjoy her drink, to drink more, even though every instinct in her told her to run.

After two sips, her vision started to fog up, and that was the last thing she remembered for a while. Unknown to her, the drink was laced with Fentanyl and codeine, two powerful sedatives. When she woke up hours later, her clothes had been exchanged for a bathrobe, and she couldn't move. Her hands and feet were chained to a wall. She was now in a dark, damp room, probably someone's basement. Fear overtook her as she realized she was no longer in control of her life. She had willingly left solid protection and a sure future for one of uncertain escape. Now she was under the control of a complete stranger. She screamed for hours, pulling at the chains until her wrists were bloody, but nothing helped. She finally sat there sobbing, praying for a miracle. If only Liam could find her... then the weight of her mistakes hit her. She'd left no trail; only her phone could trace her here. She was hoping that Liam would be worried enough to start looking for her before she was moved to another location.

The hours dragged into days. She would occasionally find a bowl of food and a jug of water inside the room, along with a bedpan to relieve herself in. Her fear turned into panic as she realized that every time she drank the water whoever it was left her, she fell unconscious for who knew how long.

She didn't know day from night, or how much time had passed.

#

Liam arrived home for dinner at the same time every night. He was quite punctual, and made sure to spend as much time with Liora as he could. She, too, was never late... except for tonight. Thinking she must be with friends — she had met a few — he ate in silent solitude. Towards bedtime, however, he began to get worried. Trying her cell many times with no answer, he called up the parents of the few friends she had. All but one said that the last time they saw her was after school. That one mentioned that he had seen her hop in the back of a flatbed truck. Liam knew exactly who that truck belonged to, since there were very few civilian cars on base. The driver was no help, though, as he hadn't known anyone was in the back of his truck.

Now on the verge of panicking, the ordinarily unflappable Colonel Rhett had finally encountered a situation where he didn't know what to do. Not finding Liora's cell in his home, he called up his communications officer. The whole base was on alert as word spread quickly that Liora was missing, possibly kidnapped. Liam was a beloved officer, and everyone stepped up to help, even those off-duty. They had trained for things like this, and were always ready for action.

The communications staff quickly honed in on Liora's digital trail; in fact, they found her cell still pinging a tower. All her social media sites were scoured for anything from her. They found her Snapchat account still active, and were able to use the locations function of that app to pinpoint where her cell was. Choppers were loaded with Army Rangers and immediately dispatched to its location. In ten minutes, they had located the trailer with the phone, but whoever had been there was gone. The evidence indicated that the occupants had fled a few hours before, leaving nothing behind but some trash — and Liora's smartphone.

With very little to go on, Liam's comms officer reported that modern social apps would often grab neighboring numbers from other phones in their vicinity, usually to push advertisements. Since Snapchat was still open, it had snared the cell numbers of the kidnappers as the last within its range. Liam's communication staff easily pulled all the relevant info, and were soon tracking those numbers — but nothing was pinging. These people were careful; probably professionals, Liam figured. It was now two days since her disappearance, and Liam was getting extremely worried and frustrated.

One of the items the kidnappers had left in the trash was a receipt to a fast food restaurant; that gave them something to go on, and it happened that the restaurant had a full suite of security cameras. Liam's team analyzed the surveillance footage from it and all the buildings surrounding the restaurant, and homed in on the time stamp to see the blue car. The faces of the people inside were quite clear. A man and a woman sat in that car, but the woman wasn't Liora; she was much older. The man was a very heavy-set white male, probably in his late forties.

Liam was getting pissed now; they'd messed with the wrong family. By this point, he strongly suspected these were human traffickers. Their faces registered as known sex offenders, and multiple potential locations of operations were listed in the relevant databases. Liam mobilized most of the Army personnel in the state, and a BOLO was issued for the two suspects.

Drones and satellites located heat signatures at the third location on their list. This house, located in the deep forests of North Carolina, should only have held a small family — but they detected over twenty heat signatures. Liam personally led the Rangers in the assault. A team of forty in Apache Blackhawks quietly touched down outside the house, and the perimeter was secured as two gunmen were taken out with silent shots by snipers. Liam's team approached the house, viewing the interior with their advanced infrared detectors. There were four adults inside, all carrying guns. *Good enough,* thought Liam, and ordered his team to take them out, shooting with armor piercers through the walls.

That was quickly and efficiently accomplished, and they rushed inside to find nineteen young girls and boys of all ages, drugged and chained to the walls, wallowing in their own filth. Liam raced from person to person before finally locating an unresponsive Liora; fearing the worst, he felt for a pulse. His heart leaped as he felt a weak throb. She was still alive! He sagged with relief.

All the kids were alive, but some were in poor condition. They were ferried in the Blackhawks to the nearest base, and nursed back to health as Liam worked to unite them with their families. When Liora awoke, the most genuine hug she had ever given was Liam's surprise. He hugged her back, feeling an emotion he rarely felt but desperately needed: love. This time he didn't hold back the tears; they wept together and hugged as tightly as she could stand.

Thereafter, Liam set out on a mission to eradicate the brand of human trash who had kidnapped her. These modern-day slave traders, human traffickers, were a threat to national security — or at least, that was the case he made to gain support from his superiors. He even believed it. The intel they gathered from Liora's rescue led to them to a network that spanned the globe. The investigation fanned out from North Carolina to Texas, and then to California, revealing a constant train of human movement, hitherto undetected, stretching across the U.S. into Mexico. From there, it reached everywhere in the world.

While Liam's initial push was driven by his need for revenge to clear his conscience over what Liora had faced, it soon became much more. The network was also a weapons and drug-smuggling web of deceit and criminal activity. What Liam thought would be a rapid push and quick eradication turned into a multi-year crusade, as his teams followed the trail of the regional leader of one of the smuggling cells.

They tracked him to Southeast Thailand, where Liam found breadcrumbs of information that hit him hard. This criminal was the same man thought to have killed his brother almost twenty years before.

#

Liora's Israeli citizenship had its advantages for her Uncle Liam. When she was old enough, at her request he used his connections to get the Mossad to accept her into their program; her being an Israeli by birth made his case more persuasive. She had the looks and the toughness to be one of the best. A person whom everyone wants to befriend and who can blend in anywhere makes the perfect spy. In addition to her toughness, Liora was incredibly intelligent; speaking seven languages, she was at home no matter where she went. Furthermore, having been a criminal in her early years, she was adept at picking other criminals out of a crowd, or, if necessary, getting close to them, personally and professionally.

At the age of twenty-four, Liora emerged from military training as one of their most valued new assets. She was stunning, with soft blue eyes silhouetted against her deep brown hair and naturally swarthy skin. At six feet tall and slender of frame, she imposed a commanding appearance in most situations. When she entered the room, people gravitated towards her. Within a year, had performed her first few missions flawlessly.

Killing wasn't her thing, but it was something she eventually had to embrace, an unintended consequence of the situations in which she sometimes found herself.

#

The intel that Liam's team had most recently acquired about the smuggling ring's criminal mastermind led them to the remote village of Phaimi, Thailand. The leader of the human trafficking group claimed to be a descendant of China's "lost" Kuomintang's Nationalist Army, and was loyal only to himself. His group had embraced terroristic ways, and was heavily involved in activities that landed him on Liam's radar. Liam's personal interest was in both pursuing his vendetta to avenge his brother's death, and in setting right at least one part of the world.

The region was difficult to gain entry into, so Liam reached out to his friends at the Mossad and requested that

Liora infiltrate them and carry out the mission. As it happened, the Mossad's interests aligned with Liam's, and thus began Liora's most difficult mission to date, one that would engage her far longer than anyone could have anticipated. The path to Phaimi would take several months to years for Liora, as she first needed to gain the trust of a Chinese syndicate that had ties to the Thailand group.

Her odyssey began when she entered the outskirts of Shanghai, looking for a place to call home for a few months. Speaking fluent Mandarin did little to help her gain the trust of the locals, so she dressed and looked the part of a poor foreigner living in the city's slums. After a few weeks, she found work at a courier service. She would have to ride packages, deliver food, or whatever was needed from one person to another, navigating a bustling city with few traffic controls. The days were long, the pay meager. But Liora persevered, keeping a log of her deliveries and an eye out for the contact she was seeking.

On a particularly rainy afternoon, she had a delivery to an office tower downtown. The package was high-priority, and required her to move non-stop or risk punishment from her employers. This was odd, as they had never threatened her before. Arriving at the office building, soaked from a ride in the rain, she quickly toweled off and made her way to the top floor. Must be important, as she was rarely allowed to hand-deliver inside office buildings. The recipient was a military man, she was certain, though he was in a suit and tie. He made small talk with her — unusual, since delivery people were considered the lowest of low class, and interacting with the upper class, which this man clearly was, was frowned upon. The small talk turned into a whole conversation; this was the contact she had been was hunting. After ten minutes, he offered her a job on the spot. The conditions were that she accept a new wardrobe and living quarters, and pay them off with the work she was about to do. Without hesitation, she accepted.

Her new job went well beyond courier duty. Liora soon realized why she had been recruited for this role: her beauty and command of Mandarin, a plus for the business clients with whom she would interact. It took the better part of a year for Liora to work her way up the ranks, as the import/export company had many layers of security in the form of management, each required the gaining of trust. Trust was a valued asset in Chinese corporations; and once gained, allowed for broad privileges.

The Mao Tung Che was a powerful organization of organized criminal businesses with deep ties in Chinese and other Asian governments. Liora, now acting under deep cover, rarely had contact with her true employers; everyone was constantly under surveillance, especially the higher up in the organization one went. She had noticed, of late, an increase in surveillance, and suspected she would soon be moving up in the organization. Her rise to power took cunning and endurance. Her skills, many physical in nature, were a valuable asset for gaining intel, and created vulnerability when the need arose to quietly eliminate certain threats.

#

Sulman Thie found meeting in his yacht off the coast of Singapore a great convenience. The open ocean would keep his secrets, with little room for drones and people to hide. The open water proved to be a mercy for some, as they unexpectedly found themselves without a boat, having to test the depths of the ocean. This day, Sulman was meeting with representatives of the Mao Tung Che organization. Hoping to solidify movement of his illicit products into the Chinese market from his Thailand base, he had recently reached out to the Mao and received a minimal response, which did not take as long to receive as he expected.

Their price was not unreasonable, he thought, but when only the head of his messenger was returned, he was not sure how he had offended them. He tried again and again, each time sweetening the offer with more cash and drugs. He sent over a dozen messengers, but the price was getting too high, as only the heads of those men he sent were making their way back to him. He tried one last time, pinning his hopes on this offer; without the Mao Tung Che, his empire would never make it past the border. His last messenger entered China in a Maybach Mercedes full of product, gold, diamonds, and cash, with the signatory being the leader of the Mao Tung Che, thinking this would ensure it was got to the right person.

Part of his messenger returned, just the head and neck, with a note stapled to the forehead with the time and coordinates of this meeting. Sulman was furious. The last reply was an act of war, and he would respond accordingly. This was his favorite boat and he despised spilling blood on it, so his means of ending this would be nonviolent.

His thoughts were going all kinds of sideways as a speed boat rapidly approached.

#

Liora, meanwhile, had heard rumors of a Thai national who was waging war on her employers. The Sulman had sent a request to do business, and the leaders were intrigued; the idea of expanding their empire always interested them. Seeing this as a way to get intel to Liam, she used their second reply to send him a message. Normally, the messengers were low-level workers, such as she had been. She knew she was taking a risk, but needed to let Liam know of her need to leave. She had personally taken the message from the courier, saying she was ordered to retrieve it. These low-level people respected authority, and this one handed over the message without any questions. She added to it during a stop in the ladies' room, and then made her way to the messenger. She knew the Mao Tung Che leaders had sent an additional message, asking Thie to meet to discuss terms, but the Sulman had returned their second messenger's head with a threat of retaliation pinned to it. They continued to send messengers, and the insults were greater each time, with each messenger killed in an inventive way.

Liora had been summoned to the leader of the organization's office; maybe her advice was needed to deal with the Sulman. A good step, she thought, maybe a chance to prove herself and get into the inner circle of power. She had purposefully minimized her looks and overall appearance, as she had heard this man was devout traditional Chinese purist and looked down upon women trying to perform what he perceived as a man's role. She would show him otherwise if given the chance. It occurred to her that they might put her in a situation where they expected her to fail, so her wit and cunning would be her most valuable assets in this situation.

The room was a darkened corner office with candles providing the ambient light. Liora entered the room when summoned, and introduced herself with a bow. The occupants didn't say a word; they just stared at her, as if waiting for her to do something. After a second's delay, she realized they were waiting on her to serve them. It galled her to the core, as clearly they had not seen her as a worthy member of the organization from the start. She bit her lip and grudgingly served them (if only she could have enacted the violent scenario playing in her head at that moment!). They motioned for her to sit, though it required her to sit at the lower table in an almost kneeling position: more symbolism of dominance from their side.

Once in position, they explained her assignment. There were no promises or hints that it was anything more than what they asked — simply get on this boat here, go there, and kill Sulman Thie. They had received a message from their government sources, who had intercepted a message from the Sulman about meeting with his associates out on the ocean. She would attend that meeting. Once she had detached the Sulman's head from his body, she was to place it in the bag they had just handed her and mail it to the address on the paper in the bag. Then she was to return to her normal duties and come when summoned.

That was it — no more, no less, very matter-of-fact. At that point, she saw the reality of her situation. They were setting her up to fail. This didn't jibe with her thoughts regarding her position in the organization. Why would they send her on this mission? This was the kind of job where expendable people were sent, not valuable assets. Her mind settled on the belief that they knew or suspected something about her past, or perhaps had intercepted her message to Liam. Realizing she had little time left in this organization, she set long-laid plans in motion.

She was lost in thought on her way home when a tap on the shoulder startled her. The tap was from a bike messenger, who delivered a coded note made of printed sugar, completely edible and easily dissolved in her stomach. Immediately she knew the source: Liam. It had to be important, as he would not risk her safety for just anything. Upon entering her apartment, she opened the canister and read the message. The contents of the note sent her to the floor, tears of anger welling in her eyes.

The immediacy of this mission was clouding her thoughts. She must somehow escape the Sulman, as she knew she was walking into a trap, and hoped to use it to her advantage. Preparation was the key. The note indicated she follow the clues at the dock. Once there, she found Liam's surprise and brought it along with her, pulling it to her boat unnoticed.

#

Liam's intel on Phaimi was a dead end. Satellite images showed that the town was a bustling center of commerce, with coastal access being the only points of entry or exit. Some of the locals were enticed to join Liam's organization, though the intel they provided proved little more than a laundry list of town grievances. Finally, a credible source had intercepted a message from Shanghai to Thailand. The message was flagged, as it had come from the Mao Tung Che, hand-delivered to a bike messenger by a Western woman of striking appearance. Definitely Liora, signaling its importance, as she knew her actions were under observation both internally and externally.

Liam had given orders to intercept any messages that Liora sent by bike messenger, as a member of his team was posing as the messenger. This was an unusual deviation of protocol, and her actions did not go unnoticed by either set of her employers. The message was cloned, with a tracker slipped in on its way to its recipient. This was the lead Liam was searching for. The message was a reply to a Sulman Thie in Phaimi, the very place he had been observing. It indicated that the head of the Mao Tung Che was willing to discuss business terms, but payment would be required up front. Once the entry and exit routes were found, thanks to his tracker, Liam hatched a new plan.

This was an unexpected turn of events, as neither side knew or suspected they were being watched and manipulated by Liam. The tracker found its way through a series of tunnels once it hit land. From there. it finally came to rest in an unremarkable house that was an entryway to a labyrinth of underground rooms. The Sulman sent one of his own men this time, loaded with cash and drugs. Liam had different plans for this messenger, however; his team intercepted him over open water, and quickly liberated his head from his body.

On the Chinese side, Liam had sent a return note to the Mao, declining their offer and insulting them with the head of their messenger. After about a week, Liam's team put the head of the Sulman's next messenger into a courier bag and had it delivered to him. The Sulman was now fearful, and sent more messengers, each suffering a similar end. Likewise, the Mao was growing intensely agitated as they received the heads of their own messengers, expecting a war to break out between them and the Sulman. The last effort by the Sulman was a rich score for Liam's team. That Mercedes full of cash and treasure would be a sweet prize once it made it back to the States. This time, Liam sent a different message to the Sulman, and passed it on to the Chinese government, along with coordinates and a meeting time.

The Sulman was enraged, as he had expected to have the red carpet rolled out and receive an invitation to the Mao Tung Che headquarters. He fully expected this latest meeting to be an ambush, and made plans to counter that. Neither side suspecting both sides were being played, the Mao group had planned to send their envoy to him, thinking they were posing as the buyers Sulman Thie was expecting — though they intended to use this as a means of eliminating some excess baggage.

Liam was in complete control of the narrative, and set Liora up for success... if she were careful and smart. His team was closely watching her movements, and noted that she was being constantly surveilled by the Mao. This would be the end for Liora if he didn't step in to provide her an escape route. Having set up the meeting between the two groups, he risked sending Liora the coded note and a means of escape. She would need to know everything.

#

Liora and six male Chinese mercenaries were in a speedboat heading towards Chongming Island, as their target lay in the open water between them and the island. Liora had the boat slow down about a half-mile from the Sulman's boat, well within sight. As the boat slowed, Liora pulled tight the gift Liam had given her. She had used a slipknot to tie the rope to his gift to the side of the boat before they left; now she pulled it against the boat as it stayed submerged. A moment later, they started advancing to the Sulman's yacht.

As she rose from her boat, Liora's hand casually pulled lose the rope attached to the gift under water. Climbing the ladder to the Sulman's yacht, she covertly slipped the rope onto a hook-hold on the edge of its decking. The Sulman's surprise was evident on his face when Liora stepped aboard; it was clear he wasn't expecting a Western woman in the midst of the Chinese mercenaries. Still, he welcomed them all onto the boat, offering traditional Chinese fare as refreshments, along with some Thai treats and drinks. After all the pleasantries were past, the bargaining began.

Liora suspected this was a show being put on for the drones that were inevitably watching. Her colleagues readily devoured the meal before them; Liora was neither hungry nor thirsty, and just nibbled at her food, keenly observing every aspect of her surroundings. Her interest and suspicions were aroused when she noticed that the Sulman and his men weren't partaking of the Chinese delicacies; indeed, they were barely participating in the festivities at all. They would raise their glasses occasionally and reach for food, but only the Thai snacks made it to their lips. In this part of the world, for a host to not eat from his own feast was unheard of.

Realizing this was be her opportunity, she began looking for signs of poisoning in her colleagues. The thing about poisoning food is that it takes a while to manifest when done properly, as the one doing the poisoning typically wants to generate maximum consumption without leaving the slow eaters unaffected. Liora's lack of hunger was a literally saving grace she hadn't expected.

As she had deduced, her colleagues soon began showing signs of illness. She needed the Sulman and his crew to believe she was also poisoned, so she mimicked the actions of the mercenaries, wanting to appear to dead to any surveillance.

Her plans were rapidly coming to fruition. Her practice at meditation these last few years paid off, as they had prepared her for this moment, where she could control her breathing and heart rate to look as if she were, in fact, dead of poisoning. Once everyone was still, the Sulman's men divided up into pairs and threw each member of the Chinese delegation overboard.

As Liora hit the water, she increased her heart rate, and utilized her momentum to drift towards the gift she had hooked to the boat earlier. Her plans going into this had been murky at best, not knowing how the situation would play out, though she knew the general outlines of what she wanted to accomplish; in any case, her training taught her to plan for every contingency. The gift she had brought along was a mini-submarine built for one person that contained state-of-the-art cloaking technology, courtesy of one Colonel Liam Rhett, U.S. Army.

As Liora approached the sub, she released the docking rope, took a deep breath, and submerged. She was preparing to enter the sub when the world went white.

What happened next was a blur of light, fire, water, and pain. Liora was fortunate to be underwater when the yacht exploded. She was sliding into the sub when the water started to boil and seemed to burst into flame around her. Her head slammed forward into the sub's controls, and she lost consciousness.

#

Sounds all around, grating and painful, blasted in Liora's ears. *No, this place isn't right, am I dreaming, must be, everything seems off,* were the thoughts bubbling through her subconscious mind. Having suffering from a deep gash in the head, the blood was streaming down into her eyes, clouding her vision as she started to regain consciousness. *Where am I? How did I get here? Why is nobody answering?* Memories started to float to the surface of her thoughts. She brushed the blood out of her eyes, screaming in pain. *My hand, what's wrong with my hand, the pain is unbearable!*

She was able to lift her head slightly before the nausea set in, looking blearily around at the cramped quarters. This place had no windows, and a damp smell permeated the air, though that was getting stale. Her training started to kick in, forcing herself to clear her thoughts, recalling how she had gotten here and what had happened. After several minutes, her last few conscious thoughts began to resurface. Painfully, she reached for the console to pull herself up. It took an incredible effort, but she finally had a view of her situation. The sub was diving, causing the pressure to build on the hull to build; fortunately for her, its forward motion was slow. The window for her to act was closing quickly as her eyes located the pressure gauge, which was pegged in the red. Not a good sign, since this was a small craft and could easily implode under too much pressure.

Instinctively, though the pain was intense, she pulled up on the controller, trying to bring to sub back to a safe level. The gauge indicated the pressure was improving, but the alarms and grating noise were getting louder. Her eyes darted from instrument to instrument, not sure what she was looking for. Then she saw it: the oxygen levels inside the sub were dangerously low. The grating noise must be the oxygen generator failing. She was now heading in the right direction, the surface, but would it be fast enough?

Laboring to take in each breath, she pushed the sub to its limits in rising to the surface. Time seemed to slow, as it usually does in intense situations, until the motion of breaking through the surface slammed her into the control panel again. *Damn, that hurt!* she cursed silently, nursing a probable broken rib. Her hands were wracked with pain as she scraped them frantically along the flooring, trying to find the hatch. Paydirt; she had it, and it hurt like a bitch twisting it open, causing her to swear as a few more bones cracked in her bad hand. The hatch led to a false floor, the pressure of the cabin holding back the water. The next step would be the hardest. To get to the surface, she would have to dive into the water and then head upward. Then what?

Enough of her wits and air were still about her to think through the options. Possibilities raced through her mind; she settled on the ones that made the most sense and were simplest to execute. She thought, since this gift was from Liam, that there had to be an obvious beacon somewhere, not to mention emergency escape equipment. She was getting frantic now; every second counted, as she knew she could lose consciousness soon. Her eyes located her target: a small sign over a glass box saying, *In case of emergency, push here.* Without giving it a second thought, she smashed her fist through the glass and pushed the button. A small pack dropped from the ceiling. She grabbed it and jumped into the cold ocean water.

With every last bit of consciousness Liora had left, she swam upward. It felt like forever before she broke the surface, blowing like a whale before gasping for air. The salty spray stung as she breathed in what she could before each wave crashed down on her. Clutched to her chest was the pack, which provided just enough flotation until she regained her bearings. As she drew in deep drafts of sweet air, her mind raced on to what to do next. She had no idea where she was, nor which direction she should go.

Calming down enough to inspect the pack, she noticed a pull cord and did the obvious, expecting it to inflate into a raft. She was surprised when she was suddenly enshrouded in foam. Now floating above the waves but totally unable to move, she had no choice but to wait.

As she thought about it, she realized that this was one of those newish rescue devices she had been briefed about before leaving for China. When activated, the occupant was encapsulated in a foam ball that soon hardened into stiffness. At one end of the ball was a navigation device, and on the opposite end was a propulsion system. The ball would eventually home in on the target to which it was programmed. On the other end, the target would be pinged that someone needed their help, and they would move toward each other.

In this instance, Liam had programmed it for an aircraft carrier off the coast of Singapore. It took the better part of two days for them to meet up.

#

Liora's eyes opened to the dim light of a Navy hospital bay. At first, she was unsure of her surroundings. As she studied the fixtures, she recognized their familiarity, and eased into a peaceful sleep. Several hours, days, or weeks later, she wasn't sure, she was visited by her Uncle Liam. "Welcome back to the land of the living, kid."

"Wouldn't have it any other way. How long?"

"A week. When we found you, there wasn't much life left in you."

"What happened? I remember an explosion, and then very little after that."

"Apparently your former Chinese employers were suspicious of you, and they used the meeting with Sulman Thie as an opportunity to kill you both."

She nodded painfully. "I suspected they might, but didn't think they'd blow us up."

"They were watching. We spotted their drones surrounding the yacht. They had a vendetta against the

Sulman, thanks to me. Enjoy the sub? I'd hoped you would get away before they bombed his yacht."

"Almost. I wasn't quite in the sub when they hit, so the blast knocked me unconscious. The door must have closed on its own."

Liam chuckled. "Yep, the sub was equipped with a lot of failsafes, but it couldn't fix a bomb-damaged oxygen extraction unit. We equipped several hours of oxygen in the sub, but those tanks were meant to be replenished from the OEU."

"I didn't think I was going to make it, Colonel."

He took her good hand in his and gave it a reassuring squeeze. "Well, you did. Now you're the living dead, which is handy. As far as your former employers are concerned, you're just so much fish food. Good thing they didn't know your real name."

"That bites," she groused. "I was making a name for myself in the organization."

"Well, I have an excellent opportunity for you. Since you're presumed dead, I can offer you a new life. You'd get a new identity and have you become an agent of the Homeland Intelligence Agency back in the U.S. of A. Your Mossad masters agreed with me that this would be the best place for you, as I appealed to their honor in having you close to family."

She looked at him skeptically. "You're holding all the cards now. Do I have much choice?"

He patted her hand. "You always have a choice, kid. Think on it for a while, and I'll return when you've regained your strength."

Liora slept off and on for several weeks before she fully regained her strength, and when she did, she couldn't get out of bed soon enough. The ship she was aboard was in warmer weather that the area from whence she had come. When she went topside, she relished the warm breeze flowing across the deck. Liam arrived in a helicopter late the next evening, bringing her a fresh Starbucks coffee in a thermos — a taste of home. He knew how to tug at her emotions.

"Have you thought about my offer?" he asked, as she savored the mocha goodness.

"I have," she said cautiously. "There are conditions. I need a bank account, a luxury car, and a place to live."

"So that's a yes on your part?"

"I didn't say that. Do you agree to my demands?"

"You needn't demand any of those things. I suspect you knew you'd be given them anyway. You've earned them, and I expect you to earn them many times over in the future."

"You're getting soft in your old age. If it means I'll be closer to you, of course it's yes."

"Good. Your first assignment will be as a college professor at UNLV. I need for you to get very close to a young professor there — he's about your age. Brilliant, quite possibly a genius. You're to learn as much as possible about his work, especially what he doesn't report. If he's anything like his father, he'll develop research that'll be of use to us, whatever it may be."

She nodded, intrigued. "When do I leave?"

"As soon as you're feeling better. Here's your new identity, Professor Liora Abrams. Your specialty is psychiatry. One of our agents using your real identity has been developing a professional network and resume these past three years, and you've published these twenty well-received papers. Learn them and know them by heart. We weren't sure if you would ever need an alias with your real name, but we created it anyway, and had your doppelganger present your papers virtually at conferences. Since you couldn't be in two places at once, obviously, this alias created the perfect cover for you."

Chapter 5: On His Own

The rain was a steady pitter-patter on the window, reinforcing Brill's somber mood. It had been two months since he'd buried his Dad — the point when Brill's world came crumbling down. His subsequent steady withdrawal from the world was a testament to his sadness. These days, he went through the motions at work, spoke very little, and lumbered into his room when home, waiting for a job to open up anywhere but here.

Jenna, Brill's Mom, was in an even deeper state of suffering. She so longed for the companionship that had been ripped from her arms. Now it was just her and Brill, and she could see him drifting deeper into in the abyss. She had been concerned for him even before John's death, as Brill had never developed many long-term relationships and was a bit reclusive. The silence was the hardest part for her. She longed for Brill to want the motherly attention she had in abundance, now more than ever.

Her heart sank when Brill broke the news to her that he was planning to move away. A job had opened up at the University of Nevada, Las Vegas. He had accepted without hesitation, without asking her, and now he was going away. She couldn't hold back the tears when he broke the news to her, but she knew she had to let him go, no matter how much it hurt.

The call from the dean at the UNLV hospital was the pick-up Brill needed to get over his father's death, a permanent job where he could get lost in his career. He was sure it would hurt his Mom, but he'd made a promise to his Dad to go somewhere far away from home. When he broke the news to her, she responded as he expected. Surprisingly, he felt more relief than loss. This was an area he would explore further once he got settled in, as he knew he should be sad to leave his only family, but the sadness just wasn't there.

Ultimately, Jenna decided to come with him, because she couldn't stand to be alone; and honestly, Brill didn't mind her company. Unsure if this would be permanent or if she would move on to another place, Brill decided to rent an apartment with two bedrooms, in case his Mom wanted to stay a while. The practice he would set up at UNLV would build on his studies in neurology. The mind was fascinating to him, as it was so heavily researched but so minimally understood. Physicians were supposed to be these all-knowing entities who could provide answers to the most difficult medical questions, but the reality of the medical world painted a different picture. Doctors could beautifully repair and engineer the body to do amazing things, but their understanding of it was still only scratching the surface of what was packed into the genetic code of each part of the body, even after a good four hundred years of intensive study. He believed he could provide contributions to the understanding of the mind, especially the way memory works.

During his first month at UNLV, he was still learning his colleagues' names and figuring out the politics of a university hospital. In a way, he was hoping the research he wanted to pursue would just fall out the sky and hit him in the head, but he knew that to find something meaningful and impactful to medicine would take some time — just hopefully not too long.

His mother had taken up residence in the spare bedroom in his apartment, and there went his social life. He was concerned for her, as she was clearly sliding deeper into depression, and was surprised that she'd reacted this way. His parents had loved each other, but he'd rarely seen any outward signs of that love during his adult years. He connected with some of the psychiatrists at the hospital to get their opinions about her. One in particular, Liora Abrams, provided the best insight, with her beauty and outgoing personality also igniting Brill's romantic interest. He expressed his surprise that his Mother was behaving this way, and Liora was curious as to why he would feel that way, since deep emotion is common for some time after a loved one's death.

Brill was confused by Liora's analysis. "I know my parents loved each other, though I'm not sure how deep a love they shared. I never really saw them express that love."

"What you've described to me indicates they loved each other very deeply, that they didn't just tolerate one another."

"I see where you're coming from, but when I was growing up they always held hands, hugged, and kissed each other. As I got into my high school years, the most affection I saw from them was a kiss when my Dad came home from work, but not much more than that. I expect they had their intimate times, though I never had a clue of it."

"Love shows itself in peculiar ways the longer people are together. Their comfort with each other means they don't always show outward signs of affection. You mentioned your Mom always cooked, cleaned, and did the laundry. Your Dad played a different role, that of breadwinner. Those are forms of love that two people can express to each other."

It all sounded good to Liora, as she was paraphrasing a book by Dr. Spock that she'd read the night before. If Brill bought it, then he would be an easy mark.

Brill didn't know how to respond. She gave him some pointers on how help his Mom as he left for his rotations, and he was grateful for that. The other psychiatrists in his department were less friendly, and offered little in the way of help.

One evening Brill invited Liora over, hoping she might be able to help bring his mother back to normal. She brushed that aside, suggesting instead that they meet up for a lunch or dinner. This was the beginning of Liora's infiltration into Brill's life. She did eventually meet Jenna, and her subsequent interactions with her did help, as Jenna slowly returned to her normal self. About a year later, Brill bought Jenna a condo in a retirement community, trying to get her to develop a new life and a network of friends.

During that first year, Brill began distancing himself from research. His self-doubt reflected his fear of never living up to his father's accomplishments. The visits with Liora progressed to more than a casual interest of her psychiatry skills, though he needed them now more than ever. With every conversation, Brill felt his connection to Liora deepening. He asked her out on several dates in the limited free time a practicing physician has. He wasn't sure what his role should be, as he'd never had a girlfriend before, and was clumsy in his romantic efforts.

These efforts were starting to take the place of the energy he normally would have put into a research program, and began bringing attention to his failures.

#

Liam read through the latest monthly report from Liora. He could see it plain as day; she was getting too close, a possibility he had considered. These twenty-somethings always put their emotions ahead of duty; their heads get clouded easily at that age, since they are full of hormones and have difficulty focusing. Liora had already used the alias his team had created to build a solid, credible persona. He could now use what she had built to get her into places where she would never be able to go any other way.

All criminals are vain; they want everyone to hear of their exploits, knowing they can circumvent the law with ease. Liam knew that with Liora's cover as a college professor who had written several monographs and papers about criminals, the quest of writing another book would open nearly any door he wanted to any criminal he wanted. One particular group that had eluded his efforts to plant a mole for years was the diamond trade in South Africa. It was nearly impossible to break into that group; diamonds were the new currency of terrorists, better than cryptocurrency. Almost anyone in the world would accept a diamond for payment; they were easy to conceal, easy to pass undetected, and easy to sell. With Liora stationed as a visiting professor at a university in Johannesburg, she could waltz right up to the front door of the diamond trade, and they would welcome her with open arms. They would tell her things in minutes that it would take years to uncover with a mole. This could be the best alias he had ever created — genius, he thought.

He sent Liora instructions that she was leaving for Johannesburg within two weeks, and should put her relationship with Brill on pause. How she did that was up to her, he told her, but she should leave the door open to come back in a year or so; then the boy would get to work and hopefully be more like his father. Liam suspected that John Everly had used the nanobots he'd pilfered on Brill, but he had no proof, and couldn't be sure why John would infect his son with them. John had become a liability when he stole those bots and then tried to cover it up. He'd had to be eliminated—not Liam's decision, but that of his superiors. If John had come to him and explained what he wanted to do with them, Liam could have made a case for him, and would likely have let him take over that research project.

Those thoughts pained Liam, as John had been so brilliant. Eliminating him had been a tragic loss, but it had to be done; John had left him with no other option. Too much was riding on that program, even now. The best he'd been able to do was put it off for over a decade, by convincing his superiors that they should milk John Everly for every insight possible before he was terminated in a blaze of glory.

At least John had been able to watch the son he'd traded his life for grow up.

#

Previously, Liora's life hadn't allowed for a real romantic connection to anyone. She spent a little time here, a little time there, then a long time in China, never allowed to use her real name. This assignment had bored her at first. Brill Everly was awkward, maybe brilliant, though she'd yet to see that side of him. She spent her free hours running, training for marathons, as she wasn't a gambler and there wasn't much else to do in southern Nevada. Of late, Brill had been a pursuing her; she didn't need her limited psychiatric training to decipher that. He had no clue that he was a target, and she was starting to fall for him as well.

This was new territory for her. She'd only been at UNLV for a year and a half, and she was making a name for herself. Psychiatry was easy for her, almost intuitive, and it opened up an emotional part of her mind that she had never known existed. She had grown up as a gutter rat and criminal, and then honed her skills and trained as a soldier and a spy in the most elite military agency in the world. Now, she was uncovering the incredible aspects of the female mind. She was surprised to find that the male pioneers in psychiatry could write such truths. The female mind, her own, had depths of emotional intellect she was eager to explore. It was now being clouded by the budding relationship she was developing with Brill.

As a spy, this could only lead to disaster for him. She knew how to survive. Her monthly reports to Liam indicated her attachment, and likely drove the response from him that she had just received. *Cut it off, but leave room to come back in the future.* His message was clear and to the point. He had arranged for her to leave at the end of the next week; she had until then to come up with the right scenario to leave Brill.

Some of the great psychiatrists provided the insights she needed. The thought surfaced that the female mind could create answers with layers of meanings, subtleties based on how her news was delivered. Her mind was positioned as the center of her universe — more like a sphere where the answers she posed would come across as direct, but layered with multiple meanings that circled around each other. Each sentence she would say to Brill would be spokes on this imaginary wheel emanating from her mind; at least the psychiatry indicated such an image, though she was still developing her personal emotional spectrum.

The scene she would play out would be to tell Brill that they needed a break. To him, it would come across that they were broken up. Later, she could use this to say that she truly had needed a break and then come back into his life, as the statement had such a range of subtle meanings. Liam was right; she was getting too close, and stepping away would be good for her. He had arranged for a sabbatical to Johannesburg, South Africa for a year or two. That would allow for enough separation that ideally, Brill would get his ass in gear and get creative. A love-smitten doctor in pursuit of a family wasn't something she could interest herself in at this point in her life.

The end began when Brill headed over to Liora's apartment to pick her up for lunch. When he entered, he gave her a kiss and hug; their relationship had progressed to the point where he was having some thoughts about their future together. This day was special. Brill was taking her out for her birthday, and had planned a full day of festivities, starting with lunch. Liora kissed and hugged him back, then led him to the sofa. She liked to talk, and Brill enjoyed everything she had to say. Usually.

"Brill, have you ever thought taking about a sabbatical?" she asked.

"Nope. My surgical rotations wouldn't allow me to leave so soon after starting here."

"Well, I have. I was contacted by some of my former colleagues in Johannesburg recently. They've started a new research project on the post-apartheid generation, wanting to understand the long-lasting impacts that have been passed down from generation to generation. They want me to join them."

"You can't be seriously considering it?" Brill said anxiously.

She took a deep breath. "Actually, I am. Look, Brill, we've been getting too close lately. I think we need a break."

"What?" he exclaimed incredulously. "You're breaking up with me?"

"That's not what I said. Our relationship just needs a break. We need some time apart to see if it will endure."

He sighed. "What now?"

"Lunch. You came over to take me to lunch."

He stood up abruptly. "No. I can't do this. You just broke up with me! I don't care what you call it," he said harshly in the face of her denials. "If we go to lunch, all I'll be thinking about is losing you. I need to go now." He turned to leave.

She reached out and touched his arm. "Brill, wait. Really, this is a break, not a break-up. It'll be a long break, but I'll call, I promise."

Brill shook his head and left. He was crestfallen. All his plans had just ended with a few words. Tears were starting to well up in his eyes as he left the apartment.

Liora said her goodbyes at UNLV, and was gone by the following weekend. Brill could think of nothing else for days. He called in sick, saying he had the flu; that would buy him a week. Every waking thought he had was about Liora. What had he done wrong? Did he move too fast? How could he go on?

After a week, he grudgingly went back to work. The daily routine was a blur for a month as he relentlessly poured himself into his job. Work would ease the pain, he learned, and of course some of his colleagues recited the old saw that "time heals all wounds." He was skeptical of that, as his father's death still hurt, and it had been quite some time since that had happened.

With Liora gone, Brill focused on developing that research program he'd put off. It was still challenging to find the right pursuit for his ideas. His first efforts were to see what he could do for Parkinson's disease. He had treated several patients with that condition, but nothing seemed to stand out where he could progress a treatment and have an impact on long-term prognoses. He thought about what his father would do in this situation. His Dad... the thought caused him to slump in his seat.

Then he remembered those coded pages his father had revealed to him shortly before his death, and all the clandestine work he had completed for the military, disguising it as Vassal. When Brill had inherited the controlling interest in Vassal Biogenetics, he'd immediately sold it for a nice profit of fifty million dollars. He knew the military really controlled Vassal, and wanted no part of it. When he offered it for sale, he was betting on the government paying whatever price he wanted for it, as he suspected they had no idea he knew of their involvement — so he priced it high, but not too high. They'd called his bet. It was a handsome payoff, and allowed him to set his mother up for the rest of her life. He hesitated to buy any other property, as he wanted to be mobile, especially now that Liora had dumped him.

Those old memories had him thinking back even farther to his difficult childhood, and his former best friend, Sirum. Sadly, he hadn't thought about Sirum in years. Sirum had also had a difficult childhood. He was autistic, but brilliant; some called him a savant, though Brill had his doubts about that, as some also called Brill a savant. Autism... Brill had seen only a few autistic patients at the hospital, as most were treated at private hospitals. His thoughts drifted to the causes of autism. It was thought to be a mutation in Chromosome 15 that negatively affected executive function, the brain's mental "control room" in the prefrontal cortex that helped one organize and accomplish basic tasks. Poor executive function also made it difficult to develop empathy — the ability to step into other people's shoes and understand both actions and feelings, which most children pick up naturally by age three or four. Other theories existed for autism's cause, but whatever the case, some of those impacted with this condition had a single remarkable ability or some other unusual brain anomaly.

These thoughts took hold, and the thread of a research program started to form.

Brill's thoughts on autism soon had him requesting that all incoming patients with Autism Spectrum Disorder be sent to him. Within months he was treating twenty ASD patients, cataloging their every nuance, observing their brains with electroencephalogram (EEG) and Positron Emission Tomography (PET) scans. He created several brain teasers to see if he could home in on which parts of the brain were driving the autistic symptoms. A good deal of research had been done in this area, but it was often contradictory, and he felt there was something that had been missed — something either so obvious or so abstract that nobody had given it serious thought yet.

As promised, he occasionally got a call from Liora, and always enjoyed hearing her voice. The pain of their separation eased with each passing month. Now that Brill was consumed with developing a research program focused on autism, thoughts of her were fading to the back of his mind, to be dealt with at a later date.

One of his autistic patients was a young boy, Adam, who exhibited symptoms of a type he hadn't seen before. When he was brought in, his mother had frantically lugged his limp body into the emergency room, pleading for help. His case would normally have been passed to the ER physician, but Brill had volunteered to work the ER that day. After he stabilized her son and calmed her down a bit, he started to collect the boy's history. His mom said that Adam was autistic; at least, that was what the teachers at his school told her. Loud sounds caused him to go into a panic, and he was a number whiz; he could do complex division and multiplication in his head in milliseconds. His mother went on to describe some of his unusual behaviors. When her son would go into his fits, he would end by clenching up and then fall back, staring catatonically. He would stay this way for hours before returning to normal. This behavior had started a month ago, and the period of catatonia before he awoke kept getting longer.

This time, Adam hadn't woken up at all. He'd been catatonic for two days, and now his mother was in a panic. Brill immediately suspected a tumor rather than autism, as this wasn't normal autistic behavior, and indicated some more serious condition. Brill sent the boy off to be scanned; but when the results came back, he was at a loss. No tumor, nor any blood flow blockage of any type. Adam exhibited an abnormal amount of activity of the slow delta wave of sleep, yet the hippocampus showed the high gamma waves of the waking state. He wasn't showing any REM activity, suggesting he wasn't dreaming; so this paradoxical brain activity had Brill stumped.

Brill read the reports for many of the comatose patients at the hospital, and found, as he closely compared each case to Adam's, that some had entered their current states under similar circumstances. Realizing that he had to try something, lest Adam remain in a lengthy coma, Brill suggested some experimental medications. He was careful not to over-promise, as a parent in this situation would grasp at any hope, and he wanted this boy's mother to understand what he was going to try. "Mrs. Coldwell, you need to be aware that the drugs I'm recommending are experimental ones that have never been applied to the anomaly Adam is experiencing. Before I suggest them, I want you to understand my thinking in trying them."

"If you do nothing, will my son get better?"

"I can't say either way. We can try to wait it out, if you want. Adam's brain shows lots of activity, and that's a good sign. My concern is that he's not responding to any of our attempts to wake him."

"I don't understand what's wrong with him, and it sounds like you don't either," the woman said helplessly.

"I don't," Brill admitted. "The brain is a mysterious organ, and autism still isn't fully understood. But we've got to try something. I won't lie to you, Mrs. Coldwell. Adam is exhibiting symptoms unlike any that I or any of the other neurologists I know of have ever seen. I've asked colleagues all over the world about this case, and none of them can offer any suggestions that I would take seriously. Most of them suggest surgery, though I don't see the need for that. It seems that his brain is wired correctly, so surgery doesn't make sense."

"So you want to experiment on him?"

"I want to try some medications that may help," Brill said soothingly. "They've been used on other brain disorders. I'm going to try to balance the signals between each state, and try to help his brain see that he's not really asleep, so hopefully he'll wake up."

The discussion then centered around the potential side effects of each medication. Later, Brill went over the potential surgeries that he might have to try if the medicines didn't work. Mrs. Coldwell was distraught, but eventually agreed to let Brill try what he thought best. She was at her wits' end, and couldn't find a reason to say no.

Adam's treatments started with a set of brain scans and continuous monitoring as the medication was administered. In an adjacent room was another autistic patient Brill was treating for different symptoms. At the same time Brill had administered the planned series of medications to the catatonic boy, he was also starting a scan on the other child. This boy, Kevin, had severe autism, exhibiting limited speech and severe developmental challenges.

The EEG was hooked up, and Brill began administering the tests he had developed, looking for some clue others had missed in their research. The scan ran its normal course, and he finished to find nothing out of the ordinary. He gave Kevin's concerned parents some drills to help their child, then he turned his attention back to Adam. The medication had now been fully administered, so Brill began a series of controlled current stimulations, trying to break Adam's mind out of its locked pattern. After an hour of these treatments, the EEG began showing a decrease in gamma wave activity.

Brill considered this a success, and repeated the procedure several times over the next few weeks. When Adam's brain activity was under control, Brill tried some limbic stimulation, hoping that the fight-or-flight response might help bring him out of his comatose state. It did. The boy nearly jumped out of the bed after Brill hit him with the treatment. His mom calmed him down as Brill pondered his success.

Upon evaluating Adam's EEG scans over the course of the treatment, Brill concluded that this case would make for a great publication — but then he noticed something odd. Right at the beginning, before any treatment began, there had been a multitude of stimulations in other areas of the brain. It looked familiar; he knew he had seen it before, but where?

He'd run hundreds of EEG's since Adam's first. He looked back through each one, trying to match the pattern, and suddenly saw it: this particular pattern was identical to that of the other boy, Kevin, that he'd been treating at the same time as Adam. It was even weirder when he realized that the patterns had occurred in both boys at the exact same time stamp, with almost a perfect image of the severely autistic boy's treatment mirrored in Adam's.

Brill thought through the possibilities. These weren't wireless devices, so they couldn't be sharing the same signal. They were in separate rooms using separate computers, yet produced the same pattern at the exact same time; but only when Brill's tests were performed on Kevin. He looked to see if he could find any similar patterns in other patients. He found that there were three others where the time stamps matched that had repeated patterns, but only when two of the autistic children were being monitored at once. Identical stimulations in both brains. He thought he might be on to something at first, but soon filed that thought away, as there were about twenty other simultaneous tests that didn't show any similarities. Coincidence could account for maybe one, he thought, but not four. Maybe a vector to explore a later time.

His work continued at a steady if monotonous pace — same treatments, same effects, with only a few successes. He needed a different theory. Lost in thought, a call brought him back to reality. It was his old friend Sirum, a voice he hadn't heard in years, in town for a convention. Sirum had become an astrophysicist, getting his doctorate in it, putting his incredible talent together with a strict regimen that kept him on an even social keel. As a boy, he had been one of the genius savants that scientists flocked to in order to study his remarkable talent for motion calculations, better than any computer's. His constant reading and prodigious memory kept him apprised as to exactly where all major (and most minor) celestial bodies were at any given time, and given his instinctual grasp of orbital mechanics, he could tell you where they had been at any point in the past without error. It was a perfect talent for the profession he'd entered. Of course, he had the typical social inhibitions that all autistic people exhibited, but hard work and his other talents helped him to overcome it. They arranged to connect after Brill was done for the day.

After Sirum's call, Brill began thinking about the autistic connection. Nearly one out of every ten autistic people has some type of incredible ability. There's an even rarer type of autism, called "the islands of genius," that is usually accompanied by severe mental deficiencies. These usually fall in a narrow range of talents, such as calendar calculating, mathematics, spatial skills, music, and art. Some savants have prodigious language skills. Some display only these skills and have severe disabilities, sometimes the result of a traumatic brain injury or a genetic mutation. Sirum was the rarest of the rare, as he had his unique spatial abilities, but not the mental deficiency that often came with such gifts; no, he was brilliant all the way around.

Brill himself had also been classified as a savant, although as far as he could tell he wasn't autistic; plus, his Dad kept him out the news and had somehow repaired any deficiencies he might have had. These genius savants intrigued Brill... and they lingered in his thoughts until an idea hit him like a lightning bolt. People like him and Sirum were so unique that they stood out from the rest. Their kind was the breakthrough he needed! If he could find the novelty in their genetic makeup and/or brain structure, he could make a name for himself.

Now he was on a mission. His plan hatched itself: he would figure out how these people had this incredible knowledge without ever having learned it. While they had to have a starting point — even Sirum couldn't calculate the orbit of Eris or Sedna without knowing of them, and their positions in the sky and distance from Earth — the actual calculations and "number sense" came naturally. Many were just thought to parrot what they saw or heard; but some, like Sirum, possessed inborne, obscure knowledge, especially of mathematics and music, without any such mirroring. Brill did, too. He could draw anything to perfection, and play any song he heard on any instrument he'd tried without ever seeing the sheet music. Brill's calculation abilities were equally impressive. His mind was so quick, he could predict a neural firing sequence in the exact order it would occur in response to a stimulus. How did he know what he knew? *Nobody* knew this information, so how could he have picked up and then mirrored it?

There had to be a deeper understanding involved, and he would trace it to its end.

He and Sirum met up later that evening, and their friendship picked up right where it had left off. Sirum had much to talk about, as it had been over ten years since they last saw each other. He was deep into his research, headed for his next great discovery. The physics community viewed him as one of their brightest. His theories on cosmological spatial dynamics were already helping to reshape Einsteinian theories on black holes and dark matter. Dark matter was the lost stepchild that most astrophysicists ignored, yet Sirum saw its true potential. It was the interstellar goo that held space together, he explained. Most saw it as the void in the vacuum, but there was more to it, he claimed, and Sirum was helping to define it and would probably win a Nobel Prize for his work someday. Equally enthused, Brill told him of his new research plan, and Sirum gave it some thought, agreeing that the opportunity was unique enough that he would help Brill out. To Brill, it felt like all the right pieces were falling into place. This was the break he needed. Now his path in life was set, or so he hoped.

Chapter 6: Finally

"Finally!" Brill exclaimed, as he excitedly told Liora about his work. He'd called her this time, as the breakthroughs he was making were astounding even to himself. The genius savants he studied all showed unique genetic mutations. The key seemed to be Chromosome Fifteen, as it was the differentiator between a savant and general autism. The genius savants who had multiple abilities lacked the duplication of chromosomes, whereas many of the linear savants, those with only one ability and lower IQs, all had a duplicative chromosome, one that was a repeat of Chromosome Seventeen copied to Fifteen. His publications had caused an uproar in the genetics world. It was the first time that pure, raw intelligence had been linked to a specific region of the genetic code. His findings suggested that proteins in the brain gave rise to intellect. The points he'd made in his seminal paper on the subject showed that three mutations on Chromosome Fifteen gave rise to the higher intellectual ability — not all intelligence, just those specific to genius savants.

The press took this to extremes, of course, saying he had developed a way to make the world smarter. It tainted the understanding of his work, and the academic community began to dismiss his findings. Brill remained unfazed, though he suspected foul play in the mockery of his work. *That damned Colonel Rhett has to be behind this*, he decided. While he was hardly paranoid, his distrust of the government was at its highest, and he knew his work would be something Liam Rhett would want to take, especially the more he learned. He started to keep duplicate copies of his work files in a safe place, but knew that wouldn't be enough.

Before long, he had difficulty obtaining further funding for his work: He faced one rejection after another, though he never tried the road his father had traveled. He couldn't stomach dealing with Rhett or his kind. Fortunately, he had multiplied his earnings from selling his Dad's company and was flush with cash, to the tune of over two hundred million dollars. He began to fund his research himself, so he could do what he liked and not be held to preset limitations. This proved to be an unwise path, as Liam Rhett became increasing interested in Brill's work, and would bring Liora back to UNLV by year's end.

The freedom of self-funded work opened the door to Brill's unique testing methods. He didn't have to report how he was doing his work, or what his results were. The university would only know that he was helping autistic patients. As he delved deeper into the dark secrets of the mind, he began to uncover anomalies in his genius savants. The tests he devised had them performing their abilities on skills the patient didn't know anything about before the test, yet invariably, they could perform the skills to perfection. When challenged with a new skill or talent, the savants would go into a coma-like state for seconds to minutes, depending on the difficulty of what they were trying to do. When they regained consciousness, they had the ability to perform whatever Brill tested them on. Could this be some sort of coded genetic intelligence? Could all humans be born with all knowledge, with only a select few able to access a small piece of that knowledge pool, related to a specific type of task?

The more Brill dug, the more frustrated he became. How could these people, some just children five or six years old, dive into their minds and come out with things they had never been taught? The puzzle gnawed at Brill's subconscious day and night. He and Sirum didn't have to go into the unconscious state before they exhibited fits of brilliance, so why did the others do it? He ran every conceivable biological test he could think of, and some he invented just for the purpose. Nothing. Every avenue seemed to be a dead end. He needed a different perspective.

Liora was unreachable, so he connected with Sirum; they were now communicating regularly, since he was occasionally part of the research. Over the phone, Sirum couldn't come up with any plausible explanation either —

and as a result, the intrigue of this puzzle started consuming Sirum's thoughts as well.

#

The lack of a definitive answer, despite the flood of data, was starting to significantly bother Brill. He'd been running all these complex experiments, but could map only the high-level electrical signals in whole regions of the brain through the EEG. His use of PET was limited, as it took a toll on the patients, requiring radioactive drugs; and he could only legally perform so many PET scans per patient, whereas the EEG was external, but lacked the specificity he needed. Knowing his limitations were only half the problem; fixing them was the other half. What he needed, or imagined he needed, didn't exist. The idea for what he wanted, however, was a starting point; and he knew that between his and Sirum's intellects, they could design and build what he needed. The question was not if, but when. How long would it take? Money wasn't really a limitation, but overcoming (or circumventing) some of the fundamental laws of physics was.

He brought Sirum to UNLV to help him. The design of the machinery was right down Sirum's alley. Spatial recognition and interpretation were his special skills, and applying it to neural signals just took some refocusing with Brill's help. Sirum knew where to start: the quantum computing industry had made great strides these past few years. It had just run up against a seemingly insurmountable difficulty, though: interference from the outside world. One of the difficulties with quantum computers is the time it takes to solve a problem. As the complexity of the problem grows, so does the time it consumes. This is an exponential problem that increases as the complexities involved grow. Quantum computers use quantum bits, or qubits, instead of bits; that is, they utilize the position and spin of a particle, such as an electron, to store data. Superposition enough of these, and they can carry enormous amounts of information. Using laser pulses, the particles can be manipulated into certain positions to store or retrieve numbers, much like bits in traditional computing.

Manipulation is one avenue, though slow. The real advance was being able to predict where the particles would be at any given time and what spin they possessed, up or down. Where they hit the wall was that a quantum system needs to be perfectly isolated from interference from the macro-world — us. This creates a paradox: how to tell the computer to do what you want it to do without interfering with the quantum manipulations, and then to have it return an answer. Sirum worked out how to solve this paradox: he would have to first translate the question he wanted answered into a quantum signal. Then, he would have to use quantum mechanics to push the signal to the computer; later, the computer would return information via the same route, and his translation device would convert it back to macro-world data. Extremely complex, yet doable... though the equipment didn't yet exist to build such a translation device.

The best equipment in the world for accessing the quantum level was CERN's Supercollider, but that would only generate quantum level effects on a massive scale, far too much for their needs. They would have to create a miniature version of the supercollider, one in which they were able to control which quantum particles were generated, and then manipulate them. Easy to say, hard to do. Building such a device alone would win them the Nobel Prize, but both knew it would get scooped up by the military long before they ever published.

This project would take some time, and Brill was impatient, but he knew his progress hinged on its success. Brill's delusion was that it would require a short time table, thinking the effort would be completed in weeks; but those weeks soon ebbed into months. He was paying Sirum handsomely to build this device, and Sirum was in his perfect world, happy as a lark. Brill's day job took the bulk of his time, and this was far out of his skill set, so he was relieved that Sirum was on his side. Brill was a great coder — it was

so much like genetics that it made intuitive sense to him —
but mechanics was not his strong suit.

Sirum took his time, as perfection is required when
working at the quantum level. The first device he built was a
macro-to-quantum translation matrix; Sirum wasn't entirely
sure how it worked, as he had made some leaps of logic (or
illogic in this case) during its manufacture, and just hoped
and prayed it would do what he wanted. How he did this had
Brill concerned. It involved access to dark matter, that
elusive substance Sirum had been mapping and describing all
these years. He hadn't figured out how to actually create it,
but found the path to access the dark matter in the Lyman-
alpha "forest" of deep space. The signals could be sent nearly
instantaneously, as quantum interactions behave differently
than higher-level signals. Translating it into reality just
required a little time and a lot of money.

The dark matter that Sirum accessed was the opposite of
antimatter, which sounded illogical on the face of it. Brill
thought *matter* was the opposite of antimatter, but it turned

out this wasn't the case. Antimatter, they discovered, was the middle ground between matter and dark matter, a simple reaction, actually, once Sirum discovered it; but a one-way reaction at first, and later a return trip. Antimatter can act like a mirror, positive on the side that faces the macro-world and negative on the side that interacts with the quantum level. Sirum found that it could translate signals both ways. People had long mistakenly attributed antimatter as the end of the line for matter; in fact, it was *not* the direct opposite of matter, but the transitional state to the quantum realm. It was the ultimate chemical reaction, the absence of energy, the final state that matter rests or unrests in within the quantum realm — the ultimate Schrödinger paradox. The two states were both energy and not energy, similar to Schrödinger's cat in the famous thought experiment, both alive and dead at the same time.

The dark matter Sirum accessed would take the signals from the macro-world — our computers and their signals — then bounce them into quantum signals via an antimatter mirror so the two states would never actually touch one another, keeping the macro and quantum states separated. The information was then returned in the reverse direction. Since energy is conserved, neither destroyed nor consumed, the equation was constantly balanced.

This was the breakthrough they needed. Building the quantum side was the easy part; again, it was just a miniature copy of a supercollider. The interface created the dark energy on the quantum side of the mirror, then relayed the signal to the quantum level, allowing for manipulation of the quantum particles and the solving of complex problems, storing massive amounts of information and then translating what it meant back into the macro-world. Sirum built two of these computers, as he knew he would need one for his own research, though Brill made sure he detailed every nuance, in case another was needed later. All in all, it took six months from start to finish. Nobody aside of these two knew about the existence of these computers, and nobody ever would, even Liora. It was a secret Brill expected to take to his grave.

"Nice work, Sirum," he sighed when they were finally ready to test it. "Looks impressive. Does it work?"

"Initial tests show manipulation on the quantum level."

"That doesn't tell me it works," Brill snarked.

"I know I can manipulate the quantum storage, so it should theoretically work."

"It looks like a giant freezer, and it's extremely loud."

"In order to stabilize the quantum field, I had to create a condition of near absolute zero inside. That requires an enormous amount of energy and extra powerful compressors, which is why it's so loud."

"Could you disguise it as a freezer? Make it so that it can store samples?"

"Maybe. How much storage would you want?"

"Just enough that it's convincing. The best place to hide something is in plain sight, after all."

That request was more challenging than Sirum had first let on, as one couldn't exactly open a door to absolute zero (-459.67 degrees Fahrenheit) on a whim. Room temperature air colliding with air that cold would cause the equivalent of an explosion. So Sirum created an interface like a submarine would use to let someone into the pressurized cabin. He made a decompression zone where the sample would be placed and a vacuum pulled; then it would be chilled and sent to a storage zone. The reverse would occur when retrieving a sample from the super-chilled zone, as it would have to be slowly brought up to room temperature. This was exactly what Brill was looking for, as its size indicated all the space was needed to create such a freezer. The end result was a work of art. It stood about the height of a normal upright freezer, but was twice as wide. The power consumption was such that Brill had to install a generator on site to provide the massive amounts of power needed. But he was delighted with the end result, as nobody in their right mind would break into a device that would instantly freeze the surrounding environment. It provided the perfect cover for their subsequent work.

#

A storm was rolling in as Brill explored the creativity of one particular math savant, using his quantum computer to map individual neural signals over an entire human brain for the first time. Lightning struck, literally, at the exact time Brill was having the savant perform a new test. The building was grounded, so Brill wasn't concerned about lightning. But this storm was different than most, as multiple lightning strikes at the same time typically sees the most powerful strike going to the ground, while the others seek the next best thing. One such strike found the antennae atop of Brill's lab and made its way to a proper ground, which happened to be Brill's patient. At the time, he had electrodes hooked up to the young man, and was testing him with a specific type of calculation, using an equation Sirum had just developed and nobody else in the world had seen. If the savant solved it, his solution would prove the existence of genetic knowledge. The type of electrodes Brill had attached to the savant's head were a conducting type; they proved to be the endpoints of the lightning strike, sending a huge surge of electricity right into the patient's head. Brill thought he had killed the young man as he rushed to his side.

He was horrified until he realized that although the patient had just received an unbelievable jolt of electrical energy, he was perfectly healthy — simply in the frustrating semi-catatonic state that all genius savants went to in order to solve their hardest problems. When he calmed down and checked his monitor, Brill couldn't believe his eyes; the computer seemed to be mapping the savant's individual neural signals to regions of dark matter in a section of outer space! It seemed that the subject's neural signals were the exact same type of signals Sirum had detected in a region of space known to contain only dark matter, which happened to involve the precise equation that Sirum had been trying to solve. How, Brill wondered, could the man's mind be in space and yet here on Earth simultaneously? It didn't make sense. It was almost like his brain was acting as a receiver for a dark matter transmission.

The savant returned with a solution to the problem minutes later, at the exact moment the computer showed that his mind signal no longer matched the stellar signal. Coincidence? *Doubtful*, Brill thought. There was a connection there, somehow; Brill just wasn't sure how, and he had no idea how to reproduce the experiment, as he could easily kill someone if he tried to pump that much energy though a patient's head again.

#

His next discussion with Liora surprised him. She was extremely excited about his new findings; but the surprising part was that she was done with her sabbatical, and was returning to UNLV in a month. That was odd, he thought; when they'd talked a month ago, she'd mentioned she had too much work to do to leave — almost another year's worth. Some book she was writing. Regardless, he would be happy to see her, and maybe pick up where they'd left off — though the seed of doubt was planted in the back of his mind. He just didn't realize it yet.

Her return filled an emotional void. He had given so much to his research and work that he hadn't realized how much he needed the emotional uplift. The initial reunion was one of bliss and blind passion. But that soon faded into the reality of two people who had gone their separate ways, and were now good friends at best. Liora easily reconnected with her work and colleagues; for them, she never missed a beat, as she'd been attending regular staff meetings remotely. Brill was glad to have her back, but it just wasn't the same. The emotional connection didn't materialize, so he continued to pour himself into his work — so much so that Liora often had to remind him that she was around. He rarely found time to visit, and they rarely went out.

The damage had been done, and Brill had moved on. Logic was always there for him, steady and reliable, unlike Liora. It never faltered or failed, and he could always return to it, as it was forgiving and beautiful in its simplicity. The female mind was too perplexing to him, even with his high intellect. The solace he found in his work was far more rewarding than any physical gratification he could have with Liora. She was no longer what he needed.

The friendship was good enough, and no longer a distraction. This was the middle ground Liora and Liam wanted anyway.

#

In time, Brill's research hit a plateau. He was still making progress on mapping the individual neurons in his genius savants, but was never able to replicate the neural signals he had observed linked to the dark matter regions of space that one time. *Must have been a fluke*, he surmised, though he kept trying. One afternoon, Sirum was visiting to do some maintenance on the quantum computer. He regularly stopped by, as it was a short drive up from Tempe, Arizona, where he resided. After several beers later that evening, Brill began a philosophical discussion. "Sirum, a thought I've had for some time keeps gnawing at my subconscious. Have you ever wondered if all the knowledge that will ever be learned or invented has existed since before time began?"

"That's deep, Brill. Have you been reading philosophy books for fun?" Sirum joked.

"Ha! That would definitely *not* be my idea of fun. They just confuse me, especially the more recent ones. But the thought keeps coming back to me... I think it was something I learned or had to read in high school, maybe John Locke... yes that was it, some thesis he published."

"I suspect it's the theory of innatism Plato developed thousands of years ago, though Plato didn't assert that knowledge was pre-learned, only reason, desire, and spiritedness. I think it was Rene Descartes who expanded Plato's theories into all knowledge being inborn, or something like that. I was a philosophy minor in college, so there's too much useless information in my head."

"Ah, I thought it was something I picked up from watching a Sci-Fi TV show."

"I loved those types of programs. Too bad they always get cancelled."

"Yes, there are several great TV shows out there — but it's not philosophy that has me thinking this way, it's my genius savants. How can they know what they know, and yet in some cases, be incapable of any other intelligent thought?"

"Aren't you and I considered genius savants?"

"So they say, but we don't fit into the same class as the savants I've been studying. Think about it. Some of these guys can barely feed themselves, like one of my recent patients, who had a severe brain injury as a newborn — a lack of oxygen during birth. He can't function without someone doing everything for him, yet put him at a piano, and he can play any song and creates his own. He's deaf, too, so he couldn't have heard those other pieces of music. Explain that!"

"I'm with you, Brill. There has to be something more."

"There's one more idea that I can't shake. What if our memories are actually points in time where our minds can go back to when we saw, learned, or heard something, and actually access it, like a form of time travel? What if memories are only stored as temporal coordinates in our brains? The genome would allow for such coordinates. I just don't see how memories, basically vivid videos of an event, could be stored in neural cells. Our brains simply don't have the storage capacity for more than ten years' worth of memories. After that, the brain would have to erase memories and no longer have access to them. That doesn't seem to be the case."

"So what you're saying is that you think the brain somehow accesses a point in the past, and pulls those images from the past in real time as they're happening?"

"That's an eloquent way of putting it. I'm beginning to think more and more that memories are points or coordinates of a time and place — temporal coordinates."

"Time-traveling brain cells. Don't publish that, Brill, or you'll definitely lose any credibility you've gained in the scientific community."

"Give it some thought. You're great at spatial mapping; add time as another dimension."

"Brill, my mind is incredible at knowing where things are at any given time, but homing in on a narrow slice of time like that would be impossible even for me."

Brill thought for a moment. "Okay, this may sound crazy... but could you build me a machine that could track consciousness when it's directed externally?"

Sirum laughed. "Hell yes, that's crazy! I wouldn't even know where to start. There's nothing to hang onto as it leaves a person's head, so I have no signal to follow."

"Well, have another beer. Maybe an idea will drop in your lap."

"In Vegas, many things may drop in a person's lap; ideas usually aren't one of them." The smile that crossed Sirum's face as he said this made them both burst into laughter.

Brill couldn't let the idea go. He knew there *had* to be a way. It just required some creativity. The next day, he was still mulling over the idea of tracking someone's projected thoughts when his Mom showed up to deliver some of his Dad's old stuff. She thought Brill needed to decorate his office, as it didn't look professional enough for her. Of course, his Dad's Nobel plaque and medal were in there, but that just reminded Brill to live up to his father's accomplishments; they'd make their way to his house. At the bottom of the box was an odd-looking rock — rather flat, with some sort of inscription on it. As he put the rock under the lights of his desk, he saw that it was a pictogram or glyph, not an inscription. He'd never seen this before. Where did it come from, and why was it in his Dad's office?

His Mom had the answer, which surprised him. This was something Brill himself had found as a young boy on their trip to Chile, decades before. Brill had no memory of that trip. She went on to recall how this rock had almost cost him his life, yet ended up saving it, as it caused Brill to undergo surgery for a life-threatening tumor sooner than expected. Eventually, Brill was saved by a bone marrow transplant, using marrow donated by, of all people, Sirum.

A transplant, thought Brill. *Sirum's bone marrow. Could it be*? It was like a light bulb went off in his head. Sirum's marrow could conceivably have given Brill the incredible mental abilities he had developed. People with bone marrow transplants sometimes began to express the genetic traits of their donors, or so one theory went. Could his father have anticipated this and used the nanobots to make sure it happened? His Dad had never said what the bots were there to do, just that they were there, and he never actually verbally said even that, just written it in code on the notes he handed to Brill shortly before he died.

The thought rattled Brill. As his eyes turned back to the stone, he noticed an odd image on it. The people looked like Mayans, he thought, or at least the images looked like those he had seen in Mayan glyphs; yet this rock was from Chile, way out of place. Those people lay next to each other in a prostrate position, and there was a balloon-like drawing emanating from their heads, reaching for the sun or sky; Brill couldn't entirely decipher that last part. This image reminded him of the conversation he and Sirum had had a few nights ago over beers, regarding the projection of one's consciousness. Was this an ancient belief, or him trying to justify his theory? The better question to him was *why*. Why would some civilization hundreds or thousands of years ago think their consciousness could project to the stars?

It was the catalyst he needed to push onward, and not let the idea drop.

There was some research on psychic connections being done at Harvard, he knew; by then, Brill was reaching far and wide for any thread that would lead him to the device he needed. The group at Harvard was more than excited to have him observe their work. A neurologist such as Brill, even with his notoriety, was still an audience, and they relished the chance to show off their work. They were trying to understand how some people could share similar thoughts without trying. They believed there was some type of shared mental link between the two people, and were using happily-married couples that had been together for at least ten years, as subjects of their research. The commonality was that one person could finish the other's sentence or say the very thing the other person was getting ready to say. These couples were reporting it often enough that the random occurrence effect was dismissed.

The researchers at Harvard had invented a way they believed could slow the mental connection enough that it could be monitored and tracked. They'd built two interconnected tanks where the subjects were fully immersed in a dense conductive medium. The substance was a gooey mixture of amino acids, sound-dampening substances, and charged particles. The subjects themselves wore earplugs and goggles, as they needed to be able to read a monitor inside the chamber. The surface of each chamber was coated with a substance that prevented even neutrinos from passing through. The only existing aperture was a tube connecting the tanks. They believed they could funnel the projected thoughts, in response to questions on the monitor, from a subject in one tank to the subject in the other. The tube connecting the tanks was loaded with billions of extremely sensitive molecular sensors. Any motion or movement at the quantum level would be detected by these sensors.

While Brill was there, he observed in real time the projection of thoughts between subjects in adjoining tanks. *Remarkable*, he thought, both in response to the results and to the equipment they had designed. Wondering how much they would share, Brill asked if he could see how the machines were designed. They were more than open; they pulled out the blueprints and gave him pointers on every detail. They had started to explain the software needed when Brill asked if they would let Sirum visit. They agreed. They were eager to collaborate, offering to build him a coupled device if he could get the funding, which wasn't a problem. He said he would think it over and get back to them, even though he had already said "yes" in his mind.

On Sirum's way back from his trip to Harvard, he was already designing a more advanced version of the tank system that might meet Brill's needs. He built the device in two months, though Brill requested additional capability after the fact, causing Sirum to make a second set, taking an additional four months. Brill wanted the device not just to transmit thoughts, but to project them outward over vast distances. This required amplification of the mental signals. The natural signals could easily be picked up by a receptive mind, but an unreceptive one would require a much stronger signal. Seeing where Brill was going with this, Sirum devised something like a wave generator. Once it received an incoming signal, it could amplify it exponentially. It relied heavily on the quantum computer to isolate the neural signals from noise, something that only quantum computing power could do, with the same timing as the transmission of a thought from one neuron to another.

When it came time to test the machine, Brill excitedly bounced from room to room, ready to put his new toy through its paces. The first subjects were the savants he'd been experimenting on for the past few years. Getting them into the tanks was a more difficult experience than he'd anticipated, as most were extremely frightened. It took some coercing from their parents, but they were eventually submerged and able to see the monitors. In the first set of tanks he had two similar savants, who took the same newly devised test at the exact same moment. They both went into the expected mental pause at the same time before their minds were ready to solve the problems.

Since they were submerged, they couldn't recite their answers, but Brill knew their minds would begin to solve the problems anyway. For the first time, Brill saw something probative, though not what he had expected. When the boys went into the mental pause, there seemed to be a projection of some sort of pattern involved, different from the ones he'd seen at Harvard. Once they recovered, the projections stopped. Thinking this was an outward projection and not a person-to-person projection, Brill had them transferred into the new tanks with a new problem. The new problem elicited a mental pause again, and his sensors picked up the outward projection. This time the signal was amplified so intensely that both he and Sirum flinched as they received it. Brill grinned hugely; he knew the projection came from his savants! Where the signal was going, however, was another matter of intense discussion between him and Sirum.

The outward signals from the savants seemed to be projected to an area of outer space densely packed with dark matter. Sirum was adamant that the thoughts were projected there simultaneously due to that being the problem they were both solving. Brill had a different perspective. "How could they be solving the problem when they're in a mental pause?"

"Maybe that pause is how long it takes for their brains to run though the calculations?"

"Unlikely, Sirum, as we were also giving the problem to other savants in a separate room, viewing their reactions and having them verbalize the results. Those boys demonstrated the solution in parts, both at the same time, indicating that was what the boys in the tanks were doing. Since we only showed them one part of the equation at time, they couldn't have had the final solution already, which is what you're implying."

"I thought one of your arguments was that all knowledge is already known, and we just need a way to express it?"

"No, I just was asking the question. Plus, these boys didn't have the final answer until they had the complete equation. They had no idea what the other variables were that we introduced at the last second."

"I see your point. So I guess that disproves the theory of innatism."

"At least this experiment does. We need more data."

Over the next few months, Brill refined the testing protocol, and found ways to incorporate musical and artistic genius savants into the testing. The astonishing part to him was that the projected thoughts were all going to the same dark-matter region, but only during the mental pause all these individuals showed, and only for the time their minds were paused. This finding led Brill to expand his research to ordinary people, graduate students mostly — basically anyone willing to spend hours in a tank full of goo. Those efforts proved futile, as these individuals projected too many thoughts, and the result was an unreadable mess. The thoughts seemed to bounce off each other and cancel themselves out. His own thoughts drifted to every aspect of his research over the last several years. What had he missed?

He was on his two-hundred and twelfth volunteer when he caught a shred of a thought. It wasn't projected to where the savants were projecting, but it was an outward thought nevertheless. *Now* he had something. He had meticulously analyzed every aspect of the volunteers, from their protein make-up down to their full genetic profiles. Now he had to find the needle in a haystack. But even with the quantum computing power he had at his disposal, the analysis took a few months. Once finished, Brill cursed at the report. The only similarity was *one* amino acid change on Chromosome Fifteen in the volunteer, and it didn't match any of the savants. Yet it was another thread he could weave into this complex pattern.

Focusing on the lone genetic anomaly, he set up a series of experiments to monitor the subject's blood continuously while performing the projection mapping. He was looking to see if there was some protein that was helping this person, which was either not in the savants or changed just enough to amplify neural signals. It took many experiments, and the volunteer was about to quit when Brill finally homed in on the answer. It was a protein: a prion, in fact. Prions teach other proteins to look and behave like themselves. This mutation on Chromosome Fifteen resulted in the formation of a prion. The volunteer wasn't willing to let Brill drill into her brain to see if it existed in her neurons, no surprise there, but Brill had high confidence that he *would* find it there if he had a chance to look. Now the trail led back to the savants. What did their genetic codes produce?

He found prions, but not the same ones across the board. They were similar among savant types, though; the math savants had close similarities within their group, while the musical ones had a different type of prions, but pretty much the same set from one musical prodigy to the other, and so on. Now he had it — though this did present a problem for his future experiments. Would healthy individuals let him inject them with prions that might cause mental disabilities, but give them a highly specialized skill? Unlikely. He would have to explore animal tests first, though his hopes weren't high for success.

His first experiments were, in fact, a total failure. Every chimp he injected with the prions suffered severe brain damage. Every prion type completely wiped its brain of all abilities, so severely that even the autonomic systems stopped functioning. Their minds basically forgot how to breath, how to pump blood. Brill was undeterred, thinking this to be a result of using human prions on primates. Luckily for him, one of his graduate students was so desperate for work that Brill viewed this as an opportunity to try his experiment in real time, despite the risks. The student chose the type of ability he would like to exhibit, so Brill created those prions. The injection of them presented no obvious problems, and the student was lowered into the tank.

Everything was going well until he went into severe

seizures. He survived unharmed, but refused to continue the

experiments.

Chapter 7: The Desert

The intense heat was beating down on late evening as Brill ran at a fast pace through the downtown streets of Las Vegas. Running was a pastime he'd picked up in medical school to alleviate the boredom of studying. The heat hung on even as late as midnight, but there was no better time of day to safely run through the chaotic streets.

He had been running farther and faster lately, trying to answer some questions in his head. Running was about the only peace he had, though the city was getting too congested for it. He began to hit the trails up into the mountains, as he needed more and more miles. This year he was going participate in his first ever marathon, and was going to push himself to the limit, whatever that might be. The trails were dangerous at night, of course, with the rattlesnakes out hunting rodents. The last time he'd run up into the hills after sunset, he'd nearly stepped on two snakes. As much as he hated the heat, he could safely hit that trail only during daylight hours.

Liora routinely joined him on his trail runs, and they'd race until one of them ran out of gas — usually him, as she was in incredible shape. This time, she had chosen a new trail, one Brill might never have noticed. He was surprised when she grabbed his hand and pulled him onto the trail; it was well-hidden, and he wasn't sure they could find their way back. It was also at such a steep an incline that he felt he would fall if he stopped running.

They hit a narrow crevice and pushed themselves to see who could hit the top first. As they crested the top of the hill, they narrowly avoided a super-high chain-link fence topped with razor wire. As they hit the top, they careened to their right, almost face-planting into a cliff. There was a narrow passage they could continue to run on to avoid the cliff and fence, and they finally hit a plateau where the rock gave way to a wide-open space overlooking the valley below, where the fence no longer hemmed them in.

As Brill passed the last of the fence before it doglegged away, he noticed a For Sale sign on it. The fence clearly surrounded government property, and that piqued Brill's curiosity. He knew the land well around Vegas, but had never encountered this hidden jewel of property. He wondered again how Liora had spotted the trail, as it was so well-hidden, then shook his head and took note of the phone number on the sign as he hurried to catch her. By the time they made it back into the city, they had covered over twenty miles, and were thoroughly exhausted.

That night, they hit the town for a buffet they felt they'd earned; calories were never an issue at their age, not after running so far. The conversation started off with small talk about the challenges of their work, and any interesting findings. As the evening progressed, Brill thought to ask her about that trail. How had she seen it, and had she run it before? She dodged the question a time or two, but finally answered after finishing the glass of wine she had been nursing all evening. "Brill, I was delighted you were willing to try out some new trails. How much have you learned of the history of this area?"

"I know a lot about the areas I frequent, but haven't given the rest much attention."

"The area we were running today used to be a mining town. The name escapes me, but it was taken over by the government during the Great Depression and has remained government property till now. Not sure why they're selling it, but the trails are fantastic around there."

"Mining? Have you seen any of the old mines?"

"No, but one of my patients, a guy who's a tour guide around here, was going on and on about how great it would be to be the lucky one to get that property. The government is auctioning it off, and he had tourism dollars in his eyes."

"Interesting. I'd love to get a close look at some of those old mines. How cool would that be, to see a piece of history left unchanged? Especially around here!"

"I'm not sure how much of the old mines or town are left, but I'm certain the government built something there. My patient said it's in the side of the mountain."

Brill scratched his head, deep in thought, "Do you know much they want for it?"

"I wasn't paying attention. Is it really for sale?"

"Yeah, I saw a sign on the fence. I memorized the number, and I think I'll call now." He did. After dialing, Brill received a message that said the Federal government was taking sealed bids on the property. There was no amount listed. *Dangerous*, thought Brill, as he would hate to overpay if he were to bid on it.

As Brill's research continued to make progress, he became increasingly worried about government surveillance. He was sure he'd gained the interest of Liam Rhett, though he wasn't sure how, when, or if he was being watched or bugged. His Dad's murder had forever cemented his distrust of the government. He needed a way to protect his work, as scenes of the future were already playing out in his head, showing the government raiding his lab, his life's work being swept away to some hidden facility similar to Vassal. He was determined not to let that happen.

The idea percolated in his head for a while to create a hidden backup lab where every bit of work he was doing was copied, unknown to anyone but himself. That desert property kept jumping to the top of his mind. How much would it cost, and would he have to build? If he had to build, then nothing he did would be hidden. It would be too obvious.

He had to see what was hidden behind that fence. He didn't want to drag Liora into it, so he found a day when she was out of town and made his way to the trail. He had a great memory, but even he had trouble finding it. He still couldn't believe Liora had found it. During their run, it was like she knew where she was going, and that bothered him. Was she secretly connected to Rhett somehow?

Once asked, that question could never be unasked, and it floated in the periphery of his mind from then on.

As Brill was running the perimeter of the fenced-in land, he found his entry point. On one hill, there was a gully that dipped just below the fence line, just enough for a man to squeeze under. It occasionally rained in these hills, and he guessed the rain had found the lowest point some time back and eroded the area beneath the fence. He didn't want to get too close in the daylight, but he would risk the snakes if he waited until night. No easy choice, he thought, so he pushed on in the heat of day. He figured that if they had heat sensors, the air temperature would mask his body's signature. Power lines passed over the fence, so he followed them to their endpoint, a small mountain about two miles ahead. *Good*, he thought; at least there would be power when he set up his secret lab.

The heat was starting to get to him by then, as there was no shade from the point he'd entered until his arrival at the mountain; it was pure desert, and it was hot, hot, hot. His water was running low by the time he found some shade under a small mesquite tree. Brill's eyes followed the power lines right into the side of the mountain. That was a good

sign, as it meant there *was* something inside the mountain.

The entrance, though, was hidden. He spent hours walking

around the mountain, climbing to the top; still nothing.

Finally, he spotted a small stream bubbling out of the rock

near the top, and went to refill his bottle. As he knelt, his

eyes caught a glimpse of a reflection off to the side. He was

so parched, he consumed more water than he thought he

could ever drink, and then approached the area where he'd

spotted the reflection. There it was: a metal door, with an

associated road and parking lot, hidden down below. There

were no cars, a good sign it was in fact abandoned. After

making his way down to it, Brill tried the door, but of course

it didn't budge. It confirmed what he was looking to find,

though: something on this land that he wouldn't have to

build. Feeling better about the place, he made his way back

to his car and called it a day.

Brill was now surer than ever that he wanted the property

behind the fence, but how much was it worth? How many

acres? He searched every archive he could find, but none had any information on that plot of land. He wanted to put in a bid, but really needed more information. There was only the phone number and a website to enter a bid, though; no other information. So Brill took a chance and put in a bid. He felt he could part with a million dollars. It might be overpaying, but it was worth it if he got what he wanted.

A week after placing the bid, he received a call saying his bid was accepted. He was now the proud owner of one hundred acres of Nevada history. One hundred acres! Once payment was received, the lawyer said, he would be sent the deed to the land and keys to the building, along with a map of entry and exit points. As promised, the documents and keys arrived several days after he electronically submitting the payment of one million dollars. He was so excited to see his new property he could hardly wait for Liora to return.

#

Eighteen Months Earlier

Liam's frustration was growing. Liora had experienced a close call in South Africa; he feared she might stray too close to the inner circle of the cartel and he might not get her back. He needed her in Vegas to monitor Brill Everly. The work Everly was developing was of keen interest to the HIA, as they could immediately put it to use. The irritation for Liam was his lack of knowledge, which was a rarity for him. Somehow, Brill had managed to keep all his secrets secret. Liam needed to know what those secrets were; and even more importantly, how to prevent them from being discovered by other interested organizations.

It took several months for him to extract Liora from her assignment. The alias he had created for her remained immensely valuable; he could use her anywhere, and wanted to make the most of her. Since she had been out of sync with Brill, Liam doubted she could get as close as she had before she left; he needed a fallback plan. If Brill was anything like his father, and he seemed to be, then he had a secret side that would sow the seeds of distrust for everyone around him. If

Liam could play to that side of Brill, he might yet be able to get what he was after... but he would have to be smarter than the genius.

Eventually a plan materialized in his mind, and Liam was confident of its success. There was an old military installation near Red Rock, part of the original Area 51 acreage, that the government still owned. Liam called up one of his old team who had served with him in Africa, now a general in charge of government assets, and laid out his plan. He explained that he would need the general to transfer ownership of one hundred acres in the north part of Area 51 to Liam's organization. He couldn't say what he needed it for, just that it was an HIA need. After some bartering — as every favor required a reciprocal one — Liam was able to get what he wanted. What he had to give up for this land would be a price worth paying, though it would be some time before his friend could collect: Liam had to loan out Liora's services to the Air Force for an undisclosed period of time.

The building on the parcel was an old Cold War-era protective capsule, a retreat for the President and other high-ranking leaders in case of a nuclear launch. It was well-hidden and fortified inside of a mountain, which worked against drone surveillance, so Liam wanted to refurbish the building before sale, and make sure he had eyes and ears everywhere. The report his inspectors sent on its condition was dire. The building was in such bad shape it would have to be ripped out and rebuilt, and there was no power source even close by. It had been removed thirty years before when the building was decommissioned. Liam took note, as he could use this to lessen the terms of his mutual agreement for the place.

What Liam hoped would be a two-month refurbish turned into a year and fifty million dollars. It wasn't cheap to run power and water to a building in the middle of nowhere. Getting supplies for his team to actually build was something the military had perfected, though, and they had no obstacles there; they just had to make the end result look older than it was. Not too old, but recently used and abandoned. In the end he had what he needed, as he always did, and he could set the trap for Brill. He would need Liora, naturally, and she would have to play her part to perfection. He had to leave enough breadcrumbs to entice the adventurous side of Brill, and make him think he was outsmarting everyone else. The property would only go to Brill, assuming he could get him to want to buy. Liora was the key to that. He would also put up roadblocks to make sure he could get the right operatives in place.

Liora wasn't so sure of his plan. Her concern was that it might start to raise doubts about her in Brill's mind. It would just seem too obvious: run on a hidden trail that even she had trouble finding, then get Brill to take notice of a For Sale sign erected in the literal middle of nowhere— who does that? That was the kicker, she thought; anyone with any sense would scratch their head about why a For Sale sign was stuck at the top of a mountain on a hidden trail. It was a big red flag to her, but Liam wasn't worried. He wanted her to completely ignore it and make no mention of it.

Everything would work out, he assured her. He knew how

Brill thought, and felt he could predict his actions with a high

level of confidence.

#

The road to Brill's new purchase was little more than a

trail. If it ever rained, he wasn't sure he would make it on the

existing track. He liked that the facility was so secluded, but

he would have to improve the road if he ever hired people to

work out here; plus, he was going to have to invest in a

hardier vehicle, as his sports car was taking a beating.

Getting the building up and running was a work in progress;

it had taken him several layers of electrical inspectors from

all levels of the government to allow power to be restored,

since it had been shut off for at least ten years. Then he

needed a certificate of occupancy, as the Feds had declared

the site abandoned. *I might as well have built a new building

from scratch,* he thought; *it would have been easier.* The

water supply was also giving him difficulty. Somehow, a

well was tapped into the water table, though there wasn't supposed to be an accessible water table this far north, and he couldn't get the state to release the water as safe to drink, meaning he couldn't occupy the building without drastic measures.

Then, one day, a consultant called him out of the blue. He claimed to be an expert in cutting through government red tape, and could guarantee that he could put the right resources in place to get the building operational within six months — for the right price. At that point, Brill would have taken anything; the building was useless without a right to occupy it and water to drink. The consultant's references checked out, and Brill was more than happy to let someone else deal with all the bureaucratic crap. He was too busy with his work to fight government agencies. *One more roadblock removed,* thought Brill. Once the building was operational, he could set up his secondary lab. For now, the new lab would only mirror or clone all his university data. He didn't intend for anybody other than he and Sirum to set foot on its premises.

A year after its purchase, having worked through all the bureaucracy and remodeling, Brill had a functioning retreat. He often frequented the desert building, though the two hours it took to get out there soon became cumbersome, so he ended up buying a helicopter and learning to fly it himself. This reduced the commute to fifteen minutes each way. At the top of Brill's mind was getting his quantum computer out to the desert facility, but he had to do so without drawing notice; luckily, his helicopter would be the perfect transport, because he'd made sure to purchase a roomy one with plenty of power. Sirum was his right-hand man with the quantum computer. Brill created a cover story for the lab, saying the "freezer" was broken and had to be sent off for repairs. In the middle of the night, he and Sirum covertly moved it to the roof of his university lab's building, and loaded it onto the copter. Brill's piloting had been getting better, and this ride was smoother than any of his previous ones, though landing in the dark at the desert lab was a first for him. They thought they had a perfect plan to get the machine into the subterranean building: there was a service platform that would transport large items from the surface to each floor.

They had successfully moved the computer to the platform, all three tons of it, and were slowing lowering it when they hit a snag. In its narrowest dimension, the computer was about two inches wider than the platform. No big deal, they decided — until they realized that the shaft the platform descended narrowed as it got deeper, until the platform was almost touching the walls on the lower two levels. The shaft had been blasted out of the mountain, and the rock was too hard to cut with a saw, so the shaft was the size it was and that was that. They didn't know this when they started, learning it only when the machine got wedged between floors and wouldn't budge. Now Brill wished they'd simply used a tape measure. "What good is it to be a genius if you can't think of everything?" he raged. After struggling to pry it free, three hours later they had movement and were able to raise it slightly.

They had pulled it up less than two levels when the lift motor quit working.

With limited options, they settled on blasting the north wall of the shaft to make a bit more room. Sirum thought he could jury-rig the winch to lower the computer from its current point, but going up was no longer an option. This was a tough decision for Brill, as blasting might mean the collapse of the whole shaft and the destruction of the computer. In the end he decided to go for it, and they set about determining the best way to widen the shaft.

The lowest floor had some hairline cracks in the rock of the north wall, and presented the best and most dangerous option. With the charges set, they braced the platform, trying their best to anchor it at Level Three, two floors above the bottom of the shaft. Squinting, Brill gingerly pressed the button to set off the charges. The explosion was every bit as terrifying as he had anticipated, with part of the upper shaft collapsing as well as the part they'd targeted. Fortunately, they'd put in place a makeshift net to capture any falling rock, though they hadn't expected as much to fall as did. Clearing the debris was a long-term chore that took multiple visits. The removal of the stones from the lowest level, where they needed to be, revealed an unexpected surprise: the blast had opened a narrow entrance, less than three feet wide, into what appear to be a natural cavern.

Then tragedy struck. One Saturday morning, Sirum and Brill were standing atop the quantum computer, trying to rig a workaround for the broken lift motor, when there was an enormous cracking groan in the surrounding rock. They dropped and held tight to the computer, staring at each other in wide-eyed shock, as they heard a rumble of falling rock below. They both weathered the quake, but the lights in shaft did not; it went dark, and the only light was the dim sunlight filtering down the shaft from above, now diminished by a rising cloud of dust. Luckily, they both had their smartphones on them, and Sirum grinned as he activated the flashlight app.

Neither of them were wearing protective tethers, because they were surrounded on all four sides by solid rock... or at least, they had been. Just when they were sure they were safe and had loosened their grips, there was another quick, sharp jolt, and the platform *swayed*, dipping toward the east. Sirum began sliding toward the edge of the computer, scrambling to get a grip all the way. As he was fighting to right himself, he reached back to push against what he thought was the solid wall of the shaft, only to find his hand full of air. A wide fissure had formed unnoticed in the east wall. Sirum slid right into it; but somehow, he managed to grab the bottom flange of the computer as he fell. That saved his life. "I'm all right, just hanging around down here," he called calmly up to Brill, almost sounding a bit amused. "But my hands are sweaty, so if you could expedite my recovery...?"

There was no way Sirum could pull himself up the smooth side of the computer. Hooking his feet into the straps holding the computer in place, Brill slid forward to a point where he could try to grab Sirum's hand — thereby causing the platform to tip even farther. With a yelp, Sirum slipped and fell two stories into the shaft they'd just cleared, striking the bottom with a meaty thud. Brill wanted to scream, but he couldn't: he had to hold his phone in his teeth as he was using it as a flashlight, so he could find handholds in the fissure, which extended a good ten feet or so into the wall of the shaft. He'd always been pretty good at wall-climbing in the gym, so he leaped onto the craggy face of the fissure and somehow half-scrambled, half-slid the nearly 30 feet to the bottom, moaning in fear all the way. He couldn't fathom living without his best friend. Sirum couldn't be dead. He'd landed on his feet, right?

The bottom of the shaft was very dark, and finding Sirum in the weak phone light was challenging. When he did, he was relieved to discover that Sirum was still alive. But the fall had mangled his legs, and he had a serious head wound and other injuries from when he'd collapsed, after striking the floor feet-first, and his head smacked into a jagged pile of rock.

That was when Sirum and Brill entered the hidden cavern for the first time. The bottom of the freight shaft was littered with debris, which was still occasionally falling from the fissure, and Brill had to move Sirum to a safer spot where he could treat him. After squeezing through the aperture with his fortunately skinny friend, Brill didn't have time to explore. Luckily, he quickly found a flat, uncluttered surface near what appeared to be an underground lake or river. The water was very cold, and Brill decided it would help slow the inflammation of Sirum's injuries; so he carefully laid Sirum in the mountain water, then took off his own shirt and soaked it. He laid that over Sirum's head injury, figuring it would buy him some time to find the medical supplies in his new facility.

To his immense frustration, the exit from the bottom floor of the damn shaft was entirely blocked by the pile of rubble. So he gingerly climbed up the rocks and the wall above to the second level, phone clutched in his teeth again, where he was able to force the door open about 18 inches. Apparently this doorway had been warped by the shaft's latest movement, and there was no opening it any further without a cutting torch. But the opening was just enough for him to get inside and get what he needed from the infirmary. He came back down the same way, with the supplies in a bag he pushed out ahead of him and then slung on his back.

Sirum was still breathing, and his pulse seemed okay. Holding him as still as possible in the frigid water, Brill affixed a splint to Sirum's neck and back. He wasn't sure if his friend had suffered spinal injuries, and had to plan for the worst. Getting him out was a priority now, as time was working against them. But how? There was no way of getting Sirum out through the building; he couldn't drag him up to the second floor, and couldn't get the door open enough to get him through anyway. Getting him up through freight shaft was out, too. It was demonstrably unsafe, and he lacked any ropes or cabling he could use to raise Sirum out from above. Neither of them had ever anticipated anything like this. And in any case, Brill didn't want the whole world to know about his desert facility just yet.

After sealing the entrance to the cave with rubble, to block out any incidental light from the freight shaft, Brill turned off his flashlight app and waited for his eyes to adjust. About ten minutes later, he became aware of a few faint shafts of light stabbing down from above as he scoured the ceiling of the cavern for any sign of an exit. Okay, that meant there were some natural shafts to the surface. Good. Hopefully one would be accessible. Now, as much as he hated it, he needed Liora's help. He'd try to make it seem like he and Sirum were spelunking and had suffered an accident.

He cleared the cavern entrance. After making his way back to the surface via the second-floor access, he called Liora. It wasn't hard to sound frantic. "Liora, I need your help! Sirum's been injured in an accident in the desert!"

"What happened?" She sounded cautious.

"We were caving near my new place, and Sirum fell and injured his head, legs, and back. He's unconscious and stabilized down in the cave. I had to leave him to get reception to call for help. Please, I need you."

"How can I help?"

"I need to keep this quiet, so it has to be just you and me. Maybe a few paramedics. He's down in a cave about two hundred feet below the surface. There was an earthquake while he was coming down, and something snapped his rope when he was about 30 feet off the ground. I don't think the shaft we came down is there anymore. But I've found some other shafts we can use. I need about five hundred feet worth of rope or a cable we can attach to the winch on my helicopter. I hope one of the shafts is big enough for a gurney. Once I'm in the copter I'll radio the hospital to have some supplies readied. I just need the cave rescue equipment from you. Please have that ready. I'll be at the UNLV Hospital helipad in thirty minutes or so."

"Since when do you have a helicopter, and when did you learn to fly one?" Liora demanded, then said, "Questions for the flight out. I'll have what you need when you get here."

"I knew I could count on you!"

After marking the entrance to the first natural shaft he found, Brill radioed his admin at the university to round up the other supplies he needed, and to see if any of the emergency staff could help. He let them know a friend of his had been injured in a cave fall, and it was serious. To his surprise, he found everything ready on the roof, Liora and two paramedics included, when he arrived. He landed just long enough to shove everything inside and take on the passengers; then he was back in the air. The flight back to the desert was spent updating the team on the nature of Sirum's injuries, what he'd already done, and what they needed to do.

Once he'd landed on a relatively flat spot near the marked entrance, they attached the cable to the winch on the helicopter and wound it up. The cable was well over five hundred feet long, so it was more than ample. Brill was the first down the natural shaft, which proved just large enough for their needs. Once he was down, Liora and one of the paramedics followed. That's when they almost suffered a second tragedy: as Liora was descending with the first paramedic right above her, the upper walls of the shaft gave way, and nearly took them with it. Brill was looking up, watching them descend; as the first rocks passed within range of his helmet light, his quick reflexes saved his life. Diving out of the way of the rock fall, he recovered quickly enough to get to Sirum and make sure that he, too, was safe from the falling debris. *The blasting of the elevator shaft must have destabilized this entire side of the mountain*, he concluded with dismay. Now movement up and down these natural shafts was breaking loose parts of it.

Their helmets protected Liora and the paramedic from the worst of the debris, and fortunately, they weren't seriously injured. They were able to complete their descent, but getting back up presented a new challenge. The paramedic immediately went to assist Brill in treating Sirum, while

Liora climbed back up her rope to see if they could exit. But as she feared, the upper walls of the shaft had completely collapsed in on themselves.

Near the top, her two-way radio enabled her to talk to the other paramedic. They devised a plan for him to search the area for other entrances to the chamber, while she did the same from beneath. If he found an entrance, she wanted him to retrieve the cable, if possible, and lower it down the new shaft. He was their only lifeline to the outside world, so he needed to stay safe. If they couldn't find a way up in the next hour, he was to call for help. She gave him Liam's special number, as she knew the Colonel would pull out all stops to get her to safety.

Though Sirum was soon stabilized, they had no way to get him to the surface. Time was working against them now; the only thing on their side was the low temperature of the lake water. It was helping to keep the inflammation down, but Sirum's body could only take that for so long before he succumbed to hypothermia. They had brought several powerful drugs to give to him, though, and those were also working to keep him alive, but he'd need surgery ASAP.

#

Liam Rhett was surprised when the call from the paramedic came in. The number he had given Liora was intended for dire circumstances only — and she wasn't the one calling. Not knowing all the details of the situation, he had to assume the worst, and sent the rescue squad from Area 51. They arrived within half an hour; apprised of the situation, they began looking for a new entrance to the mountain. They knew that the two of the people below, Liora and Brill, were HVTs —High Value Targets — and must be rescued at all costs and immediacy.

Even for these well-trained troops, progress was painfully slow. Every time they began to make progress, the mountain would shift, and their chosen shaft entrance would collapse. After the third attempt, they found a stable hole and braced it heavily before they began the rescue. It took them over three hours to get all four people below out of the cavern, and none too soon. As they were pulling Sirum out, the brace at the entrance gave way and nearly crushed him. The accompanying tremor was so severe that they were concerned the entire mountain would collapse. Once they loaded Sirum onto their helicopter, they had him at Brill's hospital and in emergency surgery half an hour before Brill got there.

Sirum's injuries were much more severe than anyone had realized. Had Brill known back in the cave, they might have taken a different approach to his rescue. The surgery took fifteen hours, with many close calls. In the end, it wasn't clear if Sirum would be paralyzed when he awoke or not. Brill utilized the time to analyze Sirum's genetic code, to see if any of his Dad's technology might help him. Sirum's mind was a great concern, as he had suffered several cracked cervical vertebrae, a severe concussion, and a fractured occipital bone — and his brain might have been deprived of oxygen for an extended time.

#

Sirum did recover, though his road to recovery was a long one. In time, he regained full use of his arms and legs, and suffered no permanent damage aside from the scars.

The need to explore the cavern kept drawing Brill back to it. He needed that place, he decided, to hide his computer. While Sirum was recovering, Brill cleared the rock fall blocking the lower entrances to the former elevator shaft, then lowered the quantum computer to the bottom and into the lower level of the facility. He then explored as much of the cavern as he could without risk of further cave-ins. He uncovered an entrance to an even larger open chamber, studded with surprisingly few stalagmites and stalactites. Brill finally got a chance to explore the body of water as well. It proved to be a very large underground lake, extending as far as the eye could see even with the brightest lights. He could easily hide a lab somewhere in this area, he decided. he just needed to get utilities to it somehow, and hide the entrances.

After most of a year, Sirum was finally back helping Brill. They worked tirelessly in their free time, what little of it they had, to build out a room in the second cavern and make it into a functioning lab. They called the cavern Avalon, as they were both huge fans of the Arthurian mythos. Exploration of the cavern yielded some unexpected pluses, as they found several deep passages to even more caverns. That would be a bonus to kill some time when he was out here working, though he wasn't sure how he was going to manage any of it with his busy surgical rotations.

Ultimately, the shaft from which they had pulled the injured Sirum from the lower chamber was used to divert powerlines to the new cavern lab. They covered the rest of the entrance with intake and exhaust fans, cementing them into a false floor, such that someone would really have to know what they were after to make their way down the shaft. The natural lake created a water source not only for the Avalon, but for the building as well. With those engineering aspects covered, they began to equip the lab with everything

Brill would need, including the massive quantum computer, which they followed by building a false wall and a hidden entrance. He could come and go as he pleased, and nobody would be the wiser.

During this period, Brill's paranoia led him to question the very foundation of information available to the world through web interfaces. He had noticed some inconsistencies in what was reported in papers and fundamental information sources like published books — slight changes here and there over time. He was consumed by a belief that the government changed the narrative to fit the needs of each administration, which was now causing him to question every aspect of everything he gathered from public sources. To prove this, he began creating periodic information clones about every six months of what was available to the public, since he could easily do this with the massive storage space the quantum computer allowed for. An algorithm he and Sirum created would compare every single word of "respectable" online sources, tracking sentence structure changes and outright omissions from update to update and then making cumulative comparisons. Time would tell if he was right.

The setup of the labs was taking a while, but it was going wonderfully. He had arranged things so that everything that occurred in his UNLV lab was immediately copied to his systems in Avalon, and in real time fed back the data he needed, as the experiments labored on.

#

These days, Brill was working on his bedside manners, as he'd recently been chastised by one of the staff for being too unemotional and distant. He took this to heart, brushing up on his people skills. Today, a patient he'd recently treated was in his office for a follow-up visit. The man, Mr. Han, had a rich history, and was eager to share his stories with a willing ear. He'd been a monk for thirty years deep in the heart of Tibet, at the Tradruk Temple in Lhokha, before he escaped as a refugee to the States when the Chinese army invaded five years earlier. The monastery where he'd lived had been a lightning rod for the Chinese drug trade, specifically the Mao group, as they used the temples to exchange their drugs for diamonds. Brill tuned him out for a bit, thinking about his next patient, but something the man said about "connected consciousness" caused Brill to snap back to reality.

Brill politely asked Mr. Han to repeated his last comment about the Dharma mind or universal consciousness, which Westerners called panpsychism. The idea was that consciousness is everywhere, and Mr. Han claimed his sect had reached a higher level of this group-conscious state than most. He was trying to convince Brill to practice meditation and focus on the consciousness of others, as reducing their suffering was what they meditated on. Brill's curiosity was piqued. "This meditative state you mention has me curious, Mr. Han," he said. "You said you were connected to those around you. Did you feel that way because you were right next to each other?"

"It was more than that. When we entered the Dharma mind state, a special Buddhist practice, I could hear the thought voices of those around me."

This Dharma crap was starting to get on Brill's nerves. Brill couldn't understand how it was possible that the lamas could display such a mass effect with just meditation. He was unconvinced that this was anything more than a group psychosis, but trying to be nice, Brill entertained the man by posing questions that feigned an interest. "Very cool. What happened next?"

"Our minds seemed to enter a place of light, where our thoughts were focused on whatever we were trying to achieve," Mr. Han said. "From there, we could see our thought stream to that effort. Most of the time it was to help some world leader or influence attitudes."

"You didn't smoke or eat some sacred substance before this, did you?"

"Dr. Everly, we were monks. We ate bread, vegetables, and fruit, and drank only tea and water. If we did not purge our bodies of the world, then those impurities would impact our thoughts."

"Sorry, had to ask. Did you ever observe an impact from your efforts?"

"Ah, I sense skepticism... actually, we had many instances of success from our efforts."

"Please, do tell."

"There was one in particular where our efforts had a devastating impact. The last few years at the monastery, we were overrun with thieves and drug traders. We took it upon ourselves to use our mind state to change this. The head of that drug group was a Thai — Sulman Thie was his name. In our Dharma state, we sought a solution to this problem instead of trying to determine a cause. The answer that returned to each of us was to direct our thoughts to the removal of this man. We set our meditative state to the destruction of him. We saw a vision of him in a boat on the ocean, consumed by fire. That thought took hold, I am sad to say, and we embraced it. Shortly before the Mao group invaded, we learned that Sulman Thie had indeed been killed in a fiery explosion on the sea. The image we saw was what happened. Knowing we caused his death shook us to the core, as we sought peace, not death."

Brill nodded thoughtfully. "Okay, so you believe you were responsible for this man being killed in a boat explosion on the sea? Wow. I'll have to take your word for that."

They continued on for a time, until Liora popped into his office to confirm a dinner date with Brill. Not realizing he had a guest, she apologized and was about to leave when the monk, who gaped and turned several shades whiter when he saw her, said something in Mandarin to Liora. Brill, staring in fascination at the monk, was surprised when she rattled off a reply in the same language without missing a beat. She immediately turned and left. Brill became concerned for the elderly gentleman, as he had barely breathed since Liora had replied to him. He finally regained his composure, saying something under his breath. Brill asked him to repeat it.

Eyes wide, Mr. Han said, "She destroyed my temple, she and her assassins. I would never forget that face."

"Mr. Han, you must be mistaken. Liora Abrams is a professor here at the university, and wouldn't hurt a fly. I'm going to ask that you stay a bit longer and have us rescan you, just as a precaution."

"She is dangerous, Dr. Everly. Do not trust her."

That comment he brushed aside, but Brill was still curious about the old man's Dharma mind concept and the meditation involved. Was it different than normal meditation? Why did Mr. Han so strongly believe he was connected to the other monks during this meditation time? Brill was eager to learn all he could, and asked if he could see a demonstration and participate.

#

In the days following, Brill found himself thinking back through the events of the past year or so, as there was something that didn't sit well with him, and he hadn't had time until now to put all the pieces together. What was it?

Something about the rescue of Sirum. He replayed every detail of the event in his mind. What was off about it? He'd brought Liora in, begging for her help; nothing out of the ordinary there. The paramedics were no issue. The cave-in was unexpected, but nothing was out of place. The rescue; that was it. That was what had been bothering him. What was it about the rescue that didn't seem right?

He searched the hospital for both paramedics, but could only find the one who'd been trapped underground with them. The other had just quit showing up for work one day. Nobody ever heard from him again. He was good friends with the paramedic who was with them, Eric, and Eric was perplexed as to why Carl would just disappear. He had reported him as missing, but the police informed him that Carl's apartment had been empty when they checked — not just of people, but of everything. No furniture, no belongings of any kind. His lease had been terminated early, and all penalties paid off. The guy just left, for reasons of his own; case closed.

Eric did mention that Carl had joked about the rescue crew that came in to help from Area 51. Some elite Army rescue crew who happened to be training nearby when the call for help went out, he said. This didn't sound right to Eric, as he was certain the military rarely concerned themselves with ordinary civilian matters short of natural disaster, and that was usually just the National Guard. Now Brill's paranoia was on overdrive. Somehow, Liora had to be involved — but how? She had been with them down below.

It was a mystery that would resolve itself in time, just not soon enough.

Chapter 8: Johannesburg

Thinking back, the transition from Las Vegas to South Africa several years before had been more drastic than Liora had anticipated. She'd always craved adventure, and had been getting bored with her assignment to Brill Everly, a brilliant but dull young man who worked too much. Her Uncle Liam had offered her the new assignment as a distraction — a year at best, he said. Just enough time to break Brill's dependency on her, and for her to inject some excitement back into her life. The UNLV job had her contemplating her role in the world, and had her analyzing her actions, sometimes depleting her of any decision-making ability at all. Damned psychiatry.

The plane ride to Johannesburg was a long one. Watching movies and isolationism wasn't her thing, so she looked to her seat companions to strike up a conversation. Liam had booked the tickets, and surprisingly had spared no expense, as she was in first class. The person sitting next to her was an older gray-haired man, his South African accent indicating he was heading home. Liora was great at finding threads of connection, as she never forgot a name and remembered every detail about the people she met. This case was no exception. It turned out this man, Conner, had lived in Jerusalem fifteen years prior, and she seized on this. Her probing questions were crafty, innocent in their delivery, and her looks and persona always prompted a response, usually with some element of truth.

Conner revealed several clues to his connections; indeed, he seemed more than eager to impress her. She immediately understood why she was in first class. A smile crossed her face as the thought crossed her mind; Liam was always ten steps ahead of her. Conner was one of the connections she was supposed to make in South Africa. He was a prominent member of the Swan family, the leading conglomerate that controlled the diamond trade. She guessed he was high enough up to be useful, too, based on the name drops he was providing. The connection to Jerusalem was all she needed; her skill at conversation helped her achieve a personal level with him, as she knew an associate they'd both intersected with in the past. As soon as she made that connection, he let his guard down and began revealing personal info a normal person might have brushed aside. She filed away these nuggets for future use.

The sixteen-hour flight was one of almost continuous conversation between the two. Liora's cover was ideal; revealing she was a psychiatrist engendered a level of trust and allowed her the ability to infiltrate almost anywhere. Shortly before touchdown, she awoke and was readying herself for what lay ahead when Conner let a clue about his true nature slip. He was now hitting on her — a bold move, she thought, as he knew he was talking to a psychiatrist by then. This made him more vulnerable. As she pretended to give in to his veiled attempts at making a quick score, the information flowed more freely from his lips. His family had apparently acquired the diamond business fifty years ago in a deal swap where they gave up their Indian poppy fields for the land containing the South African mines. They had made their fortune from the byproducts of the poppy harvest, he said; she knew that meant the opium trade, though he didn't say so. This was getting good, she thought; and now to sow some seeds for the future. They arranged a dinner date for after she got settled in for a few days. She wanted to get close, but not too close yet.

The place Liam had set up for her was a high-end apartment near the financial district. Though she now had a direct contact with the family she had been sent to investigate, there was still much work to be done. The first thing she had to do was to establish herself at the university. They were expecting her arrival, and she wouldn't let them down. The staff there provided a welcoming environment; it was easy for her to fit right in. Here, she was going to research the influence of apartheid, generations after its end. The older staff was eager to enlighten her about the era when it was in effect, and the changes made since. This cover would provide her the means she needed to roam about the

country and piece together information for her real
assignment.

South Africa was to Liora's liking. It had everything one
could desire in an advanced society, from the wealthy class
down through the working poor. It was easy for her to fit in,
as anyone with beauty and a strong personality is a draw for
people anywhere. Her time in China had prepared her to do
well here. She had to play her cover well in order to get the
information she really needed. Knowing that the working
poor care less about secrecy than they do about providing for
their families, she knew she could entice them with the right
incentives.

Her first stop was the information stored at the local
library. Everything in South Africa had once been recorded
in paper folios and notebooks, and it cost too much to make
it the old records electronic, so it just sat in a warehouse in a
library waiting to be read. This library was no different than
most, except that it was more antiquated. From the mid-
2000s forward, everything new was electronic, so few had

much use for the archaic records. She began looking for names and addresses of people who had unknowingly been associated with the diamond and drug trades she needed to infiltrate.

The first section she began researching were records of apartheid victims; then she was going to cross-reference those with land that was now diamond mines. Those folks had to have sold out or been forced out years earlier. They could likely provide descriptions of the ones buying the properties, as the names now on the properties were all members of the Swan family. If she could find a few still alive who hadn't wanted to sell but had been coerced to do so, then she would have the thread of connection she needed.

She found one record of a large farm that had been sold fifty years ago, in the Gauteng province of what was now the Cullinan mine. She noted the name and location in her journal, and checked to see if she could find any county records with the same surname. After about three hours spent poring over old records, she finally came across a purchase with the same surname in what was now the financial district of Johannesburg. A palatial estate by any standards; a good indication they had been paid handsomely. She looked over death certificates and birth records, and found several with that address. Those living there were likely the grandchildren of those on the original purchase paperwork.

In her excitement to find the clues of association, she almost missed the second purchase on that land. It was a very small house, likely the servants' quarters, and the purchase price was miniscule compared to the landowner's. It took her several more hours to find the same name in nearby cities. She hit upon township tax records indicating a purchase of a small bungalow with that same name the year after. She could find nothing else after that, but it would have to do as a starting point. Her journal was now filled with several addresses and names. It was a beginning.

A symbol indicating radioactivity on the aerial surveys caught her attention as she closed the book, but there were no mentions of anything radioactive in any of the other records.

She was able to calculate the geolocation coordinates using an app on her phone held over the surveys, as they had specific geo-coordinates called out. It was very close to the diamond mines. Armed with that information, she started sifting through the records again, but nothing special was ever noted about the location. One folio that should have contained it had several pages torn out. She could do little more than take note of what she'd found with that single reference. After quickly taking a picture of it, she placed all the notebooks and folios back on their shelves. The last thing she needed was to draw attention to her work by leaving them out for someone else to put away.

She needed to visit the diamond mine — just to see it, if for no other reason. Wanting to keep the connection alive with Conner, she set up a time for them to meet. He was more than eager to accommodate.

#

The road leading out of Pretoria to the mine was a two-lane highway with several guard checkpoints along the way, and narrow passes where the slightest mistake would send one careening over a cliff into the valley below. They were nearly to the Premier Mine when a lone road heading towards Rayton caught her eye, as it was blocked with razor wire and concrete barriers. Casually, she asked Conner why the road was blocked off. His response was that it was unsafe, something to do with earthquakes and fallen bridges. *Odd*, she thought, *why the razor wire?*, though she didn't pursue the matter beyond his response. Something to check out later.

The mine was everything she expected: highly unsafe and teeming with activity. Based on all she had heard about such mines, she was hesitant to take the tour down into the Earth, but she figured if Conner was guiding her, then they'd make absolutely sure she also survived, as he was too valuable to lose. During the tour, she had the opportunity to chat with several of the workers, making sure to get their names, where they lived, and the names of their family members. The guise of writing a book enabled her to easily gather information, as most people want to be mentioned in such a work, and tend to be less guarded in what they share. Liora found that most of them were generational; they'd followed their fathers and grandfathers into the profession. Many didn't survive past their fiftieth birthdays, as lung cancer and cave-ins caused many a premature demise. One man stood out to her: his last name was Levi, the same as the surname on the sale of the servants' house when the mine sold. This could be the lead she was looking to find... or it could just be a common name in the region. She wasn't sure, but she'd track down his family later. It should be easy, given that they lived on Pretoria's outskirts.

During the trip back from the mine, Conner invited Liora to attend his cousin's wedding. *This is it*, she thought, *an opportunity to meet the family in a raw environment, no pretentions and plenty of alcohol.* At the wedding, several days later, she made it a point to connect with all the non-family members present. She felt they were most likely to be the ones with connections leading to the pot of information-gold she wanted to find. One particular guest owned a shipping company, another was a chicken farmer, another a railroad tycoon, and another, Jim Fink, owned a mineral company. She struck up a lengthy conversation with him, finding that his family had bought their mine two hundred years earlier when they got out of the business of slave-trading. Blood money, he called it, glad to be doing something honest, implying his family were *dis*honest up until the mine. In her experience, when someone said something like "it's honest" or "truth be told." it was a good indicator they were hiding something deeper. He was bragging, and her fake interest kept him talking, as did the shots of whiskey she plied him with. After an hour of this chatter, she learned that not only was he mining gold and platinum, but that he was absolutely *not* mining uranium. "Never would I do that," he said with a wink.

That was the moment Conner rescued her from further conversation. He asked what they had been talking about for so long, and she ran down the list of things Fink had said, omitting the uranium insinuation. That had roused her interest, though, and required a follow up. Between the blocked road she'd seen before the mine tour, the statement about uranium, and the radioactive symbol on the old map, she was finding there was more to the diamond trade than Liam had let on. She wondered if he knew, or if it was just happenstance that she'd stumbled across these bits of choice pieces of information? She suspected Liam did know, but had wanted her to find out on her own. She needed to so some legwork to fit all the pieces onto the gameboard.

Now armed with a more specific mission, Liora decided she needed to locate the link between the uranium and the diamonds. The drug piece must be a small portion of the overall operation. In fact, it would make sense to have the authorities thinking this was a drug smuggling operation instead of a terrorist ring dealing in illicit uranium, with diamonds as currency. *Nice theory. Now I just need to prove it and put names and faces to the players in that ring.*

Liora had discussed with her colleagues her plans to interview families connected to apartheid, but of course the research she didn't mention to them was that all those on her visit list were connected in some way to mining diamonds and/or uranium. Oddly, her first connection was over in Cape Town, far from the mines. The family in question, the Ashtons, had served the Swan family for a number of years before they retired. They had a deep connection to apartheid, as they had led rebellions to raise global awareness of it in the late 1980s. Many in their family had been jailed and tortured for their stance, and had only recently been officially pardoned by the government. They were an obvious choice for her to visit, but it was their connection to the Swan family she was most interested in learning about and had to somehow work into the conversation.

She knocked on the door of the modest home a bit nervously. When an elderly man flung it open, she said winningly, "Hello, I'm Professor Liora Abrams from the

University of Johannesburg. I have an appointment scheduled with a Mr. John Ashton."

"You're speaking to him," the man who opened the door bellowed. "Come on in, girl, and have a seat. Would you like a tea?"

"I would be delighted."

They sat in the living room, sipping their tea, as Liora dove into a plethora of questions relating to the Ashtons' days of forced segregation and servitude before she worked in their jobs at the Swan home. "I noticed on your list of life activities that you worked for the Swan family. Did they treat you well?"

"Treat me well? Of course. This house you see is what they bought me when I was too ill to continue working for them." He smiled widely.

"It's lovely. Would you mind sharing a day in the life of the work you did for them? I like to provide all details in my book. Please hold nothing back, sir. If something is too sensitive, I can hold it out, but I need to know all to complete the story. I need every detail, good and bad."

"My wife and I were their personal administrators," the old man declared. "We're proud of the work we did for them, and they took care of us. Loyalty for loyalty, y'see."

"I see. Can you tell me about their diamonds, and how they use them?"

"The diamonds were the source of their income, y'see. Still are. They mainly sell those to the Jones Group. From there, who knows where they go? They did mine other things, though, things they kept secret— and I should as well."

"They seem to do a lot of good in the community. Please talk about some of that."

"Yes, yes, they regularly give to the Usher Charity, and they set up food banks in their name across all of South Africa. You won't find a single person who will talk bad about them. They take care of even the lowest of the low, y'see."

"Wonderful," Liora said, scribbling quickly, though she was also recording the conversation with his permission. "I do love to write a good story, especially about those who give so much back to the community."

"They do a lot of good," Mr. Ashton said reflectively, "but mixed in with that is also the bad, I suppose. Be careful what kinds of questions you ask, girl. You're an outsider here, and people will take note. I understand your desire to learn, to get that little bit of dirt to make your book sell better, but don't do it with this family, please. Everyone in this country will defend them."

"I appreciate your advice, and will take it into account. Don't worry."

Subsequently, she learned a great deal about their mining operations, and with Mr. Ashton's introductions, found other families to talk with about their time with the Swans. She knew she had to be careful, as word would soon get back to Conner if she asked too many questions, so she soon veered off to families generationally impacted by apartheid, but who had connections to the Fink family. Those who had worked for the Finks had plenty of dirt on them and little good to say. Most stated baldly that they were lucky to have gotten out alive and free of their tyranny in the end.

The bits and pieces of information she got from these families allowed her to put together the framework of a vast smuggling operation with the Swan family as the hub, and the Finks as spokes leading out from there. There were distinct firewalls between the Finks and Swans. Nothing could directly tie one to the other, at least from a business perspective. Radiating out from the Finks were connections to who knew where: her next puzzle to assemble. To do that, she needed to visit those hidden uranium mines.

A year into the book campaign and two hundred interviews later, she still hadn't found a way into the uranium mines, but she'd spooked several high-ranking players in the drug cartel that received the diamonds. They had other ties to the operation they were desperate to keep secret. Liora had set up a meeting in Swaziland with someone who claimed to have dirt on the Swans, and said they could help her answer questions she hadn't thought to ask. Her connection to Conner was humming along nicely, and she played the part of charming professor, always keeping him abreast of who she was interviewing. This man in Swaziland, though, took Conner aback when she told him about her plans.

"He's dangerous. Why do you need to meet with *him*?"

"Not everyone I talk to is going to be a saint, Connor dear. I'll be careful. Here's the address where we're meeting."

"Please *do* be careful. That country has many dangerous areas. At least let me provide a security detail for you?"

"I couldn't ask that. Imagine how it would look if I showed up with armed guards!"

"I had to offer," he huffed.

"And I appreciate the offer, love, but I need to do this alone. I'll be safe, no worries."

The trip to Swaziland was uneventful, but the intrigue picked up after she arrived in the tiny country. The hotel she checked into was one of the most elegant she had visited, a beautiful structure with hundreds of years of history. As she was settling in for a quiet night, a knock on the door roused her out of her slumber. It was a young lady standing by herself. That seemed odd, so Liora cautiously cracked the door with one hand, the other on her 9mm Glock. It turned out the young lady was a messenger from Conner, who asked if she could deliver the message she had in an envelope. Still suspicious, Liora asked her to slide it under the door. "No," the woman said, "I was instructed to deliver it into your hand, and not to let go of it until I do."

Liora cautiously unchained the door so the messenger could enter. The woman did not want to come in, though; she just handed Liora the envelope. As she did so, she read a message: "The danger ahead of you is real. When you need me, text the number inside the envelope. Since I can't deter you from this trip, be extra cautious and I'll help where I can, Conner."

The messenger turned and left without another word. Now Liora was concerned, as her visit with the informant wasn't until the next day. Luckily, Liam had given her a special set of gadgets for use in just such an emergency, what he called "skin phones." One could very easily program a skin phone to dial a single number. It was just a patch placed beneath the ear, halfway up the neck. It would dial out with a simple command or the touch of a finger, and would connect via satellite to anywhere in the world. Its position on the neck allowed it to pick up subvocalized sounds from the throat; incoming sound could only be heard by the ear on that side, as the sound was directed to the eardrum as quick vibrations. Bystanders would never hear anything. It was a clever device, and she had a limited number of them, just in case. This was clearly a time when she might need one, so she affixed one to her neck and prepared it with Connor's number.

The interview was more than forthcoming, as this informant, who called himself Albans, really did have all the dirt she was looking for. And he was eager to share — too eager. The more he talked, the more she began to realize that

Conner's warning was about to come to fruition. Only people without fear of repercussions would share so much. Albans didn't fear her, she suspected, because he was planning to do something to her. What she was learning would be worth it, however, if she survived.

Albans shared that the drugs were actually a front to get *plutonium*, not uranium, out of the country. His organization converted the uranium into weapons-grade plutonium using an old nuclear power plant in the mining region of South Africa that was supposedly decommissioned years ago. Instead, it provided power to some of the mines and regional communities. Once the plutonium was ready, they lined their drug containers with the material, and had couriers hand-smuggle them out of the country, up through the heart of Africa. The diamonds were used as currency. That is, the Finks were paid in diamonds, and then traded those to the Swans for a cash discount. The Swans would then sell those on the open market for many times their mined and purchased value. The drugs were an outgoing crop, mostly opium. Nobody would suspect the plutonium, so they generally had free rein of the continent.

When she heard Albans naming names, she knew her fate was sealed. She hoped they wouldn't kill her right away, so she was bolder in the questions she asked. "Why are you telling me all this? It has nothing to do with apartheid."

"Apartheid? A good cover for you, miss. The questions you've been asking paint you as a government agent; we just aren't sure if it's the drugs or plutonium you're after, or both."

"Really, I *am* a professor, and apartheid is why I am here. Who is this 'we'?"

"You're looking at the 'we'. My associates choose to remain anonymous. Your usefulness to us is past. If you truly are a professor, then nobody will miss you much." With that, a hand snaked around her throat from behind and placed a chloroform-soaked cloth over her mouth. She was unconscious in a matter of seconds.

When she woke, much later, she could immediately tell she was on a boat. The rocking and rhythmic slapping of water against the sides was a dead giveaway. She lay on her side with her hands and feet tied, her mouth gagged. At least she was alive; that was the first step to escaping. Eventually, they would untie her to feed her or allow her to go to the bathroom. She could still have made her emergency call with a subvocalized command, but something kept her from doing so, some thought niggling at the back of her mind.

She remained in this position for what felt like hours. Having nothing to do but think, she reviewed the events of the last few days. It was odd, she thought, that Conner would warn her, then provide her a potential means of rescue by calling an unknown number. He must have been in on it from the start. *If I call without acquiring a phone from someone on this ship, then they'll know that I had a means of communication they couldn't detect,* she realized. They were either trying to flush out a potential risk to their organization, or truly believed she was a government agent. She set herself to playing this one out, but reprogrammed the skin phone with Liam's emergency number, just in case. She could do this because the phone was responsive to specific voice commands pitched below the audible range, as it felt the vibrations in the throat.

Having successfully reset the number, she waited things out. The song *Knocking on Heaven's Door* kept playing through her mind. She hoped her situation wasn't as dire as the song indicated.

The hours of lying in the same position were taking its toll on her. Every muscle in her body ached, and she longed to stand and stretch. When the lights in the cabin suddenly went on, the intensity of them blinded her momentarily; then she was yanked off the floor to a standing position. Her hands and feet were loosened, giving her the momentary relief of blood fully flowing back to where it should be before descending into a hell of pins and needles. After that had passed, they let her clean herself up a bit and then shuffled her to the upper decks. On her way there, she heard someone mention Madagascar; whether it was a destination or a departure point she didn't know. *Madagascar*, she thought.

Wow, must have been out for days. As they brought her to the upper deck, she could see them approaching a shoreline.

Jim Fink greeted her with a smile, "Welcome, Professor Abrams. Today is your lucky day. Seeing as how we could find no connections between you and any government officials anywhere, your life has been spared, though you may wish it hadn't been."

"What the hell, Fink? Where am I?" she demanded.

"Where you are is no longer your concern. You now belong to me. You were warned to be careful, girl. That should have been a clear signal for you to not gather specific information."

"I am a college professor, writing a book. How can I not ask questions, no matter where they lead?"

"It's not the questions that are the problem, Miss Abrams; it's the answers you're getting."

Their verbal sparring went on until they docked at a marina soon after. Then Fink led her across the gangway, down a dock, and onto dry land. Her hands were still bound, but loosely enough that she could free them with a dislocated thumb when the right time arose. She was patient, knowing her opportunity to escape would eventually arise. As much as she wanted to call Liam, playing this out would gain her more influence with Conner and the Swan family. From her conversations with Fink, while she waited for whatever came next, she was enlightened to the reality of the power arrangement between the Finks and Swans. Apparently, there was significant animosity between the two families, and as with any criminal organization, there was zero trust between them. They just tolerated each other in the name of good business.

After being led through several buildings, they pushed her into a room deep within one of the buildings, with no windows and only a sink, toilet, and bed as furnishings. Clearly, this was to be her cell. They didn't count on her being a trained spy, though, or they wouldn't have left her that particular bed. It was more like a cot, but had the elements she needed. The mattress was laid over a frame made of wire — wire that could be uncoiled and shaped to her needs. Not having much else to do, she set about devising her escape. Once out, she would need to "acquire" a phone and call the number Conner had left her in Swaziland.

Several days passed as she learned the rhythm and routine of her new quarters. Once she'd determined a pattern, she saw her opportunity: when they delivered her evening meal, they would open the door and two armed guards would enter. These two seemed to be the only ones taking care of her, so eliminating them both at the same time would provide her the means of escape she needed. That evening, when they were delivering her meal, she acted as if she were in serious distress, moaning and hunched over on the bed. That brought both guards into the room, whereupon they closed the door. She had a wire in one hand, and used the other as a brace when she fell out of the bed, whereupon one guard knelt down to grab her arm and help her up. This provided the opening she needed to wrap the wire around his neck. Using him as leverage, she was able to sidekick the second guard in the throat, incapacitating them both as she rendered them unconscious. The wire then provided her a means to tie them up. She cleaned them out of their weapons, phones, money, and keys. The money was in Malagasy ariaries; she was in Madagascar all right.

Now to escape, knowing nothing about the lay of the land.

Getting out the building undetected was easy, as they hadn't set any other patrols. It was night, so the cover was good as she faded into the streets of the anonymous town. Once she'd made her way to what appeared to be an abandoned building, she used one of her captors' phones to call the phone number Conner had provided. The person on the other end of the line was not Conner; they simply asked for her need. "Rescue, please," was her reply.

"Where are you?" the quiet female voice asked.

"Somewhere in Madagascar. Near a marina."

They walked her through the process of opening the geolocator on the phone, so they could easily find her. Doing so was a risk, but what other choice did she have? Not sure whether it was another trap, she waited.

When daylight came, there were numerous explosions in the direction from whence she had come from, followed by rapid gunfire. The door to her building burst open, and at gunpoint, she was questioned about her identity. Only after providing a code, as she had been instructed, was she hustled aboard a helicopter and flown out. *Hopefully back to Johannesburg*, she thought.

The flight lasted many hours before the chopper finally touched down on a private airstrip. Exhausted, she staggered out of the copter and collapsed. She awoke in a beautiful room in a plush bed, to the scent of flowers. Having regained her strength, she refreshed herself in the adjoining bathroom and began to explore her new surroundings. It wasn't long before a servant found her and escorted her to a dining room.

She was cheerfully greeted by Conner Swan and his family. "I thought we might have lost you when you disappeared from Swaziland," he told her. "You should have taken me up on that offer for protection, yes?"

"If I had, then I wouldn't have a story to tell, would I?"

Connor smirked. "I wouldn't recommend repeating that story, as it might bring more harm than good. Time for talk later. Have breakfast first."

They shared the meal; and later, in his study, he filled her in on the events that had unfolded since her abduction. She had been out of pocket for about two weeks. The Fink family had decided to use her abduction as a catalyst to try to take a larger stake in the Swan family's business operations. They were unsuccessful, and had been systematically removed. A new ally now controlled that aspect of their business arrangement.

Liora thanked Connor and his family for the rescue, and let them know her time in Johannesburg was nearing its end. She had all the information she needed for her book, and would welcome any feedback they could provide, once she had a draft. Since they would be prominently featured in the book, they were eager to see it when she was done.

#

Liora Abrams left Johannesburg via a stop in Germany en route to the USA; she would spend a few weeks there updating Liam on the web of nefarious activities in Johannesburg, and wrapping up the remaining loose ends of the operation. Upon reuniting with him, she was about to give him a big hug when he reached for her arm and swiftly injected her with something. "Ouch, damn! That was *not* the welcome I was expecting. If I ask what that is, will you tell me?"

"I can tell you what it's for, not what it is. We have some unique technology. The injection I just gave you will protect you from the effects of that technology. When you get back to Nevada, you'll find that your doctor friend needs a remote hideaway. I want you to take him on a run and make him think it's his idea to buy the property."

"How am I supposed to do that?"

"You'll find a way. I have confidence in you. Now, tell me what you learned in Johannesburg."

After filling him in on all the details, she got up to speed on everything Brill had accomplished since her departure. He seemed to be making tremendous progress now that he wasn't hampered by emotional ties, and was fully committed to his work. Four weeks in Germany helped her to get back into the Nevada mindset, and she was soon on her way back. She had written her book in an intense burst of activity during her time there, and had already sent a draft copy to the Swan family, though they would soon be wrapped up in an international investigation into illegal weapons.

#

Nevada's climate hadn't changed a bit; it was just as hot as the day she'd left. Liora stopped by to surprise Brill, and he was in fact pleasantly surprised to see her. It didn't take long for them to get back into a rhythm, and they played off each other beautifully, so much so that Liora could sense her feelings for him returning. She was a bit saddened that he didn't seem to reciprocate, though they remained close friends.

The assignment Liam had given her was to get Brill out to a facility in the middle of the desert, and for him to take notice of it and hopefully buy it. She had to do the run several times to find the trail and the fence. Positioning the For-Sale sign was a bit trickier, as the fence seemed to go on forever. It was during her third time running the perimeter that she found the ideal place. The fence bordered the upper part of the mountain trail, a perfect resting place during a run, which made it a suitable place to put up the sign. Of course, the number on the sign would only go to Liam's organization, and only Brill would ever see the sign, so it should be an easy sell.

After she convinced Brill to do a long run out into Red Rock, she got far enough ahead of him to pull him onto the mountain trail, as he would never have been found it on his own. Everything went as planned, as she took a rest break with her back to the sign, forcing Brill to notice it as he looked at her. She could tell it caught his attention; if it hadn't, she would have brought it up later. Brill took the bait and ended up buying the property. She could tell he was soon having fun with it, as she noticed him and Sirum sneaking off in the night and on weekends to spruce it up. She was surprised when she learned he'd purchased a helicopter and was now flying it up there. Their dinner dates became rarer, and he was constantly making excuses as to why he wasn't available.

The call she received from Brill about Sirum's accident shocked her. He needed help, he told her, but he didn't want anyone to know except two paramedics and the ER surgeons. *Not good,* she thought; something terrible must have happened to poor Sirum. She quickly called up Liam, and he arranged a contact at the hospital that he would send with her. If she got into further trouble, she was to use a special phone number and code. Liam was insistent that his contact stay with the helicopter, just in case. Liora had always wondered how Liam could anticipate trouble so effectively, as the cave-in soon had her giving Liam's contact the number to call him, along with the relevant code. The situation had turned grimmer than she had first expected. Getting out of that hole in the ground proved to be an exhausting but exhilarating experience, unless you were Sirum. How that man was going to survive was beyond her, until she got out of the hole and saw Liam's folks there ready to handle everything. They had taken Sirum on ahead and were working on him before Brill even got out of the ground.

She knew Brill was doing something clandestine down there, but couldn't figure out what. There was no way they were just spelunking, as Brill wasn't the type; good cover story, though. She'd figure it out eventually, and Liam would want to know if he didn't already.

She wondered how long it would take for Brill to start questioning her actions. He was too brilliant not to notice her peculiar behavior.

Chapter 9: Travels

Brill was very interested in the old Tibetan monk's claims of connecting to others through meditation, and asked to be trained in the method. Mr. Han was hesitant to share his religious rituals with an outsider, but Brill was persuasive. Two key elements needed to be in place to make it work, Mr. Han insisted: silence and cold. The monk insisted that Brill learn the art of meditation before he would begin to teach the Dharma method.

After a few sessions, since this was a process that took many months, Brill began getting impatient, starting to think it a waste of time. Meditation was easy; learning to push his consciousness out through his mind to connect with the world might be something he could never achieve. At first, they tried using the hospital for the sessions, but the noise and distractions were too great, so the monk brought him to a local temple, where the right elements were in place. Brill's skepticism started to fade as a glimmer of success began to materialize.

By the fifth visit to the temple, Brill was starting to enjoy the experience, if only because he could spend several hours doing absolutely nothing. He sometimes had to fight to stay awake. The more Mr. Han showed up, the more crowded the temple became, though, as the monk was legendary in his religion. This particular evening, he and Brill had clasped left hands while on the floor meditating, and the whole of the temple joined in — some four thousand in total. Brill was in clear mind state, heart rate slowing, getting slower, slower, slower, until it was barely beating — *and he felt it*. Suddenly, he was there: all alone, yet not. The place he found himself in was devoid of everything but a dull gray, if color actually meant anything here. Feeling didn't exist; thought was all he had. A gentle pull was drawing him closer to something. That something was a problem he'd been trying to wrap his mind around for weeks. Here, there was no other thought, only that; so what was the solution? The answer he needed was obvious. He couldn't fathom what would happen next, as he had what he needed, yet didn't know how to return. He could feel — no, sense — another presence, a mind of great strength providing direction and freedom. Where he was had been so satisfying he didn't want to leave; he only wished he could think of more problems, as he was sure he could find the solutions here. The mind, though, was strong, and pulled him away from this bliss. That road was not where he wanted to go, but he was pulled back to his body, reconnecting his consciousness with his mind.

A hand was shaking him. "Dr. Everly, Dr. Everly. Please wake up."

Brill's eyes slowly opened, and he felt as though he had lost something dear, though the solution to the surgical problem he'd been wrestling with had manifested itself clear as day, and that was still consuming his conscious thought. "I'm awake. Why are you shaking me?"

"Dr. Everly, you were in the Dharma mind state," Mr. Han said. "We almost lost you."

"Oh." Reaching for his watch, he asked anxiously, "How long was I out?"

"You have been meditating for two days. You have not moved, have barely breathed. We are greatly impressed with your command of your body and your ability to enter the Dharma mind."

Brill blinked. Two days? Then he asked, "When I was in that state, where was *there*? All I could sense was a single thought — how to solve one problem I've been thinking of for weeks."

"That place is one you should not have been able to reach yet, Dr. Everly. It takes most of us a lifetime to get there, and some never do. It is the unity consciousness state; once there you never want to return, or don't know *how* to return."

Brill nodded thoughtfully. "When I was there, I had no feelings, just the one thought, and the solution jumped out at me. Then I didn't know what to do or where to go."

"Yes, we had to create a special bridge to find you. When we felt your consciousness go, we had to call in all believers across the globe to help find you and bring you back. Eighty thousand of us joined in collective consciousness! We joined each other's energy by sharing contacts in each temple and using our training to find you. I am strong, but have never been where you went, and my consciousness almost left the collective before I saw you. Once I had you, the path was clear to return. The how is not known; we just do it."

Later, as Brill was voraciously consuming the food and water the monks gave him, he was thinking, *This is bullshit. I was deep in my mind and would have returned eventually, despite what their religion says.* Likely, their voices and shaking had helped snap him back to reality. *But I'm sure I would have returned on my own*, he insisted to himself. Still curious as to how these people connected to each other, though, he asked, "I would like to explore your group a bit more. Would they be open to providing blood samples and allowing me to screen their genes?"

"We are an open people," Mr. Han said, "and you have achieved the ultimate state of being. You are now revered as enlightened. If you ask it, we will do it."

That was news to Brill, but he decided to take advantage of it. The genetic analysis was a thought that had occurred to him when he wondered if it might indicate a connection as to how his savants learned what they learned — a stretch, maybe, but worth exploring. Thinking back on what had happened, he decided that the experience was so unique there had to be a genetic component that allowed one to drive one's thoughts to such a clear state. If there was, he would find it. Perhaps the savants shared some gene that allowed them to go into that trance state he had experienced; he wasn't convinced he had actually been in some other place, as he could imagine it as a kind of retreat to the inner workings of his own mind. How the others got in there to get him out was a puzzle he would solve at a later time; but it had to be solvable.

This collective consciousness business remained a riddle. The modern Western concept had roots in the ancient Greek philosophies, which was probably where it had originated. The possibilities were endless. Why did everything he was pursuing seem to originate with the Greeks? They weren't the first great civilization; the ancient Mesopotamians and Egyptians beat them to the scene by several thousand years. The Egyptians, though, were a mystery that had not yet been entirely solved. They had built enormous pyramids with simple tools and massive amounts of manpower that had withstood the test of time, yet many of their secrets remained hidden. Scientists thought they had figured out some aspects of how the early Egyptians built their monumental works and what their functions were, but truth be told, modern science still knew relatively little about how the earliest Egyptians had thought and operated.

These thoughts were making his head hurt. As he glanced up from his studies, his eyes fixed on the unusual stone he'd found as a child. That stone... there was definitely something curious about it. He picked it up and looked it over, for about the hundredth since retrieving it from the box of his dad's stuff. He suddenly realized that the image was of the very thing he was pondering, and it struck him as odd: a civilization halfway round the globe was depicting the group mind or consciousness being extended out of their bodies. The ancient Greeks had never indicated they had any connections to the ancient Mayans, yet this stone was showing the very philosophy the Greeks had developed. Could it be a real thing, or just a miracle wished for independently by these civilizations?

Maybe his thought answered his own question. He needed more information, but he would have to travel, and time off for travel wasn't easy to come by for a busy doctor.

One evening, Liora and Brill were discussing his theories and his need for travel when she helped him home in on the solution: go on sabbatical. Her words rang true; he could use the time away, and just the thought of adventure made him feel some excitement. He decided to start in Tibet. Mr. Han had helped him generate some fame in Tibetan Buddhist culture, and he knew he would be well received there, making it easy for him to gather the information he desired.

The genetic analyses had come back by then, and his quantum computer had helped him handle the trillions of calculations needed to compare all twenty-three pairs of chromosomes and their potential proteins for the several hundred subjects he'd tested. It turned out that most of the monks in his group shared a high degree of similarity in Chromosome Fifteen with his savants, in the very region where he himself had experienced a mutation. The mutations associated the leukemia he had as a child. Another oddity that arose in Chromosome Seventeen resulted in a higher-than-normal production of tau proteins. Could that be the link to the ability for deep concentration? Yet another oddity was on the mutation in the PAR1 region of the Y-chromosome, which only affected males, and might be the stronger link to the savants. It had some overlap with X-chromosomes, though not as much as the Y. He decided he needed a more detailed analysis, which would be one of his pursuits in Tibet. He would sample the DNA of the higher-order monks there, comparing it to the DNA of those with lesser abilities. Hopefully, this would give him the clues he needed to proceed further.

#

His trip to Asia was a long sojourn, in several senses of the word. It wasn't easy to get to Tibet, given the tense diplomatic relations with China, and when he arrived in Asia, he stayed for a while. He was amazed by the beauty of Tibet; getting this close to Everest had him in awe. Since the country was under Chinese military control, foreigners normally couldn't visit, so he entered as a physician on a humanitarian mission. He had planned the trip carefully; his group would tour the country, going strategically from monastery to monastery. As part of his medical efforts, he could sample the population and obtain the genetic analyses he desired.

They entered the country from India through Nepal, under the international symbol for medical personnel. They knew the Chinese cared little for foreigners, but it would buy them some good graces with the locals. The first area they visited was the home of the Kirti monks in Ngaka; Brill wasn't sure why this one had to be first, but it exerted a pull on him, perhaps due to the self-immolation of some of those monks in protest to China's invasion of their country. This particular monastery also happened to be one of those most heavily observed by Chinese authorities, with CCTV cameras everywhere. Though he didn't realize it, his arrival would draw unwelcome attention, as Liam's wasn't the only government body interested in his work.

In public, the monks ignored Brill's presence; but in private, they connected with him as soon as possible after he entered the country. Two days after their arrival, his team happened upon a non-violent protest on the lamas' part, but found the Chinese Army had a different strategy in mind. They decided to make examples of the protestors, to try to discourage such behavior; and with Brill's team present, they had the audience they needed. The doctors were immunizing those at the gathering when they were shuffled along into a courtyard with no means of escape. It became clear who was doing the shuffling once they were enclosed in the courtyard: the soldiers had been nudging them to the area. The doctors made little of the movement, continuing to treat patients as they normally would, until shots rang out and people began trying to escape, with nowhere to go.

"Bedlam" was an accurate description of the chaos as the physicians tried to find cover that didn't exist. Brill made his way to an injured man who had taken a bullet to the thigh. As he was kneeling down to administer care, he was lifted off the ground, a bag yanked over his head, and whisked away through a crack in the courtyard wall. Some of the monks had been sent to get him to a secure area. The word they had received was that the Army was going to execute him and blame it on the monks. They reasoned that his doctor allies would have to serve as a sacrifice in order to get

Brill to safety. Brill had achieved notoriety from his experience in the Nevada temple, and these monks were to ensure he came to no harm, as he served their purposes better alive than dead.

Tibet was full of hidden tunnels and underground labyrinths. The one the monks had used to remove Brill from the courtyard was very old, leading to a part of the temple few ever saw. Once the bag was removed from his head, his eyes adjusted to the dim light, revealing what seemed to be some type of ceremonial chamber. The walls and ceiling were adorned with vivid abstract images. He wasn't there long enough to take in everything, but an image of painted stars stuck in his mind. They seemed to march for several hours after that. The pitch of the trail indicated they were descending; to where he didn't know. As his legs began to ache from the constant decline, they reached a leveling point where they began walking alongside an underground stream. So far, nobody had said a word to him, and he still wasn't sure if he was captive or friend.

The stream led to a larger cavern and disappeared into the mountain. This area was lit with an abundance of candles, indicative of a temple, and was filled with monks. Many were meditating, and completely ignored their entrance. One man rose from the ground and lumbered over to greet them. Apparently a monk of high importance, he bowed in a welcoming gesture to Brill, honoring him with a high title. "Welcome to our home, Great Teacher," he said in excellent English. "I am Tsang."

"Why have you brought me here, Mr. Tsang?"

"Just Tsang, please. You were in danger, Great Teacher. The village you were in was to be an example in action by our Chinese masters."

"I was helping people who were injured, and didn't need to be rescued."

"You did, Great Teacher; you were to be murdered by the Chinese. We merely showed your light a new path. Here is where you were meant to be. Please, sit and commune with us," Tsang said, handing him a cup and bread.

Brill took them both and ate the bread; he didn't realize until then how famished he had been. The cup proved to filled with strong tea. Tsang went on to explain the nature of their servitude: they were the hidden resistance. Their every waking hour was directed to thought and meditation on cleansing their land of the Chinese infiltration. "You came seeking answers to questions you have yet to ask, yes?"

"I suppose. That's a deeper logic than my brain can process at this moment," Brill replied.

"Great Teacher, the answers you seek are on the path of consciousness that leads to powerful thought. Thoughts lead to action, and action leads to change. We don't have all the answers, only the way. A path for you to follow, if you choose."

Brill loved a good riddle, but it was hard for him to process every sentence that was a riddle, as the answer to each sentence was required to process the next one — which was very tiring. He was taking in all they were saying when he noticed an image on the wall behind the speaker: almost the exact image carved on the Chilean stone he had in his office, the one he had found as a boy! Pointing to the painting on the wall, he said urgently, "Would you explain to me what that means?"

Tsang smiled. "That is said to be a representation of the ultimate achievement of a mortal soul. Actually, we would ask you to explain it to *us*. Few go, but fewer return. You are one of the few to return. We have the questions, but you have the answers, Great Teacher."

Tsang went on to explain that the image had been there since ages past. In their belief system, it was the reason they meditated — to someday rise to that level of consciousness. The heavens were of pure thought and pristine in character, what they strove for in life. If one's consciousness could reach that level, they would be in eternal happiness. For Brill to have returned, he explained, was a sign to them that their journey and his were tied together.

Where he led, all would follow.

This went on for some time, and Brill began getting frustrated with the outcome. They truly believed he could do something for them, for everyone. Ha! He could barely get his research off the ground, so how was he going to help them or anyone else?

They rested for the evening, and woke Brill in the early hours, or so he thought, as there was no daylight here. They had reasoned from their meditations that Brill's journey should take him south to Burma; from there he would be on his own, and they were confident he would know the way. They urged him to keep going south from Burma, though they cautioned him the road was fraught with danger.

After he exited the tunnels into Burma, many days later, he connected with a caravan of migrants heading the direction he wanted to go.

The villages where the migrants stopped all needed Brill's services. Being a doctor, he used his expertise to barter for food and shelter. He was able to keep this up for several weeks, making his way to Thailand and then down into

Malaysia. In the town of Rawang, Brill hit a snag in his plans. He was helping some locals who were waylaid on the roadside, and he was held at gunpoint by a group of drug smugglers. Brill was able to convince them of his abilities as a doctor, and was now bound to them until he could find a way to escape. This group was a rough bunch that stole anything they needed or wanted. Their destination was Kuala Lumpur, though their activities were soon deterred, as they must have pissed off a more powerful group. The next day his "employers" were suddenly cut down in an exchange of gunfire, leaving only himself and two of his original captors standing. Nets were thrown over them all, and they were dragged aboard a ship and chained to the wall, as the new group began questioning them.

His new captors spoke in Malay, the native language of Malaysia. Brill knew only a smattering of the language, and had trouble trying to understand their intentions from their actions. Those actions soon turned to several forms of torture. It became clear to Brill that the Malays were seeking information, and were willing to use any means necessary to get it.

After they tortured and killed his two former captors, they turned their attention to him. Since they kept repeating the same phrases to him as they had to the other two, Brill knew they considered him one of that group. They hadn't realized he was a captive, and pleaded with them in the only languages he knew well, English and Spanish. Neither seemed to work. They progressively got rougher and rougher with Brill, to the point of putting metal plugs in his ears and then hooking up car jumper cables to them.

As they attached the other ends to a twenty-four-volt battery, something remarkable happened. Instead of feeling intense pain, Brill's consciousness seemed to separate from his body. It was as if he were standing outside himself, watching what was happening, and now he understood what they were saying as if they were speaking English. He watched as they continued their efforts, only to see his body stop; yet here he was. They must have thought him dead, as they gave up and left him there. The questions they had been asking related to where "the drugs" were. They kept insisting he had to deliver the payment to someone called Conner. He couldn't move in his current state, just stand and watch.

What Brill hadn't yet learned was that the gift his father had given him so many years ago had awakened: the nanobots taken from Liam's team were now active. They were a type of warfighter defense system. Brill's father had modified them to do even more, as he hadn't known their original function, but had adapted them to strengthen Brill's neural connections so that electromagnetic radiation wouldn't harm his brain cells. John Everly was simply trying to protect his son from any radiation treatments he might need if his cancer ever came back. Little did he know the tiny molecular machines would serve Brill in other ways.

When the boat reached deep water, they threw Brill and the others overboard. Brill's "ghost" was apparently tethered to his body by a specific distance, since he moved along with his body as it moved. While Brill's body was in the ocean, it floated on currents that brought him down into Indonesia, close to Jakarta. As they neared shore, he felt himself being pulled back into his body. Regaining consciousness, he crawled onto dry land and collapsed between some bushes. This cover helped him plan his next move.

He was near the Ciiwung River, though he didn't know it then. In time, he spotted a group that looked to be heading inland on the river. In his desperation, he decided to climb aboard their boat and hide to see where it went. They must have been planning for a jungle excursion, as they had backpacks lined up on the railing. Towards dark, they were nearing a dock when the unexpected happened: the group, which numbered about ten, was reduced to three as gunfire erupted, eliminating the others. Brill took this opportunity to grab a backpack. While the survivors were returning fire, he pilfered the other backpacks of their food and water and any medical supplies he could find.

As the boat drifted past the dock, a grenade made a quick end of the boat. Using the backpack as a flotation device,

Brill ducked underwater, shielding his face. He hoped whoever was shooting at them would think him dead as he floated downstream. Nobody tried to retrieve him from the water — for good reason, he soon realized. Off to his left, he caught sight of a large crocodile lying on the riverbank, causing his heart to nearly leap out of his chest. The current worked in his favor at this point, as it pushed him to the shoreline when the river took a sharp bend. He was able to roll onto the shore, and laid as still as possible to avoid the attention of the crocs or the bandits.

Much later, after recovering his composure, he worked his way deeper into the jungle, hoping not to be pursued by hungry reptiles, eating his liberated supplies as he went. The darkness at this point was so deep he literally could not see his hand in front of his face, so he reluctantly utilized a flashlight from the backpack. The light revealed his next step a little too late as he tumbled over a low cliff, fortunately into a lagoon below. Still holding the light, he searched the shoreline for reptiles and spotted what looked to be a cave, positioned behind a light waterfall. Making his way against the current into the waterfall, he was able to climb up into the cave, which to his surprise was free of animals.

The cave was a welcome respite from his ordeal, and he was exhausted. Finding a dry spot further back, he propped himself against a wall and was asleep within minutes. Much later, a ray of sunlight hit him in the face, gently waking him. Every part of his body ached. Though he was fit, he hadn't realized so many of his muscles were lacking exercise, as they screamed in pain with each movement. He slowly rose to his feet, exploring his newfound freedom. This place had been occupied at one point, as there were shards of pottery shoved into corners, and remnants of fires long since extinguished. Brill rummaged through the backpack to find a change of clothes; he was glad the owners of the stolen backpacks had at least planned for many contingencies, as he was wet and freezing. The fresh clothes seemed to bring a little light to his dark mood.

The cave went back much farther than his meager light could illuminate. He had a difficult decision: should he leave the cave, or see where it went, searching for a secondary exit? Something drove him to choose the latter. and he began to move deeper into the recesses of the cave. The farther in he went, the drier it got, and colder. Fortunately, as he had little else to ease the chill, his new clothing retained his body heat. After what seemed like a mile, the cave hit a dead end, though it looked to have been someone's living quarters in times past.

While searching for an exit, Brill found a path higher than he could reach, as the lower part of the wall had collapsed at some point in the past. He also noticed the highly decorated walls. Whoever had lived here must have loved to paint, as the walls told an elaborate story. Several trees had fallen in over the years, generating a nice pile of dried wood. He was desperately in need of warmth, and the flint-and-steel striker he retrieved from the backpack enabled him to make quick work of building a fire. The light from the fire further illuminated the pictures that had been painted high above.

Brill lay on his back to take in the whole collection, as he was getting dizzy from looking up for so long. The more he viewed them, the less he could believe what his eyes were showing him. It seemed to be a history of a culture that had lived here long ago. The most startling part were the land images; the shape of Africa was obvious, but there was so much more connected to it! As his mind outlined the current seven continents, he couldn't believe it. He was seeing Pangea in its entirety; *Couldn't be,* he thought. That was a modern reconstruction, yet this image was likely from some prehistoric era. The progression of the image from that supercontinent to the history of these people showed images of volcanoes and people running. Next, the continents were separated; still closer than they were today, but far enough apart to indicate that whoever drew this knew they were no longer joined. The next image looked like the islands of Malaysia, all the way though New Zealand.

The images towards the latter part of the series showed multiple figures in some type of ceremony or worship; he couldn't tell. Then he saw it: the very image that had appeared to him several times over the years — the mind-walk image of the stars on the stone from Chile, and more recently the one he'd seen in Tibet. It was just the first of that set of images; it seemed to depict individuals who were either leaders or being sacrificed, again hard to tell from this far away. Those individuals had others lying prostrate beneath them, and the main individual was shown with the image of his thoughts or psyche projecting out into the sky, providing a detailed outline of the stars in that region of the heavens.

The next image started to connect the dots for him, as it showed what looked like a waterfall of varying images and symbols pouring out of that region of the sky back into the individual. The last image showed that person drawing some of those symbols for those lying around him, and then showed them building a pyramid. Excited, Brill dug a ragged pad of paper out of the backpack and used the nub of a pencil to copy down every picture, down to the last image, so he could analyze them later. The final scene on the wall seem to depict volcanic activity, followed by people in huge boats fleeing in the ocean to New Zealand. Could this painting be of the progenitors, the first inhabitants of the continents? Aside from Biblical accounts of a great flood, Brill had often wondered if there was more to that story. Most cultures had flood myths, including the Sumerians' Epic of Gilgamesh. Either this was Adam and Eve's family, or he was seeing the development of humanity from a different perspective.

Brill wondered if these people could be the original Maori, who were thought to have come from Malaysia. If he could get to New Zealand, he might be able to put the pieces in place, and start to make sense of the genetics. These people must also have been the forerunners of the lamas who had saved him in Tibet. The belief system depicted above indicated such.

After several hours of rest, he set about his efforts to getting out of this latest hole in the ground. His efforts to reach the upper level were draining, and he didn't want to have to go back and swim out; he was fortunate not to have been a croc's dinner last time. He rummaged through the backpack, but there was no climbing gear, not even a rope; guess that wasn't in their plans. Climbing the wall was too challenging, so he did the next best thing: he built a set of stairs. There were rocks strewn about the cave and along the tunnel leading to it, and he started collecting those and piling them up next to the wall. It took the better part of a day for him to build it high enough to hoist himself to the path, and it had to be good enough, since he was out of stones.

His first attempts were exercises in futility. There was nothing to grab up there, just a dusty, sandy surface, and he kept sliding back down. A new idea for escape finally came to him, but it required additional engineering, and had to be spot on. It involved using the fallen tree parts as levers — more like a plank where the opposite end would go down, causing him to rise, as they weren't long enough to help him climb up, but were just the right length to give him the boost he needed if he timed his jump right. The other key piece was getting a stone heavier than him to hit the other end of the lever perfectly. It took a few tries to get the tree branch balanced and, using another branch, to get a heavy stone to roll from his spot in the middle to the end of the branch without falling off while he walked to the opposite end at a slightly faster pace, since the rock was heavier than him. The first attempt was a failure, as he fell off the tree limb into the pile of rocks. The next attempt he hoped would work, as he wasn't sure he enough energy to roll that bloody rock back up again. As the stone rolled away from his side of the tree branch, it nearly fell off again, but kept going, and he started to rise as he walked to the opposite side. Anticipating this would work, he threw his backpack on up and waited for just the right moment to jump, as the release of his back made him even lighter than the rock and he went up much faster. This time he cleared the edge, collapsing on the trail above.

Lying there, he slowly drifted off for some rest before waking and continuing on.

He cautiously headed up the trail. The incline was narrow and steep, and he lost his footing several times as he ascended. Nearing the top, he found the jungle had grown down into the opening, yielding him several roots to aid his climb. Topping the crest of the opening, he found himself on the slope of a mountain, overlooking a lagoon. The sun's warmth was welcome, baking the chill from him as he lay on the ground regaining his strength, thinking about how he could get to New Zealand to pursue his dream images. He was in a foreign country with no money, no passport, and limited supplies, completely out of his element. He needed help.

Chapter 10: New Zealand

The only solution to his current predicament was to get to civilization, but he was in the middle of nowhere, and all he had was the backpack — which he was now able to tear apart in the daylight. Food was his driving desire at the moment. Dumping the contents of the pack on the ground didn't reveal any additional food. There was a bottle opener, of no use; a toothpick, no use; a compass, something he could utilize. He did notice the pack had waterproof compartments within that he'd yet to explore. Unzipping one pocket revealed one of the oldest cell phones he'd ever seen, an old flip-phone punch-button job. Locating the power button, he hoped for the best.

It powered up. *Now what?* he thought. He didn't speak the local language, and had no idea if there was an emergency number to call wherever he was. With the first hurdle overcome — a functional phone — he was thinking through his options for the next step when he recalled Liora giving him an emergency contact number after the cave incident. It was unlike any number he had ever seen, an eighteen-digit one, but she said that any phone anywhere would connect him to help if he used it, so he gave it a try. A series of crackles and electronic sounds told him something was happening; then, finally, a person.

"Name and location," a very clear voice said in American English.

"Dr. Brill Everly, and I don't have a clue where I am. Somewhere in Malaysia or Indonesia? On a mountain."

"Hold please while your request is processed. Do not hang up."

After about a quarter-hour wait, the voice finally returned. "Please go to an open location and wait. Do not move far from your current position. Help will arrive within a day." Then the call disconnected.

Brill was perplexed as to whom he had just connected with, and wondered what lay in store for him, but at least someone was coming for him, help or not. He was already in a clear area, so he laid back to rest while waiting to be rescued. Thinking back to the images painted on the ceiling of the cave, he drifted off to sleep. His mind was actively processing the images as he entered a dream state, and he soon seemed to be traveling to that place in time when they had been drawn so long ago, focusing on the person who was projecting their mind. Then the image rapidly blurred, and he was standing or floating, he wasn't sure which, in a place where thought seemed to collide with action. Then he heard some quiet movement; turning — he couldn't tell a direction, he just felt he was turning — he saw another person standing next to him.

It was the figure painted on the cave ceiling; he was shown lying flat on a table, surrounded by other people lying prostrate around him. This man didn't seem to notice Brill observing him. He was asking questions, which Brill now understood; oddly, though, the answers were flooding back from somewhere beyond him. They were a rush of equations, images, sounds, and actions, but Brill understood. The question the priest was asking was how to create a building that would capture their knowledge for all time. The solution that came back was how to build something that looked like a pyramid; he could see how and what needed to be done not only to build it, but to preserve the knowledge in a kind of digital library in the stone.

The image shifted to the same man at a later time in his life. Now the question was about survival, and how his people could protect themselves from the volcanic destruction as Pangaea began breaking up, landmasses going separate directions. As Brill observed these questions going out from the man, he realized they weren't really words, but thoughts; who or what was answering the question, Brill couldn't tell. Within a short interval, he observed something returning, as had happened with the earlier question. It was like a cloud rising towards him; and when it got to the man, again there was a flood of equations and images of what he needed to do, including maps this time. He could see the branching of continents and the projection of where this man was, what he was to do, and where he was being guided to go. It looked like heavy sea craft that were imaged, and the process needed to build them.

Brill woke much later, remembering in great detail what he'd dreamed. Thinking this a vision of his mind putting the facts together and creating a story to fit them, as dreams often do, he was determined to pursue it. He had learned years ago to trust his dreams, as more often than not they offered the solutions he sought. He enjoyed when he remembered a dream like this; the brain always impressed him with its ability to create something out of the abstract.

The dream got him to thinking about his research with the savants. Was he approaching it correctly? His work was so linear in its methods. Was he looking at the bigger picture? Could these savants be similar to the man in the dream he'd just had? Was that why he'd had the dream, to connect what he saw in the cave paintings to the work he was doing? He felt he was on the brink of an answer when he heard a helicopter, which jarred him out of his reverie. It was dark by then, so he couldn't see it; he turned on his flashlight and shined it upward, waving it back and forth to hopefully get their attention. He could tell, once he saw them, that they didn't need his flashlight, as they were already on a direct course for him. Seconds later a searchlight shone in his face. The chopper landed, the door opened, and soldiers flooded out. They seemed to think there were enemies around, as they took up defensive positions around him, kneeling away from him in hyperalert firing poses. Two soldiers reached down and hoisted him up, carrying him into the chopper. They were airborne within minutes, and then someone finally addressed him.

"Water, Dr. Everly? Hungry?" A man handed him a cold bottle, along with an MRE package.

"Thanks. What country do you serve? Am I a prisoner?"

"We're U.S. Navy SEALs, and no sir. You're an American citizen who has been rescued from a foreign threat. This area is crawling with drug traffickers and terrorists. Had you gone too much farther in any direction, you most likely would not be alive today. You're on your way to the *USS Abraham Lincoln*. From there, we'll get you back to the States."

"Thanks," Brill sighed, relieved. He looked up at the SEAL. "Not to be ungrateful, but how on Earth did the Navy know where I was, and why would you rescue me?"

"Our duty is to protect America's interests and its citizens, sir. We received orders to pick you up at these coordinates, and that you might be in danger. That's all I know."

They delivered him to the aircraft carrier, and from there to a base in Okinawa, where he was surprised by an old adversary. Colonel Liam Rhett greeted Brill after he had been cleared by the base's doctors. "Doctor Everly, welcome back to the land of the living. I'm glad you survived the massacre in Tibet. The world mourned your loss. We're pleased that we were able to rescue you."

"How did you even find me?" Brill asked suspiciously.

"The Nevada state police called the Army, and from there a rescue was mounted. Since I knew you and your father, I wanted to personally see to it you made it back to the States safely."

Brill was happy to be safe, but he took that statement with more than a few grains of salt.

On the way back home, Brill had time to process the events of the past few weeks. The code Liora had given him, especially. He was skeptical that it connected to any police organization anywhere, as the person he'd talked to had mentioned neither police nor any agency. He had long suspected that Liora was more than a university professor; this just proved it. Was she connected to Liam, or did that apparent connection occur by happenstance? He didn't believe in coincidence, but he'd need more proof to justify that suspicion. He wasn't ready to fully write her off — he was falling for her again — but he would definitely be more observant in the future. He was glad she apparently had connections, but if she were connected to Liam, he would never forgive her.

The welcome for Brill as he departed the plane after landing in Las Vegas was a heart-warming homecoming. News crews and loads of people were there clapping for him. His heart skipped a beat when Liora ran up, wrapped her arms around him, and gave him the best kiss of his life. Tears were streaming down his face as he gladly embraced her.

His arrival at the hospital was no less exciting. Every staff member he saw came up to shake his hand or hug him, and for many, tears were flowing. He was a welcome sight; they had mourned at the reports of his death, and were overjoyed that he had survived. He spent the next few hours telling and retelling his story until every last person had greeted him.

In the days since his rescue, he'd felt poorly most of the time, and realized he was still recuperating from his ordeal. He told his colleagues he wasn't up to returning yet, and privately decided he would spend some time at the desert lab thinking and planning for the future. The hospital was glad to have him back, but they wanted him to get some counseling and spend some time rehabbing. They said he should take the next six months off and learn how to handle the ordeal, and work through any side effects he might have. Instead of fighting it, Brill realized he could use this as an opportunity to visit New Zealand. So he cleared it with the hospital, telling them he would like to use the six months to rehab there, since he'd always wanted to visit and it seemed like a restful place. They agreed, as long as got some counseling there. That meant he had to convince Liora to come with him, as she could be his counselor.

The conversation he had with her didn't go as expected, as he thought he'd have to convince her — and he had to do anything but. Once she heard his plan, she jumped on it. Brill went on to tell her about what he'd observed in the cave near Jakarta, and how it pointed to New Zealand. He confessed he didn't see the link completely yet, but he felt he needed to go, if only to complete the puzzle.

Prior to heading to New Zealand, Brill found an archaeologist at UCLA who had a dig planned at an ancient Maori site in the South Canterbury region. When he learned of Brill's interest and his need to spend six months away, he welcomed them as part of the team, especially since he didn't have to pay them and would have a physician and psychiatrist as part of the team. The trip was long, but seemed quicker, as he and Liora finally had time to really find each other. When they arrived, they were closer than ever, both having let their guards down, realizing their love for each other.

The dig location was a virgin site, untouched for millennia, and they had plenty of work to do. The process was not what Brill expected. An archaeological dig is a painstaking process, requiring a great deal of patience and attention to detail. Once the layers of sediment lacking culture materials — called the overburden — are removed, the careful shoveling, troweling, brushing, and sifting begin, especially once artifacts or other cultural remains are located, as one doesn't want to damage anything. Even the smallest thing may be culturally and scientifically significant. It's a slow process, and Brill lost his patience with it after two days. He worked it out with the UCLA lead to connect up with other sites where digging had been taking place for several years, as Brill was eager to see the prehistory, not necessarily uncover it — as his aching back was attesting.

Another site in the Huriawa Peninsula had been deeply excavated by this point. The ancient living floors were exposed, and the excavators had recently uncovered a potential ceremonial area. Brill was seeking hair and teeth; his main goal there was to collect ancient DNA, as well as the DNA of those people's modern descendants. If he found any additional pictograms, that would just be a bonus. Fortunately for him, the new area they opened up was more of a graveyard than a ceremonial area, as the archaeologists had identified numerous human burial sites already. After helping to excavate a number of the burials, Brill saw his opportunity to collect his samples when everyone was eating dinner. This allowed him to wander alone back to the site and surreptitiously remove a few molars. Since hair was fragile and rarely preserved, the teeth were the most likely parts of the skeleton to contain preserved DNA. Tooth enamel was tough, and the roots might have leftover marrow that had long since dried and preserved nucleic acids. Luckily, the burials were located deep in a dry cave. He didn't want to be gone too long at any one time, so he repeated this ritual for the next few dinner times, taking samples unlikely to be noticed, until he felt he had enough. The locals readily donated skin cells and blood when he explained he was doing a study of human dispersal patterns through southeast Asia and Polynesia.

As the team continued to explore the remainder of the ceremonial site, they were amazed and awed to happen upon a cave full of drawings and glyphs of a kind rarely seen. This was especially fortuitous for Brill, as the glyphs clearly indicated a message left for future viewers. Fortunately, Liora had expertise in reading glyphs from many societies, one of her many interests — a minor detail neither she nor Brill told the team.

He and Liora snuck into the cave one night when the others were sleeping, as this was still an active site they were excavating and exploring, and the archaeologist in charge wouldn't allow anyone in until it was fully documented. But Brill didn't have time to wait; he was already well past the halfway point of his sabbatical. The walls of the cave were covered from top to bottom with glyphs. They took as many photos as they could, but close inspection of the glyphs showed details that wouldn't show up in the pics. There was faint artwork between many of them, and you had to get really close to see it. They had to supplement those with hand drawings, which took a while. They spent many subsequent nights in the cave.

The glyphs cut off abruptly at floor level. Curiosity got the better of Brill one night, and he got a shovel and dug carefully around the base of the wall. After digging down about two more feet, he uncovered more glyphs, though these only occurred at certain spots on the wall. The archaeologists would have eventually gotten to them, but they would have painstakingly troweled and brushed the dirt away from the wall over a period of weeks or months, and Brill didn't have time for that. When he had what he needed, he very carefully returned the dirt to its location, patted it down, and covered their tracks. Hopefully, by the time the archaeologists did their digging —which might be years from now, as it wasn't long until the end of the field season — they wouldn't notice the dirt was loose. Fortunately, it was all of a type, so there would be no telltale striations caused by different-colored soils.

By the end, they'd hand-drawn every glyph at the site, including the hidden ones connecting them, and had everything mapped in with the photographs, just in case the wall's contours mattered. They uploaded all these to their personal laptops so they could decipher them at their leisure, and Brill sent them to the quantum server back at Avalon. Finding the starting point was the challenge for this particular storyline; was it the middle, bottom, top, left, or right? Each image was a story within a story, so one could start anywhere, but it was impossible to tell if it was an ending or beginning, especially as context wasn't easily discernible.

After a few weeks of studying the story one meticulous piece at a time, one particular set of images caught Brill's eye, as it resembled part of what he'd observed in Jakarta. That might be their Rosetta Stone. The images that jumped out at him were the out-of-control volcanoes and people fleeing over water; but here, it was apparently all wrapped up in one elaborate symbol with those elements around it. He was sure that was the starting point, but the real key would be in how the painters had told the story; did it continue left to right or vice-versa, or did it go top to bottom or from the bottom up? At least they had their starting point, though, and in the end that jarred loose the logic of the glyph sequence.

The faint images between the bolder, larger ones showed a definite progression from left to right. However, that sequence only went about twelve images across, then jumped to the row above and read right to left, until it reached the end of the row, and then up and left to right, repeating this cycle in a flat S-pattern. No doubt it had seemed intuitive to those who painted the glyphs, though it seemed strange to Brill and Liora; but once they got the hang of it, their work progressed steadily. A month later, they had the complete story, and Brill concluded that had he not uncovered the images below the current ground level, key pieces of the tale would have been lost. Knowing the starting point allowed for a sequenced recounting of the life of these ancient people, who had shared the images as apparent warnings or guidance for future generations.

Until they excavated to the level of the former cave floor — and surely someone someday would — the scholars studying the glyphs wouldn't know where to begin, and it was unlikely they would ever make sense of it. Brill, after all, had an extra piece of the puzzle — he began with the exodus of these people from the Jakarta region, as he was sure that was the starting point for the story and others like it around the world. From those, they would always have their seer faced with some challenge, and then show him reaching to the stars with his mind, and a solution would follow. Many of these solutions were great buildings, monuments, ships, and the like.

The solutions they presented always included the pictorial schematics of what they did, but those always flowed from the seer.

The story progressed from that starting point and remained in the flat-S pattern for a while — then it started to branch into a circular pattern, which took a little rethinking for them to puzzle out. From what Brill could gather, the ancient inhabitants of the site hadn't painted the glyphs all at once; they'd added to the wall of images on a yearly basis for millennia, sometimes just a single series of images per year, sometimes dozens. When they were about a quarter of the way through the story — somewhere on the order of ten thousand years, as far as they could tell — another singularly traumatic event was recorded. Something that looked like a planet had fallen into the sun. The images showed the sky turning some dim color; it was impossible to tell the color after all these years, but the message was clear: the sky was now a different color than it had been. The seer of that era was shown searching the stars for a solution, but returning only a blank slate, indicating that they could do nothing.

Analysis of the later images showed what appeared to be the continent of Australia transforming from a jungle-filled landscape to a vast interior desert with only a trimming of green around the edges, much as it was today. Then they showed snow and ice covering the landscape; half the site's population and nearly all the large animals of the region died during this Cold Time, which Brill figured had to be the last Ice Age. In many a case, the images of the massive animals were unlike anything that existed today. Next, the glyphs appeared to show a rain of rocks falling from the sky, and the surviving people fleeing into caves to huddle around a fire. The Cold Time continued for an estimated thirty thousand years.

The next images displayed a greener landscape, where the people were dressed for warmer weather. What caught Brill's attention was that the seers shown were no longer coming back from the stars with great things; they still produced, but were much more limited in what they delivered. Perhaps the true seers had been lost during the Cold Time. The images no longer showed them as revered. They delivered wonderful art, but no grand buildings, ships, or technology of any kind.

As Brill was taking all this in, it suddenly hit him what he was missing in his research. What if the grand seers of the past were the progenitors of the modern savants, and the event with the sun had damaged them genetically? Based on the limited genetic analyses Brill had managed for these people so far, both ancient and modern, this seemed a plausible hypothesis. He theorized that the ancient progenitors had possessed much greater abilities than the current savants, much like he and Sirum did. Those seers had learned, by somehow communing with the stars — or was it the dark matter between them? — how to build ancient structures like pyramids and the great arks to carry them to safety. Then came the event that crippled their descendants, when a rogue planet slammed into the sun.

Liora was especially curious about one image, and made sure Brill paid close attention to it. "Take a look at this. These images seem to show a kind of deep funnel in space, where their minds are connected to the stars. Do you suppose it could be some kind of wormhole or black hole? And look at these glyphs here. If I'm translating these correctly, it looks like they're calling it a 'knowledge well.' What the hell are they connecting to?" She then gestured to another area of the wall. "This one's a real oddity. It's apparently a man holding a baby, all hunched up. The next image shows him burying the baby, and snow falling. In that same series, the people are dressed in skimpy animal skins, hunched up around what looks to be a fire. Then they close out this series with many of those same images of people being buried."

"That's odd, but this Cold Time was obviously the last Ice Age."

"But this part of New Zealand shouldn't have *had*
snowfall during that period, if we have the chronology right.
At least it shouldn't have if New Zealand has always been in
the same location during all of human history and prehistory.
They don't look like they're in the mountains, so this must
have been new for them. They don't appear to have known
how to prepare for or deal with it at all."

Brill was still trying to make sense of all these images.
Again, the one block of images that jumped out to him was
the mapping of the continents, and their drift from Pangea to
their current locations. At some point far in the past,
humanity must have been advanced enough to have been
able to map not just ancient Pangaea but *all* the continents
after the dispersal, including the Americas, which were
unknown to most of the world until less than 600 years ago.
Or had their seers gotten that information from the
knowledge well? The real surprise was what looked like an
eighth continent positioned just southwest of Australia, in the
region of ocean known as the Roaring Forties. Could there

still be a continent hidden out there? That region remained so volatile that even modern vessels avoided it. The seas were just too rough, and the currents too dangerous for submarines to chart the sea floor.

People didn't realize that some parts of the Earth were still uncharted, except by satellite. Though one would think a continent, even if it were submerged, would show up on a satellite image. He would make sure to check when he got back home.

After long thought, Brill formulated a theory, based on the image of the planet hitting the sun and its aftermath. He knew that there was a sparse collection of widely scattered asteroids in the solar system, mostly (but far from all) located in a loose belt between the orbits of Jupiter and Mars. Many scientists thought they might be the remnants of a potential planet that had been prevented from forming due to the gravitational influence of Jupiter. But what if they were wrong? What if the asteroid belt represented the remnants of a fully-formed planet that had mostly settled there after its break-up due to the stability of the wide gap between the last

rocky world in the solar system and the first gas giant, and

much more recently than previously thought?

When the planet shown in the prehistoric images struck

the sun, or passed close to it, it had been ripped apart and the

fragments spat back into the inner system in all directions.

The sky's color change might indicate a blowback from a

rash of massive solar flares, perhaps even greater than the

Coronal Mass Ejections (CMEs) that sometimes disturbed

radio waves. Think of ripples on a pond extending out from

the sun, where those ripples are dense waves of solar

particles. Those waves slammed into the Earth, bombarding

the upper atmosphere with a massive solar wind. This might

have created an energy vacuum as the solar particles began to

cool; thermodynamics would suggest they sucked the heat

out of the Earth until an equilibrium was reached. That

would have taken thousands of years. In addition to cooling,

the Earth's rotation around the sun must have taken it through

the remnants of the shattered planet, many of which then

rained down on Earth, causing further damage and perhaps kicking up enough dust and smoke to initiate a nuclear winter. How this lined up with modern times was anybody's guess, but it seemed to have coincided with the last surge of the Late Pleistocene Ice Age, causing widespread destruction similar to that of the end of the Age of Dinosaurs, though on a smaller scale.

After they emerged from that Ice Age, the local seers were less than what they had been; and Brill surmised that the solar radiation could have damaged their DNA. They could easily have suffered teratogenic and genotoxic effects, which they would have passed on to their children. If the damage to their DNA was mostly on the Y-chromosome, then it would help to explain the rise of the limited savants known to modern science, as they were mostly male, and Brill and his colleagues had mapped several Y-chromosome mutations specific to male savants.

Another revelation occurred to him, something that had been itching at the back of his mind: the savants had all the correct neural elements in place, but the programming wasn't there. Think of a computer, the most advanced possible, with trillions of lines of code in thousands of programs; yet the only program that can run and execute is a complex one that does the same function over and over, and none of the other programs ever run. Could he reprogram the minds of these individuals? They just needed a command program to access all the areas of the brain.

Brill was on a mission now, and fully believed he could turn the savants into fully functioning individuals with greater access to their minds. How would he do this? The answer hadn't yet arrived, but he knew it would, as the answers always came. He fully believed that he was one of those unique genius savants who had access to his entire mind; he just needed to make his subjects more like him.

The six months wrapped up with Brill and Liora visiting several other dig sites, though none were as productive. The extra genetic samples Brill acquired from the image cave would greatly help his analysis, he knew. While was digging down to uncover the additional images, he had uncovered a jumbled bone bed beneath the images, from which he had taken the opportunity to remove molars and dig through the femurs for marrow. In all, he took samples from one hundred skeletons in New Zealand, which he hoped included seers, and spanned the thousands of years across the change in their abilities. The genetic information would be invaluable.

He was at a crossroads regarding what to do next — and what he should about his relationship with Liora. He didn't want to remain single forever, but he wasn't sure of her intentions, and could never find the right words to express this to her.

Chapter 11: Coming Home

The flight back to Las Vegas was fraught with rough weather and severe turbulence. They didn't sleep a wink, and were on the edges of their seats the entire trip. At one point, they were in free-fall, as they hit a spot of dead air and fell for about ten seconds. Coming out of that, the jet hit a thunderstorm head-on, and lightning knocked out one of the engines. Nothing like flying for eight more hours with only three engines to make you edgy and paranoid, constantly looking out the window. When they touched down in Vegas, the passengers erupted in applause; and while exiting the plane, everyone thanked the pilot for getting them home alive.

Brill hit the ground running, as the crazy flight home had helped him home in on the solution, though he would need Sirum's help — and he couldn't tell Liora. He was starting to love her, but didn't fully trust her. The plan he'd hatched was to literally reprogram the brains of his savants using nanotechnology. The rub was that nanobots were still a thing of fiction to the broader world, even though he knew he had some in his brain. Those may have been an option, but he wasn't sure if extracting them would cause him damage. So he put a proposition to Sirum: build nanites that could map the information from one person's brain into a similar region of a savant's brain. This would result in a literal reprogramming of the latter's "hardware."

Sirum was ecstatic to see him. He'd made a major discovery while Brill was gone, closely related to Brill's work. He'd been able to create his own dark matter in the lab, and their quantum supercomputers had been indispensable in handling the massive computing power needed to control it. He had also found was that his dark matter resonated on the same frequency as the delta waves of the brain, but in reverse. It acted like a delta wave magnet, in other words, attracting delta waves across all of creation. Both felt that must explain how their savants could tap into dark matter concentrations in space. It must have what the Tibetan mystics and ancient seers had done, too.

Sirum had created one picogram of the dark matter, and had also created a delta wave amplifier, based on the tech they'd previously developed for the thought-transfer chambers. Once he put the amplifier on his head and set it to harmonize with the dark matter, the intensity of his thoughts was incredible — almost to the point that he couldn't stop thinking about a specific problem. He said it almost felt like his thoughts were increasing and being pulled *away* from him. During this experiment, he had his assistant turn his head so the amplifier was blocked. When he did this, his thought state returned to normal. Then he had him turn him back, and the effect returned, so that he was lost in his mind, deep in thought.

When Brill outlined his plan to Sirum, it turned out that the solution was closer than he realized, as Sirum had already been working on nanites on his own for the past few years. The latest generation were designed to act as delta wave amplifiers, though he intended them to stay on the surface of the skin. With Brill's help, Sirum felt he could modify them to be compatible with neurons, though he was nervous about the possibility of damage to the brain. Brill was persuasive, though, and in the end Sirum relented and began designing the equipment he needed.

This experimenting would take some time, so Brill turned his attention to Sirum's discovery with the dark matter. If it could intensify thoughts, then it might help the brain come up with the desired solution to any problem. He would need volunteers and time.

He'd made the decision on the way home from New Zealand to quit practicing medicine and devote all his time to his research, as this was where his true passion lay. Once he returned, he ramped up his work at Avalon to determine the genetic mystery of the savants and the progenitors. The work at the university lab was where he would try to clone information from the brain regions of volunteers, mostly graduate students, and begin programming the appropriate sections of his savants' brains. In secret, he built his equipment in Avalon, the cavern facility that contained his quantum computer, so that it would allow him to experiment in a place where he was certain no outside eyes would see.

It all started with the genes. Brill treaded cautiously until he had all the historical genetic samples analyzed. He realized that he'd been operating blind before, with only fragments of information. The complete story would soon emerge, he was certain, as he believed his theory made too much sense not to work, even though science often has rude awakenings in store for scientists with that type of arrogance.

His team first determined the chronology of each sample. Then they began piecing together the genetic material from each sample, as even a sample a few hundred years old had significant degradation, and some of these were upwards of eighty thousand years old. By then, Brill had hired the best of the best of the world's geneticists, including an odd set of twins from, of all places, Swaziland. With no limits on their creativity and an ample cash supply, his researchers were able to advance the science of ancient DNA recovery to accomplish the near-impossible. One of the challenges they had to work out was how to recover a fossilized image of DNA. Think of a sculpture placed in mud, where the mud hardens around it and, over time, the sculpture itself dissolves away. You now only have the cast of what the sculpture looked like on the outside, with none of the interior details, making it difficult to reverse-engineer what goes into each spot.

The fundamental chemistry of DNA is composed of just four bases: cytosine, guanine, adenine, and thymine. The first two always pair up, and the second two always pair up. These base pairs created a three-dimensional helical structure that formed the image they were trying to decipher. Where they couldn't decipher sequences from the prehistoric samples, Brill's team made the assumption that those who suffered from autism and had the savant ability had most of the right genes in place. This gave them the framework to build most of the Y-chromosomes. They had to make further assumptions in the regions that were prone to mutation. They borrowed the recombinant properties of B-cells, the region of somatic hypermutation, understanding how those cells code for antigens to make antibodies, and used the same approach to the variable regions of the Y-chromosome. They also made the assumption that the individuals who had genius savant abilities had Y-chromosomes with this region of somatic hypermutation, allowing the brain to constantly adapt and create the genetic material it needed to go beyond the capabilities they had at birth. These were big assumptions, but allowed for the degrees of freedom needed to account for the susceptibility to a massive bombardment of solar radiation.

As with most mutations, the result of radiation exposure is an unintended mix and match of incompatible genetic material, causing deterioration of the original code. The misconception that some mutations result in superhumans is a wish by science fiction writers; reality has a different story to tell, and the story of the savants appeared to be one of harmful mutations passed down from generation to generation. Long ago, they had possessed a nice mix of the genetic diversity of our population, and they were able to access the infinite intelligence the human mind is capable of achieving. Humanity had it for a moment in our history; then nature took it back.

It took the better part of a year before they finally had what they believed were the sequences to key chromosomes for every sample, those being the Y, Seventeenth, Fifteenth, and Thirteenth chromosomes. The next step Brill instructed his group of experts to achieve was to repair the genetics of already fully differentiated cells that were no longer dividing. The challenge with neural cells is that they achieve their final states at a very early age. Once there, a person can only lose intellectual capability, not gain it; the brain begins to shrink past the age of 25. If you're at a disadvantage to start with, then your intellectual capability has limited potential compared to someone who has more active neurons with stronger genetic instructions. If the neural cells of the savants could be retrofitted with the proper code, then they could be trained to activate in the way they were meant to.

In theory, they had the concept, but putting it into practice was beyond their realm of thinking. Brill challenged them on every aspect of their work, pushing many of them to quit, as they couldn't see the bigger picture, having thought they were only doing fundamental research. He kept pushing those who remained to apply these concepts to human neurons, but they were fearful of the consequences of getting even the most minute details wrong.

In response, Brill set up animal experiments on primates, mostly chimpanzees and bonobos, at his remote facility. His scientists had free rein to experiment as needed, no review boards and no paperwork needed. If they wanted to try an experiment, Brill let them try. The first experiments he pushed them to complete were for the creation of savant-like behavior in the primates. This was a challenge on many fronts, requiring them to perform germ-line mutations, which the scientific community has long shunned. But not here;

Brill encouraged it, even demanded they perform the required procedures. He wanted to prove his theory that high-intensity solar radiation caused degradation in the Y-Chromosome in primates... but first they had to genetically engineer the starting-point genes from the prehistoric record.

Creating the starting point to prove his theory was exceedingly challenging. He gave them Sirum's Y-chromosome code to help fill the gaps, knowing it most likely wouldn't contain the radiation sensitive region, which proved to be the case. Frustrated at their lack of progress in this area, Brill eventually decided to return to Jakarta to try to dig up better-preserved genetic material. All he'd been able to get from New Zealand were teeth and femur marrow samples. He would need to enroll Liora and her connections, as this was dangerous territory, and he would need protection. Liora met up with Brill in his university lab at his request. "What's so urgent that you had to pull me away from my patients?"

"I need to get back to a place close to Jakarta."

"Why?"

"I never told you the complete story of my escape."

"You barely escaped with your life, I know that. Why would you want to go back?"

"When I was out in the middle of nowhere, I came across this cave that was once inhabited by an ancient civilization. The paintings on the walls of that cave led me to New Zealand."

"Cave paintings? Is that what you want to go back and risk your life for?"

"No. I need to get at the graves that I now believe were there. More specifically, I need to obtain any marrow that may have been preserved in the bones of the people in those graves. Then I need to immediately sequence it, as it's very fragile and won't handle preservation."

She frowned. "What could those bones have that you can't get out of the ones from New Zealand?"

"Remember those images in the cave in New Zealand? The ones where the planet was shown hitting the sun?"

"Yes, you were very excited about that."

"Excited, yes — because that depicts a turning point in human evolution. What I think happened is that our ancestors prior to that event were exceedingly intelligent, and then the event occurred and bombarded the Earth with massive amounts of radiation for an extended period of time. The radiation caused deleterious mutations in those people. They still had *some* intelligence, but it was severely diminished. I think the fragments of their prior abilities eventually gave rise to the people we now call autistic savants. From then on, I suspect the autism genes were passed from generation to generation, every now and then creating a savant. Those were artistic geniuses, as the images depicted people with such skills, but nothing more."

She sighed, and crossed her arms across her chest. "If I understand you correctly, you think there's some of the unmutated genetic material still in the skeletons in Jakarta, assuming they actually exist, and you need help getting there? How do you think I can help? I'm a psychiatrist."

"Liora... you have connections," Brill said slowly. "We both know you do. Remember the number you gave me in case of an emergency, after Sirum was hurt?"

"Yes. It was a number to the state police, just in case you had another cave-in."

He glared at her. "Let's quit pretending. I called that number when I was trapped in Jakarta on the mountainside. Shortly after I called it, U.S. Navy SEALs showed up."

"They must have forwarded your call based on your geography." Liora shrugged.

"Why are you still pretending you didn't know what would happen when I called that number? It clearly indicates there's more to you than you've cared to share."

She looked him straight in the eye and told him, "Brill, there are some things in my past I *can't* share with you. And I won't. Those parts of my life I can tap into when needed, but *this* is my life now, and I'm here to try to share that with you."

He nodded sadly. "I won't push you to tell me what you don't want to, but I need you to help me get to Jakarta with a team, and for you to get us that protection while we're there."

"I'll see what I can do. No promises," she said icily.

"I hope you can, but I'm going either way. I'd rather have your help, but I can't afford to wait on it."

Later that day, Liora called Colonel Rhett and explained the situation. He was cautious about sending too much of a presence into that part of the world, as it would alert their enemies to Brill's quest. He did agree to send an elite squad to watch over Brill's team, but Brill would have to get to the Philippines first on his own. From there, he would take them aboard an aircraft carrier patrolling the region, and could put them ashore anywhere in Indonesia.

"That would be perfect, Uncle Liam," she told him, pleased.

"Liora, you have to realize that time is growing short. Brill's work has attracted the attention of too many groups around the world. Brill doesn't think anyone but me is watching, but that's not true. He's been suspicious of me since his father was killed years ago. What he doesn't know is that I've been protecting him, holding the wolves at bay."

Concerned, Liora demanded, "What's Brill doing that's gained the attention of terrorist organizations?"

"It's more than terrorists, Liora. There are several foreign powers who would love to take what he's learned and put it to their own uses. They're keyed in on his mental manipulations. The Harvard group has been publishing continually since Brill helped them out, and they keep giving him credit, which has put the spotlight on him."

"How can Brill be protected?"

"Speed helps. You need to push him along faster. If this quest to Indonesia will help him out, then we'll make it happen. Anything Brill needs, all he has to do is ask. When you're in Jakarta, plant those seeds, and make him worried that his work is in jeopardy of being stolen. Hopefully, that will cause him to pull out of the public eye, and may give him the time he needs."

#

It was much easier to get to the bottom of the cave in Jakarta with the aid of a helicopter and drop lines. The team had a military escort every step of the way, which made disinterring the graves they found there easy. As Brill had expected, it was as much a cemetery as the image cave in New Zealand. With every hand holding a shovel except for the two men who were guarding them, they'd soon uncovered upwards of thirty skeletons. This next part was tedious; Brill had to meticulously collect teeth and drill into long bones to look for rare fragments of preserved bone marrow. Several times they uncovered marrow, but the answer they sought evaded them. Every skeleton was a bust. Further digging over the next few days didn't uncover any further graves.

Brill was about to give up in frustration; they'd been at this for three days now, and nothing more had been uncovered. Fortunately, he'd had had the foresight to bring along a ground penetrating radar unit, which could detect irregularities in the soil that might indicate more burials. To

Brill's displeasure, however, the sediments in the cave were too dense for it to work properly; it penetrated just a few feet. He wished Sirum could have come along; he would've fixed the machine to probe deeper in no time. Eventually, Brill gave him a call on a satellite phone to ask for suggestions.

Sirum helped them engineer a simple amplifier to boost the signal. Brill's spirits improved after that, but he lost hope again when even the improved device failed to detect any new graves. Toward the end of the outing they had one more area to scan, and finished that with nothing positive to show for their efforts. Brill plopped down against the wall of the cave in exasperation. As he did so, it gave way, and nearly trapped him in a pile of rubble. This was literally the breakthrough Brill needed, as it showed him that part of the cave's ceiling had fallen in, and that they had missed one area due to a cave-in forming a thin wall, sealing off one piece of the graveyard.

The area had been cut off from air and water for who knew how many thousands of years, and a quick reconnaissance located several mummified corpses. They began to extract every piece of cellular material they could find, including hair and skin. The ossuary contained a mix of male and female corpses. They sequenced them all with their portable equipment over the next few days; while the Y-chromosome from the males was the main target, the females gave them additional information they wouldn't otherwise have had.

They had nearly completed the final sequence when the team suffered the attack they had feared. Drug runners had spotted their helicopter, and sent a group to take out what they perceived as threat. The criminals had no idea they were encountering an elite military unit, and it was easy to hold them back for the time needed to rescue the scientists. Brill's fire-team rushed down to extract them, but Brill refused to go, insisting he needed 30 more minutes. They agreed to wait as long as possible, but then they would leave with him in tow, willingly or not.

With five minutes to go, they came under air assault. As Brill's team finished up, they took fire leaving the cave. The two scientists Brill had brought along were both killed as they tried to board the chopper; the price for the new data had suddenly become unaccountably high. It pained Brill deeply to have to pay it with human lives, but he knew that this might be his only chance to get the answers he needed. Any price was worth it, he decided; he was willing to lose everyone, including Liora if it came to that.

His guards were holding their own, but were soon overwhelmed between the air attack and missiles sent against then from a boat on the nearby river. They had to call in additional support from the aircraft carrier. As they took cover, heavy artillery from *Abraham Lincoln* bombed the area, allowing them the window they needed to board the chopper and get airborne.

On the way back, Liora was constantly in Brill's ear, planting the seeds of doubt and increasing his paranoia. "Brill, do you think that group that attacked us was after your work?" Although she knew they had nothing to do with that, being only concerned with owning the drug lanes, it was a valid excuse to do what her uncle had instructed.

Brill looked at her blankly. "What? How would anyone know about my work?"

"You did some groundbreaking work with the Harvard group. They're still publishing on it, last I looked. Maybe they're telling people more than what's in their publications."

He sighed. "Maybe," he said uncertainly.

A seed of doubt can be just a word or two when someone is already paranoid. That did it for Brill. He built on that thought the entire trip home, slowly piecing together bits of information until he was certain someone was out to steal his work. When he returned to Vegas, he began to pull most of his work out to Avalon, keeping only his human research at the university lab. He was beyond cautious. From that point on, he never made a cell phone call again, as he was certain the Internet server nodes the government used to filter all Internet activity were also filtering cellular activity. He worked with Sirum to develop a quantum phone, one that could never be infiltrated, as its software worked in quantum units and was unlike anything that currently existed. Of course, the recipient also had to have a quantum phone in order to talk to them. He gave one to Liora, and Sirum had the third. Three was all he thought he needed, since those two could then relay any messages he needed to the broader world. If he needed to talk with the university folks, he did so at his university lab. He now stayed in the desert at night in Avalon, and travelled back into the city to work on his subjects to progress the human element of his work.

The genetic elements they had obtained from Jakarta gave them a clearer picture of not only the Y-chromosome, but also the X. His team of geneticists had no trouble building the new complete prehistoric chromosomes. They found the Jakarta Y-chromosome was larger by several million base pairs than any modern-day Y-chromosome, mapping a region they suspected to have susceptibility to any type of strong radiation. Now they had to build it into the primates.

While observing their work, Brill realized something he hadn't anticipated. If he had just looked at the animals to start with, he might have seen it earlier. They were covered with hair. How is solar radiation, even massive amounts of it, going to do the same damage to hairy creatures as it does to relatively hairless humans? It wouldn't, he was certain. Fur would absorb and reflect more energy than bare skin would. Where this was going made Brill uneasy. The answer to his problem wasn't an accepted form of research on any country's soil.

He needed to experiment on human beings.

He wasn't sure how he would do so. *Nobody* would let him play with their DNA to "fix" them, just to damage them again in order to prove a theory. Nor would anyone willingly become autistic. This was a last-resort idea, so he turned his thoughts back to the primates. It finally hit him: give them medications that would cause them to lose their body hair permanently. It would be easier than shaving and re-shaving them.

The other challenge Brill had put to his team was in the engineering of fully differentiated mature cells. He'd assembled a group of brilliant scientists and knew they had it in them to rise above their self-imposed limitations. Ursula and Misuli, the Swazi twins, were exceptionally intelligent women. They were experts in primate reproductive biology, and were having trouble with the direction Brill was taking. His tactic was to push them harder, as he felt they could do more and better. They screened every viral cassette they could get their hands on, and found that an oddly-named retrovirus called the Human Foamy Virus could be engineered to infect every cell in the body. They began experimenting with signals that would take the virus straight to the brain and transform the genetic material of neural cells.

The first series of experiments were a success, though they hit a snag with the sex-chromosome reengineering. They couldn't push genetic material into those chromosomes, only mutate them, but even that couldn't introduce large scale changes. Their solution was to engineer the sex chromosomes on the bench, and manually introduce them into mature cells. This allowed them to provoke the mutations, though ultimately, it would require a great deal more work than Brill had hoped.

Brill was becoming fanatical about the speed of their work, pushing his team to their limits and constantly shouting about their lack of results. The first wave of experiments was a dismal failure, as nine out of the ten primates — two chimps and eight rhesus monkeys — died within hours of treatment. The cycle repeated itself, but they were continually learning and modifying their approach — until the breakthrough finally came, about a month into the transformation of the primates, when they had a complete Y-chromosome transformation.

They were set to begin the solar radiation mutation experiments when the unexpected happened: the primates with the initial set of mutations began learning at a rapid rate, especially the chimpanzees. Simple learning at first, but a change nonetheless. They were even picking up math skills, amazingly enough. The team felt they had overcome a major hurdle, and were now eager to see how quickly these primates could raise their intelligence.

Brill stopped by unexpectedly soon after, not having been updated yet. He saw his people performing these experiments and became furious that they were wasting their time, as he didn't yet realize their profound discovery. He was adamant they begin the solar radiation experiments — but every researcher refused his command, each insisting he review the data first. When Brill finally calmed down and listened to them, he was profusely apologetic, realizing he had pushed the team to inadvertently stumble upon the building blocks of intelligence. It was basic, but intelligence nonetheless. He gave the team the green light to continue to engineer all the primates, as they had many different types to work with.

They labored tirelessly for the next few months, but could only replicate the intelligence in chimpanzees and bonobos, humanity's closest relatives. None of the other primate types showed any improvements; indeed, most rapidly deteriorated, dying within days of treatment.

Some of his team were good friends with Liora, and they complained constantly to her about Brill's erratic behavior. Her efforts to win over the group had gone better than expected, as they considered her one of the team.

Brill was trying to understand what to do next, as he had only half-proven his theory. Their work indicated that the ancient genes gave rise to *some* form of high intelligence, though he'd have to perform experiments on humans to confirm this. Unfortunately, the next part of his theory would require him to destroy a few of these remarkably transformed subjects; the doctor in him vehemently opposed this, yet he needed an answer. But an answer for what?

Lost in thought, he jumped a foot high when the door slammed behind him as Liora burst in and demanded, "What the hell is wrong with you?"

He blinked, confused. "What?"

"Your team is on the verge of rebellion! Your constant yelling at them and pushing them to perform unethical experiments is breaking them, and then you expect them to keep quiet about it!"

"They need motivation," Brill protested.

"Is *that* what you call it?"

"They were on the verge of a great discovery, and needed prodding along."

"The way I heard it, they *had* made the great discovery, and you were screaming at them for being too slow and doing unnecessary work!" she raged.

He crossed his arms and said calmly, "My vision is correct, and I need to prove it. Even it means sacrificing a few of our success stories so we can study them in more detail."

"Brill, you need to go easier on your team," she told him flatly. "Otherwise, they're gone. And where do you see this work going? Will there ever be a point where you feel it's complete enough to share with the rest of us?"

Suspicious of her abrupt line of questioning, he answered cautiously, "The human element is where the work meets the world," then fell silent.

Looking a bit perplexed, she prompted him. "You'll have to explain that a bit more."

"All in due time, Liora. My immediate need is to show that the ancient genes will deteriorate when exposed to massive amounts of solar radiation, and hopefully result in a gene pattern similar to the savants."

"That's crazy. Why would you want to destroy this brilliant work?"

"To prove my theory. Then the *real* work can begin."

She shook her head sadly. "I don't understand. I thought this *was* your work."

"You'll see when the time is right."

"You're assuming I'll still be here. That any of your team will be."

He dismissed that comment as frivolous. *Everyone will see* was the thought resonating in his mind. There was too much at stake. He suspected Liam Rhett was somehow connected to Liora's questions, and he would keep her guessing. Leading her down a false path was a start. If he kept her thinking it was only about the genetics, she wouldn't understand the real gem of his work. He had his answers with the primates, and his theories were confirmed. Now it was time to move the work from the primates to humans. This was the tricky part: experimenting on people, misleading them about what he was going to do to them. If it worked, they would be smarter. Perhaps even superhuman.

If it didn't... well, that was a bridge he didn't want to cross. It had to work.

Chapter 12: Infiltration

Connor Swan had followed Liora's work closely after she left Johannesburg. Her book about apartheid was a real hit; he loved the connection she had made from the historical attitudes to present, plus she had a few chapters in there focusing on him and his family, and was well pleased with what she wrote. Still, he had placed spies at UNLV to monitor her activities for the first few months after she left. Their reports back to Connor showed a clear connection to the rather infamous Dr. Brill Everly, and they noted that she often accompanied him in his private helicopter, to where they didn't know. Brill and his research intrigued Connor now that it was on his radar.

Liora's efforts to get in tight with Brill's team created an opportunity for Connor's spies. They noted the routine: every other weekend the researchers hit the Vegas strip, so his people seized the chance to find out more, as they were ex-KGB and very good at their jobs. It didn't go unnoticed that

two of Brill's team were from Swaziland, which made them
prime targets for Connor's people. It was during the second
outing of one particular month, when the Swazi twins were
off by themselves, as they so often were, that his spies used
the opportunity to plant tracking and listening devices on
them. They used multiple copies of each, just in case one was
lost, discovered, or destroyed. The easier one was a piece of
jewelry they gave to each of the ladies. Acting as if they
were hitting on them, and pretending to be a bit drunk, they
pressed on each of them a lovely necklace, saying they'd just
won them at the poker tables. The necklaces were readily
accepted, as were their advances. The ladies were eager for
companionship.

The trackers led to a place in the middle of nowhere. They
were able to trace the route to an underground building of
twelve stories or more, but the signal was lost thereafter.
Spotting the helicopter and observing Liora and Brill coming
and going made them hungry for more information. Having
established a relationship with the twins, they were able to

arrange for an illicit tour, timing it just right, when neither Brill nor Liora were there.

Connor read the resulting reports with great interest. It seemed the underground building was an animal genetics laboratory. Apparently, Everly and Co. were trying to engineer human intelligence into chimpanzees. If they succeeded, the application of their methods to human beings would be highly therapeutic, and highly profitable. The lure of gaining access to the technology was too much to resist, and it ate away at him. He carefully planned his next move.

#

A week later, the Swazi twins, Ursula and Misuli, unexpectedly received an urgent call from their family back home. The news was anything but positive. Their parents had been abducted, and the ransom was for them to get Brill to hire two specific individuals from South Africa. Otherwise, their parents would be executed.

Fortunately, they were in a place in their research that gave them the opportunity to ask Brill to bring in a few new people. They concocted a story about needing experts in two subdisciplines, and they knew just who to recommend. At first, he was reluctant to bring new people onboard, but relented once they made their case with excuses backed by their failures.

Brill was skeptical of the twins' claims that they were unable to complete the primate-to-human transfer. They claimed they lacked skills in those specialized areas of human biology, and needed the two South Africans, with whom they had dealt in the past, to get them over that hump. The background checks passed, though, and the new researchers' publications were solid enough that Brill brought them in for interviews. They easily answered his tough questions, paving the way for their entry into his program. Little did he know that these two were imposters, lookalikes taking the places of the real researchers. The men they had taken the places of were currently incommunicado.

#

The South Africans blended well with the group. They weren't actually skilled enough to complete the needed work on their own, but were able to coerce the twins, and the researchers whose identities they'd taken, to provide them with the answers they needed. There was now steady progress being made on the transfer of the primate mutations to a human recipient, and they played a key role in its development. The bulk of the work prior to their arrival remained a mystery to the moles, however, causing them to search every hard drive and storage device they could find. During their search, they came across a place where a door used to be. It was explained to them that there had been an earthquake sometime back that had caused a cave-in and massive amounts of damage. That satisfied their curiosity for a while.

But they were thorough in their efforts, and explored everything both inside the facility and topside. In time, they found the clue for which they were searching: high-speed Internet cables that disappeared into the mountainside. They soon located the entry point, and it was clear that it had been sealed off intentionally. This signaled to them that there was more to this place than what they were finding. They used their excellent people skills to get the information the hard way: by asking question after question, and slowly peeling back the layers of secrecy until the full picture came into view.

Connor Swan was pleased with the reports he had been receiving from his moles in Brill's organization. The work was astounding, more so than he had first hoped. Several of the building blocks were missing, however, preventing him from appropriating it and implementing it. He would need a whole ape at least to reverse-engineer the technology, and preferable a matched pair of them. His spies hadn't been able to isolate the full sequence of DNA modifications that had achieved the intelligence boosts. They had pieces, and had concluded that no single person in Brill's organization knew the whole story. Each made contributions, which Brill Everly himself then put together in an order that only he knew. It was clear to Connor that he would either have to acquire the entire group of scientists to replicate Brill's work, or try a new tactic.

Once he knew the timing of their next group event, he would make his move.

#

The next meeting between Colonel Liam Rhett and his niece was contentious, to say the least. Liam had wanted Liora to push Brill into a series of failures. The work he was doing was becoming more and more valuable; Liam saw the potential for many advances in military technology, but the bigger picture was the threat to American security if someone else got hold of it, and he wasn't about to let that happen. The plan was for Liora to take some skin patches she'd picked up in Germany and place one on each of Brill's test subjects. Liam needed intel, and this was how he was going to get it. Maybe he could figure out Brill's secrets if he put his spy tech *inside* the test subjects.

#

Liora was getting closer to Brill again; not because she had to, but because she *wanted* to, and her feelings for him were growing. This particular conversation was one of many that made her start to love him. Brill was explaining the research he was doing with the chimps and bonobos. Some she could follow; much was beyond her. She knew the basics of genetics, but what he was describing was too deep, even for most experts in the field. This was what she loved about him: his ability to take an abstract area and make it into something profound. She wasn't sure she could continue to do Liam's dirty work anymore.

Her thoughts drifted back to the conversation at hand.

"Don't you realize that we're a technology-rich society, but an intellectually deficient one? Liora, hey, are you daydreaming?"

"Not sure what you mean?"

Repeating the question and continuing to expound upon it, he said, "People have all this advanced technology in their possession daily, yet fewer than one in ten understands how any of it works. Take the smartphone. Do you know how it works?"

"Of course. You look at it and it turns on. Then you find the app you want and click it."

"You just proved my point. It's not *how* to use things that matters here, but the understanding of how they work! That smartphone uses advanced technology of several different kinds. Biometrics. Then there's the way it moves data from your phone to a server node, then out to the server node wherever the information you desire is residing. Then the process is reversed, and you almost instantaneously get what you need. It uses advanced two-way radio telephony to connect calls. I could go on and on, with example after example. It's not just our country, but everywhere. People rely so heavily on smartphones and computers to tell them everything, they don't even understand basic technology anymore. The *how* of what makes things work or the theory behind it is the deficiency."

Liora was perplexed. "Guess I never thought of it that way, but it won't change my habits or make me try to learn the theory of why things do what they do. We have experts for that."

"That's a pity. I'd love to find a way to make people learn about the technology before they use something, but I know it won't happen. We want instant gratification, and everything has to be simple to use."

"From a psychiatric perspective, I can see your point, but I think it's more simplistic than that. It's Freud's theory of the id. It's the unconscious mind that's driven by basic instincts. Those are what push us to the easy path when faced with a choice of difficult or easy."

"Maybe, but I think it's a dependency on authority. We tend to defer decisions to those in power, and technology is no different. We view technology as the thing with all the answers."

"So we want to be told what to do? We're saying the same thing, just in different ways."

"Yes, but it's fun to argue." A smile crossed his face.

After long consideration, Brill had allowed Liora to visit Avalon, which only made sense, as he'd opened it to his researchers, despite not intending to at first. Liora had spent more time than usual there recently, as the primates fascinated her — and because Liam had ordered her to get closer to Brill's real work. The people there loved her company, as they got no other visitors. Brill let them work four twelve-hour days and then have three days off. The team liked that at first, but soon tired of going to Vegas every weekend. The more adventurous went to Lake Tahoe or Salt Lake City, but that eventually got old too. None of them had spouses and kids, so they enjoyed the single life, but the evenings lacked the excitement they needed. Liora used her psychiatric skills to probe into their psyches. One of her assignments was to make sure none of them were spies, as Liam had intel that several foreign powers were trying to get their hands on Brill's work.

The scientists at the facility all knew her cover profession, which at first made them suspicious that Brill had sent her to keep them in line. That perception was easy for her to get them over — she and Brill were obviously romantically involved— but their intellects, and their unusual work, made them cautious by nature. To overcome that, she took them out on the town. This strategy worked well, as it only took a few beers for most to welcome her into their confidence. It soon became clear, though, that two of them though were of a different psyche, and wanted nothing to do with her. Those were the ones she immediately wrote off, as any true spy would never take that tactic. She would know; she was, after all, one of the best in the business. One particular scientist, though, was too charming for her liking. If anyone was a spy, it would be someone like him, but she wasn't sure there *were* any infiltrators. She took the time to get to know him better, but there were no obvious clues. Then she saw it: Joe wasn't a spy, he was just easily manipulated by one of the women. Ultimately, Liora didn't think any of them were spies.

This was all well and good until the new players joined the game. The South Africans were an elusive pair. Connor had warned them of Liora's cover profession, and how they needed to be extra cautious around her. Of course, she quickly took note of them and monitored their habits. Why Brill had brought them in she couldn't fathom. She had Liam vet them, and they were solid. The pair didn't say much at any time, but said even less when she was around.

She didn't suspect their duplicity.

#

Brill was pushing his team again, but less so now that they'd made such remarkable breakthroughs. He was spending more of his time at the university labs, eager to see if he could get his volunteers to mimic a savant's mental acuity and thought processes. The genetic work on the primates was in its infancy; if he could get them to develop the mental abilities of a savant, or at least close, then he felt he would progress much faster than pushing a fully-developed human mind to have inherently honed thoughts.

Savant minds were so much more than he could characterize: brilliant in single applications, with the unique ability to know things they normally shouldn't. Where they got that knowledge remained Brill's greatest quest. Were they truly communicating with dark matter in deep space? Was it some interaction of the mental psyche with the quantum level that gave them such abilities — or something else?

The application of the genetics to humans was tougher than he'd expected. The subjects in his program were willing participants in the work; at this point he had everything approved and sanctioned through the university and all relevant government entities. The participants all had terminal illnesses, and any effort to improve their condition was hope they otherwise didn't have. Brill truly was trying to cure them, but also trying to reengineer their chromosomes, which he was convinced would let them tap the knowledge and energies that the ancient seers and, to a lesser extent, modern savants accessed. Most had some form of cancer, so his chromosomal engineering was producing some benefits...

at least to a point. But it seemed to him that the work was plodding along with little progress.

During the trials, several of the patients succumbed to their cancers. The postmortems showed no introduction of the changes he had been attempting, for either the cancer cells or the neurons. He wondered if their immune systems had blocked the treatment somehow. Several other patients were showing signs of mental deterioration, indicating the treatments were having the opposite effect than intended. Brill suspected something was missing on the primate DNA, some sequence his team hadn't viewed as important. This was something he felt he needed to handle in person, so he headed out to Avalon one weekend, when he knew the team would be gone and he would have free run of the facility.

Meanwhile, the South Africans weren't making any progress in getting the full genetic sequence. They were never alone with the primates, as there were always too many people around the primates. They debated their options, realizing their best one was to steal two specimens. They couldn't risk taking more, as it would be difficult enough to get those two out, and they would be missed immediately. They only had a brief window of time to implement their plan, and timing was be crucial. As the weekend approached, both men pretended they were coming down with colds, allowing them to back out of the trip into town.

That Friday evening, the pair tried to catch two chimps as they roamed their habitat, but the animals were very aggressive in the evenings — and they learned quickly that the wiry chimps were much stronger than humans. In order to obtain their specimens, they decided, they would have to neutralize them all; if they took down individual chimps, the others would protect their downed brethren. The primates' habitat opened into the solar radiation chamber, which was a large room full of mirrors. The apes loved going in there, as looking at themselves was one of their favorite pastimes. The only entrance was through the primate sanctuary.

The South Africans had acquired some ketamine, an animal tranquilizer, the previous weekend, but could only get enough for two shots. They decided to take a male and a female, so they could be sure to get all the genetic mutations the team had been developing, as nobody had the full picture of what had been done since the start. They found a pair engaging in social interaction; ideal specimens, as they might well mate once they were out of the facility. They were able to tranquilize them, but there were still many chimps and bonobos — so-called pygmy chimps — in the sanctuary, and they needed to lure the rest into the solar radiation room. They had hidden the apes' favorite treat in a time-release box in that room, using it as bait to lure them in. The treat — sardines, of all things — were like honey to a bear. As soon as the top of the box opened, the smell of the sardines had the animals scrambling over each other to get to the mirror chamber. Once all were in, the door slammed shut, and the infiltrators set the radiation generators to full power.

It was about then that Brill dropped in to run through the data and pull some genetic samples from the primates. He wasn't expecting anyone to be there. As he descended the

elevator, unbeknown to him, the service elevator was
heading up with the South Africans and their prizes. When
he stepped into the primate sanctuary, he thought it odd that
none of the primates were in their enclosure. They were often
very active this time of night. As he searched the facility, he
came across the sealed radiation chamber. The autolock was
engaged, indicating the generators were pumping in
radiation.

Brill ran to the control terminal and frantically cut the
power. The radiation generator had a thirty-minute ramp up
to full bombardment, the last resort Brill was planning for
these experiments, and the timer indicated it had been going
for an hour and a half already! It would take another half-
hour to get the radiation levels down to normal, and he didn't
know how he could stand the anxiety. He knew the primates
were probably dead already, and couldn't fathom how they'd
been sealed inside and the generators activated — except as
an act of deliberate sabotage. But nobody except his team
was even supposed to *know* about the primates, much less the

mutations they had introduced into them. He would investigate further once he was able to get the primates some treatment to reverse the damage, if that was even possible.

Meanwhile, the South Africans had emerged from the mountain with the chimps, and were shocked to find Brill's helicopter on its pad. They had already loaded the chimps onto a flatbed truck they had hidden in the brush, planning to drive them to a rendezvous point in the desert, but changed their plans when they saw the newly available transportation. One of the men had been in the South African army, and knew how to fly this type of chopper. Once they got the chimps loaded aboard, they were about to take off when one of the men decided it was best to go back down into the facility and eliminate Brill. Otherwise, the missing helicopter would soon be missed, and they needed more time to meet with their contact.

They quickly made their way back down to the sanctuary. Seeing the radiation room door open, they cautiously peeked inside to find Brill examining the primates. All they had to do was shut and lock the door, then set the radiation generator to full power again. They then made their way back up to the helicopter and were off, to meet with their contact in the Nevada desert.

#

A few hours before, Liam Rhett had received an alert that Brill's helicopter had left Vegas, headed for the desert facility. The Colonel had long ago hidden trackers and bugs in the helicopter, and had the building itself fully and permanently bugged during construction. This latest event was outside Brill's normal routine, so Liam took interest, deciding he would review the footage when he returned home. He was out to dinner with his wife at the time, and didn't want to interrupt the evening.

As they were finishing dinner, Liam's phone chirped with another alert. This time Brill's helicopter was headed out into the open desert, away from Vegas, not toward the city as would be expected. He immediately suspected foul play. Pulling up the helicopter video feeds on his phone, he saw two men he recognized as the recent South African hires in the copter, with two large crates stashed behind them. This was the break he had hoped for, as he'd long wanted to acquire some of Brill's apes for himself; an ironclad opportunity had never arisen till now. But if the South Africans had Brill's helicopter, then something unpleasant must have happened to Brill Everly. He wasn't ready to have Brill eliminated, so he had to act. Tapping into the building feeds, he found Brill in serious trouble.

Fortunately, the radiation generator was one of the pieces of equipment in which his people had installed remote control switches. He had expected to use them to turn the chamber on remotely, not to turn it off; but it was a simple matter of issuing a command. After shutting down the unit, he scrambled a team from Area 51 to intercept the felonious South Africans, then called Liora to meet his medical team at the lab, telling her Brill needed her help immediately. His medical team would stabilize Brill and then transport him to the university lab. From there, Liora would take over, and Brill need never know Liam had been involved.

Little did Liam know that the radiation Brill had been exposed to awoke the dormant nanobots in his system again. They saved Brill's life, preserving his mind and putting his body in a form of stasis.

During his subsequent recovery, Liora rarely left his side, as he was in dire straits. She took over the direction of his research team, giving them what amounted to busywork to do, not really sure of the direction Brill wanted them to go. She was certain now that she was meant to be with Brill, but her loyalties to Liam still took precedence. As it turned out, the solar radiation he had been exposed to — massive amounts for an extended period — did cause a serious mutation in the Y-chromosomes of his germ and somatic cells, proving Brill's theory about the male primates. Unfortunately, none of the chimps or bonobos survived the high radiation doses. Had they survived, he could have monitored how their newly-found intelligence had changed, but that contingency never materialized. Brill himself had suffered serious damage, which required a lengthy recovery period, but retained his intellect mostly unharmed.

During that time, he had ample opportunity to analyze the events of the past few months. Something didn't sit right with him, a nagging suspicion at the back of his mind that just wouldn't go away or show itself fully. How the hell did he get trapped in the radiation room? That wasn't possible without human intervention. The next question was, how had he been rescued so quickly? The timer showed he was only in there for a few hours. But the bigger question was, how had he survived that much radiation when all the other primates were dead? It should have killed him as well, especially since chimps and bonobos tended to be more rugged than humans. This bugged him, as it shouldn't have been physically possible for him to survive.

As if those questions weren't bothersome enough, there was the issue of the two missing chimps, his missing helicopter, and the thrice-dammed missing South Africans.

Someone had wiped all his video surveillance files of the event. No one except he and Sirum knew of his quantum computer, however, which kept a backup of everything, just in case something like this ever happened, though he'd never anticipated something of this magnitude. Those files were in its memory core, which he couldn't access from his hospital bed or apartment; he would need to use a terminal hardwired into the computer, ideally the one in Avalon, now deep in the cavern system. He couldn't get there, as he couldn't move from his hospital bed for a long while.

About six weeks into his recovery, Liora brought news that his helicopter had been found, crashed in the desert. Investigators had recovered the decayed remains of the South Africans and the two chimps. She shared video of the recovery of the crash site — but it was clearly staged. *Wrapping up loose ends,* he thought. The dead chimps were *not* the remains of Fred and Wilma, as the team called the pair that had been stolen; they were bonobos, not common chimps. That turned his suspicions to Liora, as she pointed out the details in the video feed, almost as if she were trying to convince him it was all wrapped up now.

Brill needed to understand his ability to survive the massive amounts of radiation he had been dosed with. Had his Dad's treatment protocol when he was young triggered something miraculous in his body's ability to heal itself, similar to how he survived the torture by the drug runners and left for dead? He shouldn't even be able to see, yet his eyes were undamaged. When he was finally released from the hospital, Brill isolated himself to research his survival, starting with his Dad's private notes and the coded papers his Dad had given him shortly before he was killed. They were kept in John Everly's special lockbox, which Brill hadn't opened in years. At first, he just pulled out all the papers and read them thoroughly; but that wasn't enough, even the coded messages. Knowing his father had been at least as careful and paranoid as he was at the end, Brill studied each paper more carefully, and took a closer look at the lockbox itself. He had never before inspected it, thinking it was just a storage box; but now nothing was beyond suspicion. Within minutes, he'd noticed an oddity about the box: the bottom of the interior seemed to be slightly higher than the exterior bottom of the box. Not by much, but enough to indicate it had a false floor. He couldn't figure out how to open it, however, as there were no latches nor any indication of a door.

Just when he was thinking of giving up, he ran his fingers down the length of the interior one last time, and a sharp piece of the flooring pricked his finger, causing blood to flow. As the blood soaked into the box's flooring, there came a faint *ding,* and Brill realized his blood was the key he needed to unlock the hidden compartment! The side of the box flipped open to reveal a thin space containing an old-fashioned high-density thumb drive, a flat ALS light, and a few papers. The papers appeared blank until he shined the light on them, whereupon the writing jumped off the pages in a three-dimensional matrix. It was the code his Dad had created so many years ago; instead of simple two-dimensional linear writing, his father had added to it a third dimension so that a dense sequence of text literally came to life right before his eyes. How this was possible, he didn't know.

As Brill flipped through page after page, he got a partial picture of what his Dad had done to save him, including all the work he'd done for Liam Rhett on the prisoners at Guantanamo Bay. According to the papers, the thumb drive contained all the technical details on each of the advances his Dad had made. This information didn't exist anywhere else in the world, as far as he knew; everyone had thought his father's work for the military had been lost when he was killed. Every computer he had ever used had been scoured in great detail by Colonel Rhett's team, but nothing was ever located.

He immediately hid the drive, of course, as he dared not use it until he could access the quantum computer. The papers he kept, and read in detail. They revealed that he had been treated with prions to repair his immune system, had been genetically reengineered, and had also been treated with special nanobots created by Liam's team at Vassal. When Brill saw the details of what those treatments could do, he started to piece together how he'd survived. The prions were tightly integrated with his DNA, which helped protect them from radiation. The nanobots he was less sure about, but he concluded they'd somehow protected his neurons and the rest of his nervous system.

After several months in recovery, Brill finally made his way to back to Avalon, gathered his team, and offered them a difficult choice.

Addressing his team, "I'm sorry all your work was destroyed," he began. "I know those chimps and bonobos were like family to many of you. I also know many of you would like to get back to the real world on a regular basis — but I have a special offer. I'm starting a new phase of my research, and I need volunteers. Those of you willing to volunteer for my program will be paid five million dollars each. Those who decline will receive a severance settlement of one million dollars and will be required to sign a rather draconian non-disclosure agreement. The choice is yours."

Someone asked, "What does this research involve?"

"Good question. It will build on the work you've done here, but could be dangerous. More than that, I can't say."

"Count us in," both Swazi twins said.

Not everyone took the deal. Those who didn't soon departed the Vegas area. Brill set them up with bank accounts with the money pre-loaded into them; they were free to do as they wished, except talk about or build off the work they had done for him. That group had loaded up all their belongings, ready to call Brill to pick them up, when an unmarked bus showed up, the driver saying he was their ride. They loaded up and gave no thought to where they were going, as all believed it was the Vegas airport. The ride to the airport should have been a two-hour drive. The bus was loaded with a cooler of beer and plenty of food, so nobody paid much attention when the ride went well beyond two hours. When someone finally looked at their phone, they brought attention to the driver that they should have been at the airport by now. The driver never even looked back at them; he just kept on driving.

After four hours of travel, they came upon a lone, guarded gate in a razor wire-topped fence that went on for miles. Their jaws dropped as the next events unfolded. The bus passed right through the checkpoint and picked up speed. The "Groom Lake" sign they spotted, along with their multiple USAF escorts, brought the group to a high state of agitation, and they began demanding the driver turn them around.

Shortly after, the bus pulled into an aircraft hangar, and the scientists were ushered out under gunpoint. Blindfolds and handcuffs were placed on each of them as they were loaded onto a plane and hustled to a secret location.

#

Brill now had ample time to pore through the video feeds on his quantum computer. He saw the South Africans tranquilize Fred and Wilma, then lure the rest of the apes into the radiation chamber before setting the radiation generators to max. It irked him to see them at his desert facility at the exact same time as he was there. They were clever, going up in the service elevator as he was going down the main. He zoomed in on their actions when they reached the surface. As they exited, they retrieved a truck, loaded the unconscious chimps onto it, and were driving off when they stopped. They hit reverse and made their way to his helicopter. After loading the chimps onto the chopper, they returned to the facility. He guessed they hadn't known he was there until they saw his helicopter; then they must have changed their plans and decided to kill him, just as they had done to his primates. It was clear they had trapped him in the radiation chamber, set the machine on full, and left him to die.

The ensuing events were harder for him to follow. Somehow, the radiation generator had turned itself off. As he kept watching, his jaw dropped as he saw an Army medical crew arrive, minutes before Liora entered the facility. This just about destroyed him emotionally. He'd suspected Liora was somehow associated with Liam Rhett, and this confirmed it. How else had the Army even known of his plight? How else had Liora known to come and rescue him? They must have infiltrated his facility electronically. He searched for hours before finally coming across the external outputs and incoming signals, which were well-hidden and used a channel that mimicked static. Had he not had the Avalon computer's quantum analysis capabilities, he would never have found the pirated signals. Where they went he couldn't trace, but it was clear someone had viewed all his video feeds and sent a deactivation signal to the radiation chamber's generator.

The presence of the medical team had not been mentioned in the chain of events that led to his rescue and evacuation, not even by Liora, who knew without a doubt that they were there. What was most troubling to Brill was that he now had a clear link between Liora and Liam. She had demonstrably betrayed his confidence, and he concluded, with a sinking heart, that she had been sent to infiltrate his life by the murderous Colonel Rhett in the first place, all those years ago.

Everything made sense now. He would never trust her again.

Chapter 13: Division

Despite his crushing disappointment with Liora, Brill was eager to begin the next phase of his experiments. It had been years in the making, with global travels, harrowing escapes, and near-death experiences galore, so much more than he had ever dreamed might happen to him. The recruitment of volunteers had worked well, as he paid far more than any research program ever had before. Over five hundred people show up for the first day of screening. Brill was looking for a specific type of genetic profile, and having an abundance of volunteers helped to meet his needs. The tricky part was finding his target group: people who had autistic genetic attributes, but weren't fully autistic. He already had his savants control group, and now he had ample volunteers, given all these unsuspecting eager souls.

Brill's moral standards were eroding further the longer it took to get to the next phase. This was his darkest moment, which didn't bode well for his human subjects.

The consciousness transfer pods they had designed had been significantly modified by Sirum over the years. Under Brill's direction, they were modified to project the psyche out of the body and track it — not just from one person to another, but into the unknown. They were hoping it would move into the quantum level, as they assumed the energy from the mind was attracted to some opposing energy in the quantum level of the dark matter, and relayed back to the person they were connecting with on those fundamental thoughts, as with the married couples saying the same things at the same time. Bridging this to higher-level thought transfer had been a focus of Brill's for years, though less so than increasing intellect, as that seemed more practical to him. The goal of their work had been to force enough energy into the brain to displace the conscious will. The difficulty was finding an individual whose conscious will was aligned to one thought or line of thinking, as most people's minds were so scattered with multiple thoughts that not much could be latched onto to push out of the head. This was where the savants were of such value, and was how he was going to

merge his research of them with the primate research. He

was hoping to genetically engineer them to such high

intelligence that their thoughts would be so strong and

directed that they could be pushed out of their minds into the

quantum level, and then tracked.

Before long, Brill's human experiments with healthy

people had been underway for three months. They seemed to

be making progress, little by little. Liora had stopped by the

lab to meet all the volunteers at one point, but Brill didn't pay

her much heed, as he was busy prepping the treatments.

During her visit, she made it a point to shake everyone's hand

and, with the other hand, clasp their wrist in a double

handshake. The method to her madness was to place a skin

patch on each, as Liam had directed her to do many months

ago. This was the tipping point that Liam had warned her

would drive Brill to greatness. She was reluctant, but

complied under Liam's constant pressure. She suspected that

there was more to her uncle's story than simply monitoring

the treatments, but she couldn't pin down what his end goal might be.

By then, Brill had realized that not all the patients responded to the treatments, and those who did remained simply themselves. No change for better or worse. He couldn't figure out what the problem was. What had he missed?

#

Liam soon saw the opportunity to acquire all of Brill's work, and discredit him in the process. Now that he had the chimps and many of Brill's former team, he just needed some final pieces of information. Liora was key, as he needed those skin patches implanted into Brill's subjects. The patches contained a special kind of nanobot that could be controlled using very simple signals sent through electrical lines. Anywhere there was an electrical outlet, Liam could control the bots. He needed to know what Brill's treatment was, and the order in which it was administered. His instructions to Liora were clear: get the patches on each of Brill's patients.

"What will they do?" she asked, as she flipped them around in the palm of her hand.

"It's better you don't have line of sight to that. Just know that they'll help advance my program and protect our country."

Liora was less than enthusiastic. "Isn't there any other way?"

"No, the time to strike is now. When Brill starts human trials, I need you to place these on each of the subjects' hands. They'll dissolve immediately and won't be seen."

Liora was reluctant, but as always, she followed Liam's orders. She didn't have the gumption to stand up to him, not now, even when she knew it would work against her.

Once the skin patches were placed on the research volunteers, Liam's team had full control of anything Brill tried to introduce into their bodies. The patches contained nanobots that would attach to anything injected, analyze it, and relay back to Liam's team what it was. They could sequence DNA, or measure metabolic compounds and inflammatory cytokines. They also let Liam control people at the cellular level and, if need be, reverse any changes Brill was trying to introduce, or make any other internal changes he wished. Brill had no control when they were active. Liam's team would let some of the changes take effect, but shut down the ability of the genetics to do anything.

#

Progress was slow, much more so than Brill had expected. In one team staff meeting, they were developing future treatment options when a nurse rushed in to get help with some of the patients she was monitoring. Several of them had gone into convulsions. This was disturbing to Brill, as none of the treatments had been targeted to the neural cells. For the patients to have seizures, something must have been triggered, especially since three of them were experiencing the same complication at the same time. He and his team immediately administered anti-seizure medication and started

PET scans. The brains of all three were simultaneously going through a cascade of failures, all in the same areas of the brain. Brill was very alarmed now, as this might point to his illicit treatments. Proposed solutions were limited on how to mitigate these effects.

As the patients labored on in their peril, the staff brought in more experts to help. Every effort was met with a different setback, and their conditions continued to deteriorate. After two weeks of this back-and-forth, all three patients died within minutes of each other. Per standard protocol, the program was halted until a cause could be determined. The postmortems didn't reveal any conclusive evidence that it was Brill's research that had contributed to their deaths. After some heavy debate, Brill was able to convince the university to allow him to continue. Only his former genetics team members were left, as all the others dropped out of the study in fear for their lives.

Brill restarted his work cautiously, searching hard for any anomalies. His research on the savants never missed a beat through all this. He was making progress on improving their intellects. The genetic modifications were taking hold, and he was incrementally improving their breadth of skills. He believed he could fully reprogram their brains; he just needed the right template. This group's research program had continued unhindered, as the university didn't see any problems with it.

Liora was looking for Brill one afternoon when she happened upon him treating the savants. "I was hoping to catch you for lunch. I didn't realize you'd started up your research again." She seemed a little uneasy, he noted.

"This is my control group. They're all autistic savants receiving the same treatments."

"Didn't the university shut you down on this, too?"

"They looked at my work here and agreed it was safe, allowing me to continue."

Realizing she'd missed a group of patients, she waited until they were walking out the door when she made an excuse to go back. "I'll meet you in the lobby. Need my purse if I'm going to get back into the building."

"Okay. I need to stop by my lab anyway. Meet you down there."

She turned in the opposite direction from Brill. She then doubled back, watching him step into the elevator. After waiting for it to go down several floors, she returned to his patients. Pulling the pack of skin patches out of the locket around her neck, she placed one on the right hand of each of the subjects. As the last one dissolved into a young man's skin, she wondered what role she was really playing in Liam's grand plan.

#

Brill was able to recruit two new patients for the study group without health problems, as everyone wants a chance to be smarter. With those individuals he was extra careful, keeping them completely isolated from those in the first round, as he suspected outside interference. His goal of attaining savant-like intelligence in non-autistic patients hinged on genetics and thought-focus though the transfer chairs. The new patients responded to the genetics, as did all the patients now. Brill wasn't sure what had happened to the three who had died, but noted that the commonality was that Liora hadn't visited the lab since this new round of trials had started. His suspicions were confirmed by their lack of issues.

With all the genetic changes in place, he started on the thought-transfer to see if he could mimic the process savants used to attain their superior single-focus intellects. The new transfer chairs that Sirum had upgraded were soon ready for action; he'd also made an even more powerful, special transfer chamber for himself, hidden inside Avalon in the desert. He used paired patients in the chairs, as he was hoping to connect them to each other and see if he could push one's consciousness outward. He hoped this would allow him the ability to use one mind to see what the other was experiencing.

At first, all the patients seemed to be increasing in intelligence; a simple test showed that much. The only patients he was able to connect to each other, however, were the Swazi twins. While Ursula and Misuli were connected, he gave the others a new treatment containing modified prions, of the kind his father had made and used on him so many years ago.

The twins were deeply connected to each other when all hell broke loose. It started with moaning, then screaming, and cries of terror and pain. Every other patient — all eight still left in his program — were simultaneously writhing in agony. Brill couldn't believe it; this shouldn't be happening! He forgot about the twins as he tended those in pain. Frantically, he called Liora. "I need you right away!" he shouted into his phone, as he leaned over to inject a painkiller into one man. "Something's gone terribly wrong."

At that moment, each of the patients rolled onto their right sides and began heaving uncontrollably. "Brill, what are those sounds?" Liora demanded as she headed out the door of her office.

"Those are my patients. All my patients, except for the twins… Shit, the twins!" He turned and sprinted to the transfer chairs.

"What do you need from me? Be there in five minutes."

"No, no, no," he moaned, trying to power down the chairs, "the twins are in too deep!"

"I'm here now," she called as she burst through the door of his lab.

"Over here," he motioned. "I need you to push this button and hold Ursula's head down." Brill then quickly jumped over to the other chair to mirror Liora's actions with Misuli.

"Ready. Tell me what to do."

"Counting down. Three, two, one. Push." They both pushed the disconnect buttons. Nothing happened. Brill was getting frantic now. "Dammit, they should have woken up!"

As he said this, the Dean of the UNLV School of Medicine and several of his staff came hurrying into the room. "Dr. Everly, what the *hell* is going on here? We received reports that your subjects were being tortured!"

"No, Dr. Devlin. They all dropped in pain around the same time. Not my doing."

"According to your staff, this happened after you injected them with something!"

"Here's the medication I used," he said, handing the Dean a vial, which didn't happen to contain the prions.

Face red, Dean Devlin snapped, "I've seen enough! Your lab is effectively shut down, Dr. Everly, and all your university privileges are revoked!"

"You can't do that! I just need a few more days to finish up here!"

"Dr. Everly, you are to immediately leave this hospital, and are not to return until we call you. Your affiliations with this institution are hereby suspended. Do not set foot on the university grounds again until given permission, or you will be arrested."

The university police prepared to escort him off school grounds.

"Just a moment, please," Brill requested, motioning Liora over to him and whispering in her ear, "Please roll those chairs to my helicopter and fly them with the twins in them out to my desert facility, and please bring along those blue-topped vials over there." He pointed to a counter across the room. Nodding, Liora closed the lids and darkened the covers to the chairs, as the dean and his lackeys hadn't noticed anyone in them. Moments later, the police locked down the lab after getting the patients into hospital rooms on another floor. The twins remained unnoticed in the transfer chairs.

Later that evening, Liora snuck back into the lab with Sirum. They disconnected the chairs and got them to the freight elevator without being noticed, since Liora had cut the video surveillance to the whole building just before she and Sirum left her office. Brill had wanted those special blue-lidded vials, but she couldn't find them, so she grabbed whatever vials she could find. The tricky part was getting the transfer chairs loaded one at a time onto the new helicopter Brill's insurance had paid out for. The first went smoothly; the second didn't go as planned. The wheels got caught on a guide wire, slamming the chair to a screeching halt. Sirum had to run to the helicopter and retrieve a tool kit, as the wire was tangled up in the wheel shaft and the only means of extrication was to completely remove one of the wheels.

Liora, meanwhile, kept fretting that they should already be airborne, as the guards would soon come by on their hourly patrol. She took up a defensive position in order to intercept any guards who might surprise them; in fact, she had just set herself in a darkened alcove when a guard strolled through the door. He never got the chance to turn his head to see Sirum, as Liora whacked him over the back of the head with the heel of her boot, which was enough to render him unconscious. Shortly after, the chair was repaired and loaded onto the helicopter. When the guard came to, he radioed in that he'd been hit in the head and Dr. Brill's helicopter was gone. They had no proof, but issued an arrest warrant for Brill, as they assumed it was his doing.

#

By the time Liam Rhett got word that Liora had placed the first set of patches on Brill's patients, his team had already started gathering data. Soon, they were hitting one roadblock after another. Nothing seemed to work, so they upped their efforts. They started using the nanobots to extract the treatments and send the collected data back to them. At first, the extractions only disrupted a few neural signals, nothing major. As Brill's treatments got more complex and worked their way into the brain, however, their extractions began causing severe damage. They didn't actually care what happened to Brill's patients; they only wanted the information. They soon started seeing more complex DNA introductions, and moved to block them and extract them as they were injected into the patients. However, they didn't anticipate that the rest of the treatment would try to do what it was supposed to do, which was to infect neurons. When that happened, patients died as a result of their interference. Liam's team was close to getting what they needed, but fell short of the final pieces of information they required to put the puzzle together.

Then, due to Liora's continued betrayal of Brill's trust, data started coming through from a new set of patients. These individuals were dramatically different in their biology and minds. The nanobots tried to extract information from them as before, but failed to find anything of use. Liam questioned Liora intensely on why the patches had been placed on this group. Upon learning that they were an exclusive savant group, and Brill's control group at that, he was more determined than ever to find out what changes had been introduced to them. They could be the key to unwrapping this riddle.

Liam's next step became clear after he evaluated everything that had happened thus far.

#

Brill *knew* that his human trials had been deliberately sabotaged, as the primate work had never had issues with gene incorporation, and the savant control group didn't have issues either. He just needed to analyze the samples once Liora brought them back, assuming she did. Luckily, she did return, with everything except the vials. The chairs were a plus; he needed to get Ursula and Misuli back to normal. The twins seemed to be in some type of deep coma, and he wasn't sure where to start, so he analyzed every aspect of their shared condition that he could. The thing that jumped out to Brill was the treatment the twins had received. He was using them as a positive control, and had given them identical treatments. One worked, and one didn't. As Brill dug into the details, analyzing every aspect of their biology, he found nothing, not a single clue.

In his haste to find the errors, one morning he left several of their lymph samples in a heat chamber. By the time he remembered them, they had completely dried out. Normally, he would have incinerated them and moved on, but this time he prepared them and put them under a scanning electron microscope. As he peered at the dried-up images of dead immune cells, he noticed an oddity, something he never would have seen on a living cell — something that looked like an appendage protruding from its interior. This microscope allowed for a spectral analysis of metals and other elements in addition to its high magnification. Zooming in on the region, the microscope picked up traces of gallium and indium, two rare earth metals that would never be found inside a T-cell. He had seen this ratio before... but where?

The memory didn't surface until he recalled his father's notes, the ones he'd recently uncovered. He quickly realized that gallium and indium in the observed ratio were key elements present in the nanobots his father had discovered in the Guantanamo experimental subjects. It was clear someone had deliberately sabotaged his work by putting the same kinds of nanos into his patients; the only question was who.

Liora was the obvious culprit, but he had no proof.

Fuming, he decided he'd put more thought towards that later, as his first order of business was to get the twins back. He and Sirum reconnected the chairs, which backfired on them, as Liam's team immediately took control. As soon as the chairs were powered up, both women went into seizures. Liam had ordered his team to clean up their trail, which caused the nanobots in the twins to dissolve disastrously. Brill, of course, knew that more was going on than just the activation of the chairs; he suspected nanobots were wreaking havoc, and needed a way to stop them. He needed those prion vials that Liora had been unable to retrieve. Though he no longer trusted her, he needed her help one last time.

He schooled himself to control his anger and distrust as he asked again for her aid. "I need to get into my university lab," he told her.

"Why? They'll arrest you as soon as they see you."

"Only if they catch me. That's where you come in."

"What do you have in mind?"

"They'll likely be monitoring the airspace around the university, so we'll have to fly in below radar and park the chopper near the monorail. We can get in through the underground tunnels beneath the tracks. It'll be tight, but should allow us to access the hospital via the laundry facility on the lower level."

"Then what?" she asked, unconvinced.

"I'll lean on your expertise there. I need to get into my lab and get the vials you missed."

She pitched in, as she always did, and they were able to fly into the area undetected to land near the last monorail stop. Once there, they entered the service tunnels as planned. It was a tight fit and slow going, but they made it into the hospital undetected. Liora had brought a gel she claimed would somehow provide the cover they needed. Curious, Brill just went with it. Soon, Liora was searching the lower levels for the power junction. She didn't tell Brill what she'd had brought, but it was something she'd acquired from her time with the Mossad. Once she found the power junction from the city to the hospital, she would pour it in and hope for the best. It was supposed to soak into the wires, cutting off the flow of power without actually dissolving or breaking anything. This should shut down the entire hospital, forcing it to go to emergency power. There would be a brief delay between the time the power died and the emergency generator kicked in, but battery power would keep the critical areas of the hospital running until the generator started working.

They would only have about ten minutes. Hopefully, it would be enough.

As she prepared her sabotage, she told him, "Once I release this, I hope you know what you're looking for. You'll be caught if not. Now, put this on," she said as she handed him a hospital gown. She quickly changed into nurse's scrubs.

"Just get me to my lab and I'll find it," he growled.

Once the power died, they made their way to the stairwell, and entered the lab on the fourth floor. The vials he was searching for were nowhere to be found, although he looked everywhere. "They must have moved them," he reported. "I need to check the savant lab."

"Brill, it's too dangerous. Time is our enemy, and there will be nurses and doctors there."

"I can't leave without the vials, Liora."

They had just entered the savant area, where everyone was sleeping, when he saw his prize. After they put away the vials, they were turning to leave when they saw flashlights shining on the opposite door. The lights made it hard to ID who was holding them, until Liora spotted the night vision goggles. *Liam, has to be,* she thought, cursing inwardly. She hadn't known for sure her uncle had planned a raid of this facility, but had suspected he might at some point. Fumbling through the dark, she soon landed upon her goal, a wheelchair. She had Brill sit in it and loaded him up with blankets before pushing him out the other exit, pretending he was her patient. The soldiers, to her surprise, gave them the once-over and let them pass, her set of fake credentials easing the process. They had almost cleared the last hurdle when the lights came back on in the whole building. They were casual in their approach to the stairwell, until Brill was spotted and recognized by a keen-eyed sergeant at the other end of the hallway. He was just entering the door when the sergeant yelled at him to stop, radioing in that he'd spotted one of their HVTs. Brill rushed down the stairs to Liora, grabbing her hand and yelling that they had to run, he was made!

The service tunnel they entered a moment later was a slow crawl, but they made it to the end without being caught, though as they exited, they could see lights well behind them. It seemed to take forever to get to the helicopter and get airborne, even though it was only a few minutes. Brill thought they had escaped, not really thinking through who might be after him.

#

Liam's plan was continuing to come together wonderfully. Once he received confirmation that the twins were located at

Brill's desert facility, he issued orders to eliminate that loose end. The next part of his plan involved a trip to Las Vegas — the university hospital, specifically. He'd had enough of trying to find answers remotely via the nanobots. With Brill out of the way, he decided to confiscate all the savants Brill was treating — for national security reasons, of course — and bring them to his team at Area 51. It would be far easier for his team to pull samples on live patients, and nobody would even know that they were in his lab.

It was purely by accident that the timing of Liam's covert operation coincided with Brill's and Liora's visit to the hospital. As his team was sweeping the hospital, a report came through that Dr. Everly had been spotting escaping the laboratory floor. What could the man want so badly that he'd risk getting caught? That thought would have to await an answer, as Liam saw this as an opportunity to further discredit the young upstart. He would blame Brill for the kidnapping of the savants, a story that would resonate with the university officials he'd already suborned. Liam couldn't believe how easily Brill was playing into his hands.

Once the savants were secured, he gave the order to raid the desert lab.

Chapter 14: On The Run

Their trip to the desert was met with no resistance. As they exited the helicopter, Brill and Liora rushed to the twins. Brill added a carefully measured solution to the vials before he injected the twins with his serum. It took about thirty minutes before Ursula and Misuli started coming around. Brill's serum included a prion-dissolving solution that helped counter the effects of Rhett's nanobots.

The twins were in his recovery room when the facility's alarms went off. Brill looked to the security cam feeds to see that the black ops team had followed him here, and were trying to enter topside. This was a contingency Brill had planned for, and he wasted no time in executing it. He had prepped an EMP pulse to fry all the electronics in the building, which would work in his favor, as standard night vision goggles were susceptible to the type of EMP pulse he would set off. This was when he had to break ties with Liora, as he was certain all this was partially her doing. He turned to her coolly and stated, "Liora, please stay here with the twins while I set charges to blow the elevators. You can still leave by the stairs. This is where we part ways. For good."

"What? Why would you break up with me here, now? After all I've done..." Tears filled her eyes, and she made no attempt to hide them.

Brill hardened his heart. "Exactly. After all you've done, Liora. That's a covert Army strike team, just like the one that helped us after the cave-in. How did they know we were at the hospital? Why did my research fail so catastrophically? Why did the university cut me off and lock me out? You were always right in the middle when things went wrong, weren't you, Liora." It was a statement, not a question.

"I, I don't understand. Why would you say that?" Sobbing, she reached for him; he shied away.

"My patients, Liora. They were all fine until you visited them. Then they all fell ill, and all my treatments stopped working. Too convenient, and too much of a coincidence. Did you really think I was that blind, that stupid?"

"Brill, no. I'm in love with you. I didn't do this."

"I don't have time to debate it. If you do love me, then you'll stay here and hold Rhett's goons off while I escape with what I can. An EMP charge is about to go off; that'll help."

With that, Brill disappeared into the shadows with Sirum, who had appeared seemingly out of nowhere. As for Liora, she decided she wasn't going to comply with Liam's wishes on this. The twins didn't need her help, so she looked for a way to slow his team down. Once the EMP was engaged, she knew, nothing electronic would work, unless it was shut off beforehand. Looking around the lab, she spotted a power generator. Quickly running over to it, she powered it down, hoping it really would restart after the EMP charge went off. The stairwell had enough metal in it that she figured she could create an oscillating pulse up and down it between the rails. That should be enough to incapacitate the troops.

A moment later, the EMP charge detonated as promised, and it was unlike anything she had ever experienced; it seemed to jar her head back and forth, causing great pain in her dental work. It must have done far more to the troops, as they should have been bursting through the door by that point, but nobody appeared. She regained her composure, restarted the generator — it worked just fine — and she worked to attach cables to each of the stairway's hand-rail. Her booby trap had built to a max charge by the time she set it on oscillating mode between A/C and D/C, and set it to pulse again in two minutes. That should hold them back for a while.

Expecting Brill to have escaped to his supposedly secret cave, she set off to find the entrance to it before the military spotted her.

#

Brill was torn between his desire to have Liora with him, and his need to leave her to her masters. The old adage of "Keep your friends close, and your enemies closer" played strong in his head, so after the EMP went off, he and Sirum looped back to get her. They found her running towards the cave entrance. She'd been there to help rescue Sirum, so Brill concluded she had guesstimated where the entrance might be. That, or the people she worked for had told her where it was. He stepped out of the shadows, bringing her to a skidding halt. "Come with us."

"I thought you left without me."

"Changed my mind. We built an entrance here," he said, as he uncovered a hidden door. Had he not shown her, she might never have found it. After they entered the cavern, the entrance sealed behind them, completely obscuring its location. As they headed toward the underground lakeshore, she saw a boat concealed along the shoreline; one more thing she might never have found. Brill handed her night vision goggles, but even they had trouble interpreting the environment around them, as they require some incidental light to be fully functional — and the only visible lights this deep were a few colonies of phosphorescent microbes lining the cave's ceiling. As they entered the boat, Brill pushed away from the shoreline and engaged the electric motor.

The eerie quietness and darkness made Liora uneasy, though it seemed to her that Brill knew exactly where he was going, so she trusted him. She was aware that Brill now knew, or at least strongly suspected, that she wasn't who she claimed to be. If he knew of her relationship to Liam Rhett, though, he covered it well. Though it hurt, his distrust shouldn't have been a surprise; ever since his rescue from Jakarta and their return, Brill had given her many signals that he didn't trust her. The hospital raid to obtain the vials distanced him even more, so much so that he was at least initially willing to leave her behind. She knew he wouldn't do that unless he thought she was connected to the team invading the facility.

With this revelation, she decided to do what would have been unthinkable a year ago. She was going to tell him everything, and hope he would forgive her and allow them to start over. It was a longshot; she knew there was a high likelihood he would distance himself from her and never speak to her again once they'd managed their escape.

#

Colonel Rhett was pleased to have acquired the savants, and to be so easily able to blame Brill for all that had gone wrong. The good Dr. Everly was now wanted on multiple counts of kidnapping and wrongful death. Liam's team had tracked Brill's helicopter back to the desert facility. Liam was in no hurry to acquire him, though, as time was on his side. He had a full platoon deployed for complete recovery of everything in the desert facility. He would take it all, acquire Brill *and* his savant friend Sirum, and extricate Liora from this assignment at last.

Surprisingly, his team encountered more resistance than they expected, including casualties when they hit the booby-trapped stairs. That told Liam that Brill was buying time, most likely to try to escape. He knew of the cave system; his med-assault team had been there during the rescue and had mapped out the first cave, unknown to Brill. It would have surprised Brill even more had he known there was a hanger door built into the rocky ceiling. Back in the 1950s, the

Army had used the lake cavern to store secret aircraft. It was the only place they could find where they believed the Russians couldn't monitor what they were doing. It was by happenstance that Liam had learned of this; one of his mentors had told him many Cold War stories, including ones about this base after he'd learned Liam had purchased the property and subsequently sold it off. That door would be difficult to open after all this time, but appeared to be his only option, as his team couldn't locate the entrance Brill had so cleverly built. He sent them to the emergency manual crank for the hangar door, and his team finally managed to get the gears turning — slowly — to drive the opening, after the liberal application of many gallons of oil and grease. It took them six hours to open the overhead door, but they finally succeeded. His team then descended into the cavern, looking for any trace of Liora, Dr. Everly, and his associate, Dr. Sirum Lars.

#

Two years earlier, Sirum and Brill had mapped the underground lake and its tributaries in every direction. It was a grand adventure, undertaken for completely paranoid reasons. But as the saying goes, even paranoids have enemies; and after seeing his father die, Brill knew Liam Rhett and his rogue program would never leave him in peace. One branch he and Sirum had taken, out of the fifteen they tried, led to a roomy alcove with an opening to the surface. After prepping the location for use, they had moved the quantum chair, made specially for Brill, and the quantum computer there. To power it all and keep it connected to the hospital, they'd run power and high-speed data cables to it. It was six miles from Avalon, taking Sirum and Brill a few months to run the cables — a very slow, painstaking process. The cables they had dropped onto the bottom of the lake, so that nobody could follow them to the chair. Now Brill was headed there with Liora and Sirum.

During the slow ride there, Liora dropped her bombshell on him. "Brill, I have something to confess," she said, in a voice meeker than anything he'd ever heard from her.

"I'm listening."

"Years ago, I was adopted by my uncle after my Mother died."

"Oh, is that right?"

"Yes. He brought me out of Israel, My Mother and I were natives of that country. My father was his brother. They were both U.S. military, and he felt obligated to honor family."

"Military, huh?" Suspicions quickly crossed his mind.

"I spent my teenage years growing up on an Army base, learning military ways."

"So, you *are* connected to the military. I have a strong suspicion who your uncle is. Why don't you tell me?"

"Yes. You have a history with him. His name is Colonel Liam Rhett."

"*That* dishonorable bastard. Did you know my father treated *his* father for cancer? Helped extend his life by five years. He paid my father back by having him murdered. Then he went after me. Do I mean nothing to you, Liora?"

She took a deep breath. "I owed him my life. When I was older, and had military experience of my own, he asked me come and... motivate you, to help you to become more than your father had been. Though I never met John Everly, Liam was highly impressed with him."

"Don't even go there," Brill growled. "I just told you Liam Rhett had my Dad killed."

"I don't know the story there. I didn't, I mean. I can only be who I am, though, and I'm tired of not telling you everything. I wanted to tell you now so I can help you, and not have you constantly worried about my motives."

He snapped irritably, "Enough of your lies, Liora! You knew I was falling in love with you, and then you just left. Went to South fucking Africa. Now I can see you did it because I was just an assignment to you. Wasn't I?"

He fell silent, very conscious of Sirum's bright eyes as he followed their argument, and peered ahead into the darkness.

Liora protested, "I didn't want to go, but I had to. Liam is basically my father, and I trusted his judgment."

"And when you came back, you sabotaged my work. Because he told you to. You *murdered* people for him. My people."

"...I didn't know, but yes."

He turned to her and said bitterly, "Damn, you're a cold bitch. Cold to the core. No heart and no love, I see. How do you expect me to just forget?"

She sighed and said in a slightly quavering voice, "Brill, I don't. I wouldn't expect that. Some memories are burned into our souls. We need them to help us learn and grow. I'm truly sorry for the pain I've caused you and I'm asking — no, *begging* for your forgiveness. Let's walk a new path and see where it goes."

"Liora, I can't. Your actions have ruined my life and my life's work. Just hearing you admit to it is like a knife in my heart, and it hurts every time I go back there in my mind. We could have been *so much more* with you there working with me, not against me. The piece of me you took with you back then is something that I never got back, can never get back. Just like my trust in you."

Tears were streaming down her face now. "Just give me a chance. I won't let you down."

"You've had *plenty* of chances, even if you didn't know it. I gave you chance after chance not to be who you actually are." Now Brill's eyes were welling with tears. "No more, Liora. You're proven yourself unworthy of my trust. You didn't just ruin my life, you ruined others, too. You've caused innocent people's deaths. When we get to where we're going, I want you leave and never come back. I never want to see you again. I can't keep hoping for you to be something you're not. In that room, there's a stairway that leads to the surface. Up there is a car you can take back to the city. Sirum will join you once he connects me."

"What? You're staying?"

"I have to finish my work. If I'm right, my intelligence will far surpass that of Einstein, Newton, and Hawking combined by the time I'm done. Once the chair takes hold, and I'm able learn to focus and hone my thoughts, my intellect may increase infinitely. Once I learn how to do that, I'll exit the chair and take the other car hidden up there."

They both fell silent, and shortly after, they arrived at the deeply hidden location. Not too long before, Brill and Sirum had installed heat-dampening shields to protect against the very surveillance Liam Rhett was now unleashing. They hoped the covers over the chair chamber would prevent drones from locking in on their heat signals, at least long enough for him to accomplish his task. After they docked the boat and pulled it into the chamber, they quickly raised the heat shields and plugged every opening they could find. They covered everything except the powerlines coming up from the lake.

Once the chair was powered up, Brill stripped down and clambered into it; Sirum proceeded to hook up an IV, and the various electrodes and neural connectors. "Sirum, old friend," Brill said in a low voice. "There's one more thing I need you to do. Those vials over there" — he pointed to the table — "please hand those to me, and I'll inject myself."

"I can do that for you," Sirum said as he handed Brill the vials and a syringe.

"I can't ask that of you. If something goes wrong with the treatment, I don't want you to have that on your conscience for the rest of your life." Brill then proceeded to inject the contents of the vials into the IV port, one vial at a time.

He then said calmly, "Liora, please go. Don't come back." With that, Brill closed the dome over the chair, and she and Sirum were left in total silence. She collapsed to the floor, sobbing; Sirum reached down to place a comforting hand on her shoulder. After several minutes, they left Brill to his quest. Where that would lead Liora didn't know, but in her heart, she knew she would return to him someday.

The trail to the stairway was a narrow corridor plagued with several sharp twists and dripping water, slippery most of the way. Upon finally finding the rock-hewn stairs, they carefully began the climb. Sirum had run theatre floor lighting up the stairs, providing enough illumination to find them.

They were about two flights from the surface when the lights went out.

#

Liam's team had scoured the entire cavern for signs of life, with nothing useful to show for it. There was plenty of electronic equipment there, including a number of computers, all of it "bricked" by the EMP charge Brill had set off. They loaded it up and flew it out anyway. Eventually, in an obscure, unlit corner of the cavern, his team noticed cables that disappeared into the dirt floor. Curious, they began to pull them up. There wasn't much dirt there, so up they readily came. The team pulled and pulled until they were at the water's edge, whereupon they reported to Liam their findings, which indicated to him that there was another working area in the associated maze of underground tunnels. He couldn't leave until his questions were answered, so he ordered the team to send out drones to patrol the waterways leading to the lake. With their infrared detection, they would quickly locate any heat source, giving Liam his prize.

His team spent hours directing drones through the tunnels large enough for a human to escape through. Seeing only failure in this effort, Liam finally ordered his team to retrieve the damned drones and sever the cables; four hours was enough wasted effort. He'd cut his losses and destroy the site, and that would be that.

Once the power was cut, his team planted explosives throughout Avalon and the main building. Once away and at a safe distance, they watched as the facility imploded and collapsed into a pile of useless rubble. Liam figured that if he couldn't get Brill, then he'd seal the bastard in and let fate take its course. He was confident enough with his acquisition of the savants, chimps, and Brill's team.

It never occurred to him that he was leaving his niece there to die as well.

#

When the lights went out, Liora grabbed for Sirum. "We need to get back to Brill. If he's still in the chair, he won't be able to get out, and he'll suffocate!"

"I was going to go back anyway, just to be with him," Sirum admitted. "He may not want me there when he ascends, but I won't leave him, ever again." Liora quipped.

They held onto each other's hands, as the trip down was far more dangerous than the trip up. They both had headlamps, which helped, but each step down had to be carefully monitored, lest they hit a patch of moss and fell. After what seem liked hours, they finally made their way back to Brill, just as the earth shook, as if in a massive quake. Luckily, the ceiling held. Everything was dark as sin; there was no power anywhere. Brill and Sirum hadn't yet had the chance to build in backup power supplies. After a brief struggle, Sirum was able to get the dome of the chair chamber open.

#

Once the injections took hold, Brill could feel the changes taking place inside him. His mind was metamorphosing faster than his thoughts could process. Clarity of thought was taking over; and something else was happening as well. He seemed to feel his body lighten until it was levitating. It hit him that it was the chair helping him focus his consciousness to the quantum level; it must be due to the dark matter that Sirum had embedded into the chair conduits. That levitation sensation must be his thoughts coalescing into a single projection. Playing with this new ability, he put a thought out there, desiring to learn about the nanobots. It was a science where he lacked complete understanding, except for rudimentary skills and the data from his father's notes; but the thought was something he could sense as it started to take on a life of its own. The other things rattling around in his head went silent; only this one thought was there. Not just the *idea* of nanobots, but everything about them: what they were, where they came from, and everything that made them tick. As he focused on the thought, it seemed to draw him in, pulling him farther and farther away from his mind and body.

As he felt he was approaching the thought, he could sense it growing in size. Then he "saw" it. The size he perceived was not the thought itself, he found, but all the solutions about the thought, more than what his mind had initially asked for. This was what these thoughts were, and what they would become: a solution to all questions. *Infinite knowledge* was the term that occurred to him. He must still be connected to his body, he decided, as he felt the pull to draw in what he was "seeing." This was pure knowledge, the source of every savant's ability, the well the ancient seers had plumbed.

His psyche glanced slightly beyond this growing thought/solution when he saw there was so much more to this place. Not just one solution, but *all* solutions, to most questions. But why would he think or know that? He was now questioning himself. The event that he began to focus on now was how he would go back to bring this knowledge to humanity. This place, this quantum level, must be a sounding board for all intellect. Here, people's minds were able to reach the abstract solutions that no computer could ever reach. This must be the essence of human thought, perhaps all sentient thought in the universe: the core of sentient being. He felt he was learning so much; how much he would remember was yet to be determined, as he hadn't yet solved the problem of how to get the information back to his conscious mind. But all solutions were here, so that must be here, too.

As he was ruminating over the multitude of possibilities, something began pulling him back. The thought of and solutions to the nanobot issue began fading into the distance. He could now see where his body was. How? Somehow, he was *outside* his body, watching as the power failed and one machine after another shut down. He had enough presence of mind to know that his body would die if he didn't get out in time. The heart monitor didn't go out, as it was battery-powered; all it did was let him watch as the rhythm of his heart slow and stopped.

Then nothing. Complete darkness, and he knew his body had only minutes of life left. Once his heart stopped, his brain would soon die of oxygen starvation, unless the nanobots saved him one more time. Time no longer had any meaning to him as it unfolded. He saw Sirum and Liora enter the room. He watched as Sirum opened the canopy and pulled his body out of the chair. They both tried administering CPR, but nothing happened. His last image was of Liora holding his hand, wailing with grief.

Whether it was because of boredom or something else, whatever he was now turned back to the nanobots thought/solution.

His new presence seemed to stop at the edge of this place. The descriptions that were flooding him were of an infinite plane of existence where thoughts and knowledge collided. He watched as the nanobot thought/solution entered a great whirling depression in the middle of the space, something that resembled a giant whirlpool. The thought/solution had substance and structure as it entered the whirlpool. What he was looking at took the form not of a black hole, but of a white hole; it was completely illuminated. As he more closely examined the illumination, he could see that these were thoughts, resembling neural signals — some were his, mixed with those of others. The central cone of the whirlpool was also illuminated. As he approached it, he could see what looked like subatomic particles, or at least what he imagined subatomic particles looked like. He saw the thoughts collide with those, and take the form of equations, or something of the like.

Now he understood. This was the quantum scale, maybe even inside his quantum computer; he wasn't sure. These thoughts would bounce off the quantum particles, much like computer code inside a silicon chip. The center wasn't knowledge itself, but was a connection point for those select intellects who could enter this place. What returned were all possible solutions to the question or to the problem being asked, if the connected minds had solved it in the past or were solving it in the future, as time had no relevance here.

With so many thoughts entering this place, there were an infinite number of solutions available. What he'd thought of as a library was more like a computer. Somehow, the ancients had accessed this place, this quantum level, probably through their genetic abilities to project their thoughts here; but how did they get back?

That answer didn't readily come to him, for some reason; so after some measure of thought, he returned to the nanobots thought/solution. It was different now. More knowledge had been added to it, as there had been questions before that had yet to be asked; the solutions to those questions appeared only when they *were* ready to be asked. This place and image had some familiarity to him. The name came to him: one that was not readily recognized, as it was ancient, something from a long-dead language. Then a translation came. This was The Knowledge Well, the very image he had seen painted on a cave wall in New Zealand.

He felt neither joy nor surprise nor satisfaction at the realization. No emotion here, just familiarity. He was lost in this place. Since he had no emotion and no desires, he just was, and his curiosity was all that remained. So many questions that needed answers. So he began to ask them, lost in the deluge of knowledge.

#

Liora watched as Sirum pull Brill out of the chair. He wasn't breathing, so they started CPR and tried to give him oxygen. No pulse, nothing. They tried and tried, but nothing worked. Brill was gone. She held him as tight as she could, wailing and crying. She would never let him go. It wasn't supposed to end this way.

They sat in silence as their world collapsed, with Liora saying over and over, "Brill, please come back to me."

In time, she thought she heard a faint answer.

THE END

Made in the USA
Columbia, SC
15 August 2020